THE ARGUS DECEIT

ALSO BY CHUCK GROSSART

The Phoenix Descent

The Gemini Effect

THE ARGUS DECEIT

CHUCK GROSSART

47NORTH

Text copyright © 2017 by Chuck Grossart

Published by 47North, Seattle
www.apub.com

Amazon, the Amazon logo, and 47North are trademarks of Amazon.com, Inc., or its affiliates.

ISBN-13: 9781477819647
ISBN-10: 1477819649

Cover design by Cyanotype Book Architects

Printed in the United States of America

To the believers

PROLOGUE

Watseka, Illinois
Saturday, July 23, 1994
2:05 a.m.

The bright light was the first sign.

Connie opened her eyes and watched the light slowly creep across her wall, crossing her room from left to right. Cars did that sometimes, their headlights shining through her window as they passed the house.

Funny thing was, she couldn't hear a car.

The light stopped for a moment, then slid toward the corner of her room, fading away as it moved.

It was dark again.

She sat up in bed, rubbing her eyes and wondering what had woken her. She didn't remember hearing any noises that could've jolted her from her sleep. It must've been the glow from the headlights that woke her up. It was gone now. The night was perfectly still.

It had been a hot and sticky day, and the temperature hadn't dropped much. She'd kicked her sheet off while sleeping, and it lay crumpled in a pile. Her nightie was all wet, not the *accident* kind of wet, as she was a big girl now and didn't pee the bed anymore, but she was covered in sweat. A breeze came through her window, and even though the weather was hot, she still got goose pimples on her arms. She reached down and grabbed her sheet, pulling it up toward her chin as she settled back down in bed.

She closed her eyes and reached for Mr. Bear, but he was gone. He must have fallen off the bed. She turned on her bedside lamp and squinted against the bright light. Sure enough, he was on the floor. She wished she didn't have to reach down to get him, with the shadows under her bed providing a perfect hiding place for all sorts of monsters and creepy-crawlies. Her dad said monsters weren't real, and there was nothing to be afraid of under the bed, but *still*. He was big and could fight them off, so of course he wasn't afraid.

She snatched Mr. Bear from the floor (quickly) and reached to turn off her lamp. Her alarm clock said it was past two in the morning; she'd *never* been up this late before. She turned off the light, hugged her stuffed bear tightly, and snuggled back under the covers.

She wasn't sure how much time passed before she opened her eyes again, but it couldn't have been long, as her eyes still hadn't adjusted to the dark. Her room was pitch-black.

Their trailer was at the edge of the park, and outside her window lay farm fields, acres and acres of soybeans. That's what her dad said they were, anyway. If they were anything like green beans, she wondered why anyone would want to grow so many of them. She hated green beans.

In the summertime, the music (what her mom called it) from the fields was constant, the crickets singing all night long. She was used to hearing their songs, a background noise no longer noticed until it was gone.

The crickets stopped chirping. Just like that. It wasn't a noise that woke her this time; it was the *lack* of noise. The critters would stop chirping if startled.

If something was close.

She sat up and looked to her window. Her curtains were hanging straight down. Even the breeze had stopped. She tossed her sheet aside and stepped out of bed. For a second, she stood there and listened, gripping Mr. Bear's arm tightly.

Quiet.

In the next room, though, she could hear her father snoring.

Something wasn't right. She took a tentative step toward her window, afraid to peer outside but knowing she was going to anyway. She cupped her hands against the screen, inhaling the dusty metallic scent of the thin aluminum mesh.

The sky was clear, stars twinkling above. No moon. No clouds.

The field was dark, but she could see lights from the farmhouse way across the field where Becky Coleton lived. Her family had a big light mounted on a pole outside their barn, which would switch on when the sun went down and turn itself off in the morning. A mercury vapor light, her dad called it, or something like that, which kept most of the Coletons' yard lit at night.

Connie wished her family had one of those, too. Especially now.

She watched for a minute, looking to see if she could tell if anything was out there, but saw nothing.

A cricket began to chirp. Then another. And another.

Whatever had startled them was gone.

Connie sighed, realizing she'd been holding her breath. *There's nothing there, quit being such a baby.* She turned away from her window.

Then, a bang.

She gasped, nearly jumping out of her skin. A quick shiver jolted through her body. She stood perfectly still, afraid to move.

And the crickets were silent once again.

Her heart was pounding, and she could hear herself breathing.

Another noise, not as loud this time. The front door.

Someone was trying to get inside. A burglar. A robber. A bad man.

She stared at her doorknob, wanting to run and wake her parents, but fear kept her still. She couldn't open that door if there was a bad man in the house. *The window.* She could remove the screen and crawl out if she had to. She turned toward her window and stopped.

At first, it didn't register. She'd even taken a step before she realized

someone is someone is someone is

there was a shadow outside her window. Someone standing just outside, looking in.

At her.

She covered her mouth with her hand to stifle a scream as the shape darted to the right. Gone.

She heard her mother's voice, soft, muffled through her bedroom wall.

Then her father's voice, deeper. She heard the floor creak as he stepped out of bed.

They'd heard the bang, too. Connie stepped to her door and twisted her doorknob, wincing at the loud click as the latch released. She mustered her courage and opened her door, trying to keep the hinges from squeaking.

She heard her parents' door open and saw her father step down the hall past her room.

"Dad?" she whispered.

"Connie, were you up a second ago?" he whispered back.

She couldn't see his face, just a large shadow in the hall. She stepped out of her doorway, close to him. "No. I heard a noise and I think I saw—"

"Shh," he said, patting her shoulder while he stared into the darkness down the hall.

Connie grabbed his hand as he started to move. "Daddy, don't," she whispered.

He looked down and smiled. "Be my brave girl and stay in your room, honey," he said, giving her tiny hand a squeeze before he stepped into the darkness.

Connie stepped back into her room but didn't close her door all the way. It was going to be okay. Her dad was awake. She was safe. But she was worried. There could be a bad man out there. She turned back toward her window, hoping she wouldn't see someone looking in like before. There was nothing there, but she didn't want to stay in her room alone. She opened her door wide enough to poke her head through and heard her mother whisper, "Come here, C Bear." Her mother was standing in her parents' bedroom doorway, white T-shirt visible in the darkness.

Connie opened her door all the way and quickly went to her mother, wanting nothing more than to get away from her open window and from whoever might be lurking outside.

Or trying to get in.

She hugged her mother's bare legs, warm from sleep. Connie was shivering, and her teeth chattered as she spoke. "I heard something, Mommy," she whispered. "And I think I saw someone outside my window."

Her mother drew her closer. "What did you—?"

They both jumped at the sound of her father's voice.

It wasn't loud. He didn't cry out. But it was a surprised sound. Startled.

And then nothing more.

Connie held her mother tighter as they huddled together in the doorway.

After a few long moments of silence, her mother whispered, "Jack?" Then louder: "Jackie?"

The house was silent. And it shouldn't be. Not now.

Connie hugged tighter when she felt her mother move. "Stay here, C Bear," her mother said. "Close the door and don't come out, okay?"

"Mommy, don't go."

"Listen to me. Stay in our room and don't open the door. Understand?"

Connie felt the first tear slide down her cheek as her mother gently pushed her inside and closed the door. Mommy and Daddy always came running when she was scared, but this time they'd left her alone. They weren't supposed to do that. "Mommy?" she said quietly. Connie was really shivering now and hugged Mr. Bear tightly. The seconds ticked by, marking every moment of silence as she shifted her weight from one foot to another, feeling the urge to pee.

The door wasn't closed all the way, and she stared through the crack, hoping to hear one of her parents say that everything was okay, there was nothing there, and they could all go back to bed. The shadow she saw in her window was nothing more than her eyes playing tricks on her, they'd say.

Everything would be okay.

In the morning, she would watch cartoons and have a big bowl of cereal, like every Saturday morning.

Bad things happen to other people. Not to her family.

A noise.

Not a voice, but something else.

A gurgling. Clicking.

A sound Connie couldn't place.

"Mom?" she whispered. "Mommy?"

She heard a moan. Her father's voice. She grabbed the doorknob without thinking and opened the door wide. She stepped into the hall, one foot following the other, into the shadows.

you're my brave girl you're my brave girl

Something was wrong. Her dad was hurt. Maybe they were both hurt. Her heart pounded away in her chest as she moved toward the living room—she was so scared—but couldn't stop. "Daddy?" she said, her voice quivering as her body shook with terror.

brave girl

She could see them, standing side by side in the living room. Two shadows.

Connie ran her hand up the wall until she felt the light switch. She flicked it on.

Her parents stood motionless, arms at their sides. Their heads hung down, like they were asleep. And they weren't alone.

Connie felt a warm trickle run down her leg as Mr. Bear slipped from her hand, thumping against the floor.

She turned to run.

But didn't get far.

PART I
THE DANCE OF THE FOUR

Chapter 1

BRODY52

Joshua, Maine
Friday, October 25, 1974
5:34 p.m.

The sun was on its way down, right on schedule.

He couldn't recall the last time he'd actually watched the sun set, though. There wasn't a need to, not anymore. Those were moments best shared with someone else. Now the orange glow behind drawn blinds marked nothing more than the end of one more day of pain, piled upon all those that came before it.

She wouldn't like the way he was living, of that he was certain. She hardly ever closed the blinds. Or kept the windows closed, for that matter. "Let the outside in, Brody," she'd say.

Let the outside in.

But the outside had taken her from him, so cruelly, and he was content to let the outside remain just that. Out.

He was becoming an old hermit, holed up inside his house. Maybe in a few years he would be a Howard Hughes–esque recluse, unkempt beard and hair hanging to his waist with yellow nails thick and curling.

And why not?

He didn't have much to live for. Not without her.

No, Felix probably wouldn't let that happen, bless his soul. The man had been in their employ for decades and would never leave Brody's side. Felix felt the pain of her loss just as sharply as Brody himself had, in a different way. She hadn't been his lover, his wife, the mother of his children—two boys who no longer called. If Felix harbored any of the same suspicions as Brody's own flesh and blood, the man never showed it. He was a professional servant, cut from a cloth woven during a more genteel time. His job was this house and what was left of its family.

And Brody Quail, widower at the age of fifty-two, represented the remainder of the broken pieces of the Quail family of Joshua, Maine. Felix was the broom and dustpan, and he was trying to clean.

Brody supposed he could fire the man, forcibly breaking his chains and allowing him to seek employment elsewhere, to get on with his *own* life at least, but he didn't have the heart to do so. He doubted he could fire him even if he truly wanted to. Felix would probably smile, say "Yes, sir," and continue to go about his daily rituals. He and Felix would likely remain in this cesspool of an existence until the bitter end, whenever, and *however*, that sad result came to fruition, two lonely men bound by the memory of a once-happy family now shattered.

As the day's brightness faded with the diminishing sunlight, Brody opened his side drawer.

He'd been a cop once, a life that seemed so far away, made real now only in the reflection of his haggard face in the blued steel of his Smith & Wesson Model 27. It had been his service weapon, back in the day when a six-round revolver and a billy club were the only weapons a police officer had to carry and seldom had to use. A pedestrian endeavor, his father would say, a life meant for others, not for *his* son.

Brody joined the police force in spite of his father's wishes. The act was a personal accomplishment, something earned, not a handout from his father. When the time came to step up and take the reins of the family's holdings, though, Brody did what was expected of him. He took off the uniform and stood at his father's side.

Brody became a rich man because of that decision. But none of it mattered without her.

He fingered the rough, checkered grip of the revolver, felt the comfortable heft in his hand as he removed it from the drawer, six .357 Magnum rounds nestled in the cylinder. He always kept it loaded now.

Loading a weapon took time. Precious seconds. Time that could have made a crucial difference that night when his heart was ripped from his chest.

Seconds. The course of a life decided on the tick of a clock.

Tick. She lives.

Tick-tock. She dies.

He swiveled his chair to face the windows, trying to banish the past. The memory would never go away, though. The memory would haunt him for the rest of his days. He held the pistol in his lap and stared at it.

It could be his way out, if he wished.

One shot. Not necessarily clean, but quick and most likely painless. A second to raise the pistol to his temple. Less than a second to pull the trigger.

"A fine weapon, sir," Felix said from behind.

The man had a preternatural ability to appear whenever Brody wondered about the one-way ticket the gun provided. He swiveled around and placed the gun back in the drawer, then slid it shut. "Sneaking up on a man with a loaded gun isn't a smart thing to do, Felix."

"Yes, sir."

Felix stood in the doorway, a tray in hand. He wasn't a large man, rather thin for his height. Gray eyes stared out beneath a balding pate framed by gray at the temples.

"Your evening meal, sir. If you'd like, I can take it downstairs to the dining room."

Brody motioned for Felix to place the tray on his desk. He hadn't eaten at the dining table since Rebecca passed. His dear Reba. "Thank you, Felix." He had to give Felix credit for trying.

"This is the last of the roast from yesterday evening, sir," Felix said. "If you would like something different . . ."

"No, Felix. This is perfect." Felix was quite the chef, but cooking for one less person in the house meant leftovers were common. Brody didn't mind. He hadn't cooked a meal for himself in years, so he was grateful for Felix's culinary skills.

"Very well, sir. Unless you require anything else, I will retire for the evening."

Brody nodded, reluctantly. He nearly asked Felix to bring a plate up here for himself, but Felix would never allow such a breach of protocol. Their relationship, though close, was still one of employer and employee, and Felix would keep it that way. "Thank you, Felix. See you in the morning."

Felix turned on his heel and was gone, leaving Brody alone with a plate of leftovers and his thoughts.

Brody glanced at the clock; ten minutes until six, a little over an hour before the old timepiece would chime seven times, and he would make his way downstairs. It was what he did.

Chapter 2
BRODY10

He watched the second hand slowly sweep toward 12 and then jumped from his desk at the first sound of the bell.

Afternoon recess wasn't very long, but it was his favorite. Not only did it smell like summer outside, but afternoon break meant he was closer to the end of the day, closer to the end of the week, and best of all, closer to the end of the school year. Almost three months of glorious summer vacation beckoned, which in May seemed like an eternity before the last week of August, when he'd start all over again. As a fifth grader.

Ten-year-old Brody Quail followed Rich Gable and Gary Thompson down the hall and out the double doors to the playground. The sun was warm on Brody's face as the three boys ran across the pea gravel toward the grassy part of the playground, dodging the smaller kids who were racing to the swings and jungle gyms.

Afternoon recess was only twenty minutes long, and they had a game of Smear the Queer to finish, except they couldn't call it that around Mrs. Carlisle, one of the teachers who prowled the playground during recess. For some reason, she didn't like the name. Around her, they called it Annihilation. The teams from earlier were already forming up, a combined fourth-and-fifth-grade team against the sixth graders. John Bullard, one of the bigger sixth graders, was tossing a football from hand to hand, the rest of his team lining up behind him. Bullard had tackled him once, right after Brody got the ball and before he could toss it to one of his friends. Not only had Brody had the wind knocked out of him, but he was sure he had heard his ribs crack. Brody was small for his age but didn't let his lack of size hold him back. "Sorry, kid," Bullard had said. "You gotta be quicker with the rock." Bullard could have easily ruled the playground with an iron fist, as there weren't many other kids his size, but instead he was a gentle giant. He'd helped Brody up and even patted him on the back. Coming from a sixth grader, that was pretty cool.

Rich was the de facto leader of Brody's team. He was bigger than any of the fifth-grade boys and the most athletic. They huddled around Rich, forming a circle just like the NFL teams did on Sunday, with Rich down on one knee, all eyes on him.

"Pass it quick and keep it away from Bullard. Try to get it to me, Gary, or Lance." Lance was a fifth grader who could run like the wind. "Okay, ready, break!" Everyone clapped their hands at the last word and spread out to receive the kick. During lunch recess, the sixth graders had scored three times, and they were ahead 21 to 14. It was time to get some revenge.

The rules were simple. The team with the ball had to get it to one of the fences by moving it however they could—passing, tossing, handing off, whatever—without getting tackled. Touch the ball to the chain link, and it's a touchdown. Fifteen guys on either side. The game was fun, fast, and physical; tackle, not touch, because touch was for wussies. And best of all, the girls liked to watch.

Brody glanced back toward the school and saw all the sixth-grade girls, along with the girls from his class, sitting Indian-style on the grass and trying to look disinterested. Debbie Wilson was there, too. God, she was pretty. Brody imagined himself getting the ball and crashing through the sixth graders right in front of her, heading toward the fence and scoring a touchdown.

A tug on his arm. "Brody?" His little brother, Murphy. A first grader.

"Not now, Murf."

"Can I play?"

"Scram, Murf. Get off the field."

"I wanna play, too."

Brody took his brother by the arm. "Not yet, okay? You'd get squished. Go over there and watch. Just stay out of the way." Brody watched the smile fade from his brother's face.

"Mom says you have to play with me."

"Not *now*, Murf."

"Ready?" Bullard called, getting ready to punt the ball to their side.

"Hey, Quail! Get your brother out of here." That was Rich, staring at him. So was everyone else. Brody felt the heat rise up the back of his neck.

"Get off the field, Murf, now! Go watch."

"I'm gonna tell Mom," Murf said as he turned and ran back to the playground.

Gonna tell Mom. Murf's favorite saying. Brody loved his brother, but the kid could be a royal pain in the rear. Like now. Brody waved at Rich.

"Okay, ready!" Rich yelled.

Brody crouched and put his weight on the balls of his feet, his ready position, as his dad called it. With a boom, Bullard sent the ball into the sky (he sure was a good punter), and it tumbled down to Brody's right, directly to Gary, who cradled it in both arms and took off running. Brody ran toward him, staying off to his left and slightly behind, keeping his head on a swivel to stay out of the way of the bigger boys. Getting run over without having the ball was embarrassing.

One, then two sixth graders draped themselves on Gary's shoulders and dragged him down. He tossed the ball to Sean Williams, who was hit immediately, tackled around the legs. Brody was close. He held his arms out for the ball, and Sean saw him.

The ball came bouncing toward him. And so did everybody else.

Brody caught it and ran, weaving his way through arms grabbing at his shirt. He was quick, hard to catch, one advantage of being smaller. Out of the corner of his eye, he spied Lance (the fast one) off to his right. Someone pulled his shirt. He was going to go down. Brody tossed the ball at Lance as he was tackled, his head hitting the ground. Just like in the cartoons, Brody saw stars. Tears filled his eyes and he moaned, rolling on the ground.

don't cry don't cry don't cry

Brody opened his eyes and saw Lance flying toward the west fence, a bunch of sixth graders trailing behind, none fast enough to catch him. He was going to score.

Brody picked himself up and cheered as Lance jinked past the last sixth grader in his way and slammed the ball against the chain link. Brody turned back toward the school and saw Debbie Wilson.

He froze for a second, unsure if he was actually seeing what he thought he was.

Debbie was smiling, and those big, beautiful brown eyes of hers were looking right at him.

Brody stole a quick glance behind himself to see if she was looking at someone else, but there was no one there, not close enough anyway. The guys were all surrounding Lance, slapping him on the back.

When he turned back toward Debbie, she tilted her head slightly, still staring right at him, and Brody was completely lost. Done for. Melted.

Brody smiled back, but his moment of bliss quickly faded as he spied Murf heading off the playground and toward the road.

In a second, Brody took it all in.

Mrs. Carlisle, who was supposed to be watching, wasn't.

Murf had his head down, and he was walking straight toward the street. And there was a car coming.

Brody ran.

Chapter 3
BRODY26

Brody slapped two bills on the bar and grabbed his field jacket from the back of his chair.

Another end to another useless day. And in a few hours, he'd start all over again. He wasn't sure how he'd gotten to this point, but here he was. A one-armed freak. A baby killer. A guy doomed to work a crappy job in a crappy town in the middle of crappy nowhere, with a past no one wanted to hear about and a future as bleak as a winter sky.

Things had looked bright when he first joined the Army—not drafted, thank you, but an all-American, true-blue volunteer who raised his right hand and took an oath, just like his dad and uncle before him. He'd serve, do his part for Lyndon Johnson and country, come home to a nation that would appreciate all the sacrifices he'd made, and make a new life.

"G'night, Brody."

"See ya, Jimmy," Brody replied to the bartender, nodding his head in silent appreciation to one of the few men who called him by name. Jimmy had served in Korea and still looked like the Marine he'd been all those years ago. His hair was still cropped close in a crew cut, and his arms could crush a man's head like a walnut (which was why there weren't any fights in Jimmy's bar, at least not ones that lasted long). Jimmy had firsthand experience coming home to a country that didn't care about what you'd done, didn't want to hear the details of what happened to you, and would rather ignore the whole unsightly mess of an undeclared war. Jimmy *understood*. To most others, the people on the street who stared at his pinned-up sleeve, Brody was a monster, a murderer who went across the ocean to brutalize helpless yellow people who had done nothing wrong.

They weren't so helpless, Brody had learned. Especially the ones who'd made sure he left his arm there, shredded to pieces in the mud, a personalized keepsake for the Viet Cong, suitable for mounting on the wall of one of their damned rat tunnels.

Nobody liked soldiers these days. Especially those pussies who never went over there, staying nice and safe in a classroom, listening to some punk spout off about Plato, or some other weird dead guy, using college to protect themselves from the ugly war across the sea. They called soldiers like him "baby killers."

Brody was in college, too, when the war started heating up. He enlisted, though, once he had his degree in hand, wanting to be a grunt like his father and uncle before him. They'd fought the Nazis and the Japs. He'd fought the NVA and their Cong buddies, in a very different kind of war. He'd done his duty, but everyone at home seemed to *hate him* for it. There was no getting around the fact that he'd been there, either. For one thing, he was missing his left arm, which practically screamed *Look! A Vietnam vet! He got what he deserved, goddamned cripple!* Because of that, he decided to wear his Army field jacket as often as he could. *That's right, I was there. That's right, I lost an arm. That's right, I killed people. Don't like it? That's right, screw you.*

Brody stepped into the night air and took a deep breath. The sky was clear, and the temps were supposed to plummet into the teens before morning. He gathered his coat closer with his right hand and began the walk to his apartment a few blocks away, his breath swirling into the darkness.

Returning from the battlefield wasn't like this for his father, bless his soul. He'd fought the Nazis for three long years, crawling from Sicily, through France, and into Germany itself. Came home with barely a scratch. And the country took care of him.

His uncle Clem had fought in the Pacific, a Marine. Survived Guadalcanal, Iwo Jima. Came home with a Purple Heart. And the country had taken care of him, too, right up to the moment they planted him in Arlington.

In Brody's case, the VA had patched up his stump of an arm, the Army gave him an Honorable, and let him walk out the door. Right into a world of shit. The country was different now. People like him were objects of scorn instead of returning heroes.

And maybe everyone was right.

He'd killed, with his rifle and his knife. More than once. And for what? Did North Vietnam represent the same threat as the Nazis and Japs? Brody didn't think so. Not anymore.

The snow crunched under his boots. He was halfway home but was being followed. Two, maybe three, behind him, about twenty yards back, getting closer. He resisted the urge to turn and confront them. He took another deep breath to clear his thoughts, wishing he'd stopped after his third on-the-rocks double. He slowed his pace slightly.

Let them come.

Maybe Nixon would fix everything. He sure seemed like a stand-up guy. He'd promised an honorable end to the war during the campaign, whatever that meant. Maybe he'd load up every B-52 they had and blow the North back to the Stone Age. That'd be honorable enough, because nobody would ever have to go back to that stinking place and come home with fewer appendages than when they left. Or not come home at all.

One of Brody's followers crossed the street, walking fast. The other two were right behind him now, maybe fifteen feet away. Once these two stopped him, forcing him to turn and face them, the street-crosser would come up from behind. Brody would be surrounded.

No use waiting anymore. He stopped and listened as the two gents behind him skidded to a halt. Brody didn't turn. He wanted them to make the first move.

Five seconds. Ten.

The guy who'd crossed the street wasn't sure what to do, hiding in the shadows and waiting for Brody to turn around.

Talking wasn't going to do much good, but Brody gave it a shot anyway. "Walk away."

One of the guys behind him laughed. "Say what?"

Brody turned. One, a black guy, tall and skinny, the other, a white guy a little more built, but Brody had them weightwise. They both had their hands in their jacket pockets. The street-crosser slipped on the ice halfway across the street and fell on his ass. Back turned, Brody heard him get up and step up on the sidewalk. If this was Chicago, Brody would be a little more worried, but this was Garland Trail, Nebraska, for cripessake. These guys were wannabes. Skinny, Muscles, and, behind him, Clumsy.

"I said walk away. You don't want to do this."

Skinny looked at Muscles, and Brody recognized his laugh. "And how you gonna stop us, soldier man?" Skinny said.

Soldier man. None of these guys had been to Nam. If they had, they might have backed off once they saw his sleeve, but no, he was just another baby killer. A cripple. An easy target. "Make your move," Brody said. Deep down, he wanted to say something about being able to take all three of them with one arm tied behind his back, but he figured they wouldn't appreciate the humor. He was too tired, anyway.

Skinny pointed a finger at him through his pocket. "Maybe I should just shoot your white ass."

"That isn't a gun. Your friend doesn't have one either." The ice crunched behind him. Brody tilted his head to the side. "And if your friend behind me gets any closer, he's going to regret it."

"All we want is your money." Muscles, this time. Brody could see he was nervous. Jumping a one-armed vet wasn't going to be as easy as he'd thought.

"Then come and take it, tough guy," Brody said. These three had done this before but were rattled. In the next few seconds, they'd either back off or make a move.

Brody watched Skinny's eyes shift to his partner, the one at his back. Brody sighed and readied himself. They weren't backing off.

Chapter 4

BRODY16

The president had been shot.

They'd announced it during class. One of the office aides came into his Algebra II class and whispered into the teacher's ear. Brody watched the blood drain from Ms. Walter's face and knew something terrible had happened.

Within the hour, rumors were running rampant. Reagan was fine; Reagan was dead; the VP had been shot, too; the secretary of defense, Weinberger, was dead as well; the Soviets had done it; the Sandinistas and the Cubans had done it; on and on. Brody was in study hall, and everyone seemed to have an opinion. A couple of kids were even glad, spouting some crap about how Reagan deserved what he got, he was going to start a war, blah blah blah. Brody figured their parents must've voted for Carter.

Brody sat with his regular group of friends—Kyle Hufford, Jason Beard, and Tim Kolak. Study hall (held in the cafeteria) was supposed to be a place where students could catch up on homework, but instead it was more of an opportunity to catch up on the latest gossip. For Brody, though, it was an hour of the day he relished, because he got to be close to Joan McNally. Joan had gone to junior high with Jason and every once in a while would come over and sit with them. Brody hoped today would be one of those "once in a while" times.

Mr. Hufford came in at the start of the hour (Kyle's dad—how it must suck to have a dad as a teacher) and let everyone know what the news was saying. The TV in the teachers' lounge was tuned to ABC, and Frank Reynolds was delivering the facts as best he could, first reporting Reagan had *not* been hit, then that he had been, then that James Brady was dead, then that he *wasn't* dead, but rather in critical condition.

The recent news was all pretty scary. Nothing like this had ever happened during his lifetime, and Brody wondered if he'd recall this day like people did who were his age when Kennedy was shot.

Joan was sitting one table over, facing in his direction. Brody tried not to stare but couldn't help himself. He'd noticed Joan in the halls at the beginning of the school year, and at first glance she'd taken his breath away. She was small, a little over five feet tall, with honey-blond hair that barely reached her shoulders. Her eyes were a light, warm brown, almost the same color as her hair. She wasn't drop-dead gorgeous, like Carla Franchetti, but was so cute Brody had a difficult time looking away.

"Dude, are you listening?"

Jason slapped his arm to get his attention, and Brody realized he'd been staring again.

"Yeah, I'm listening."

"Bullshit. I saw who you were looking at. What did I say?"

"You were talking about Reagan." Safe bet, because that's all anyone was talking about.

"Okay, so do *you* think the Russkies did it?"

"I don't think they'd be that stupid."

"No shit," Kyle agreed. "If we found out they tried to kill him, we'd nuke the living shit out of that place. So if it wasn't them, who?"

"Your dad said it was some guy named Hinckley." Brody glanced in Joan's direction. She was looking at him. He looked away quickly. "From Evergreen." His neck was warm.

"I know that's what he said, but do you think he was working for somebody? Like Oswald was working for the CIA or Castro or some shit like that?"

"I don't know, man," Brody said. He shifted his glance to Joan's table and noticed she wasn't there. Before he could look around the room for her, though, he felt Jason scoot over, making room on the bench for someone else.

"Hi, Jason."

Joan. She sat down right beside him, straddling the bench and facing Jason. God, she even smelled incredible, all warm and flowery. All Brody could see was the back of her head, but that hair of hers was only inches away. It was a strange feeling and hard to describe, but it felt like a low-voltage current flashed through his body, as if every nerve ending he had was saying, *Whoa! She's right there!* The feeling only lasted a second but still caused him to catch his breath. He tried to keep his eyes from wandering, but they had a mind of their own. She was so small, almost delicate in a way. She was wearing a concert T-shirt, probably the Journey one he'd seen her wear before, which ended at her button-up jeans, which hugged the curve of her—

Brody looked away, trying to keep cool, and caught Tim Kolak's eyes from across the table. Tim was smiling and did the *hubba-hubba* thing with his eyebrows. He'd seen Brody giving Joan the once-over, and Brody felt himself flush. They all knew he had a raging crush on Joan and loved to rib him about it. Kyle, Jason, and Tim all had girlfriends;

Brody Quail, 16-year-old sophomore at Forrest J. Gerber High School, didn't.

Brody had kissed a girl before (more than one, actually), but other than that, he was definitely not in the same "experience" league as his friends.

Joan had a boyfriend, too, which sucked. A junior. Wrestler. Brody didn't know his name, but he'd seen him with her before. He wasn't a small guy, either. Brody was crushing on a girl who had a boyfriend who could easily kick his ass.

"Isn't it scary?" Joan said. She swung her other leg over the bench and put her notebooks on the table in front of her. "Todd thinks it was the Russians who did it, because they're scared of Reagan."

Todd. That was the wrestler's name.

"Brody doesn't think so," Tim said. "Tell her, Brody."

Joan turned toward him, and for a moment, Brody was lost in her eyes, so big and bright. She wore just enough makeup to be pretty. Her lips were parted, ever so slightly, and Brody imagined how soft they would feel against his. There was that shock again, a rush running through his body.

"Oh yeah?" Joan asked. "You think Todd's wrong?"

Brody cleared his throat. "I don't think they'd dare try to assassinate the president of the United States." His voice actually cracked, like a little kid entering puberty. She held his glance, and Brody tried to look away but couldn't. He cleared his throat again. "I don't think they'd be that stupid." In a way, he'd just called Todd stupid, too, and that was awesome.

"Who do you think did it, then?" Joan asked.

"Kyle's dad said it was some guy from Evergreen." Brody's throat felt tight, and he was hot all over. His voice didn't crack this time, though, which was a relief. "I'm sure they'll figure it all out once they have a chance to question him."

He wanted to keep talking, to show Joan he was smarter than her big, bad wrestler dude, but just like that, she looked away and turned back toward Jason. "You've got Krichek for third period, right?" she asked.

"Yeah," Jason answered. "Why?"

"He said something about a test next Friday, but I didn't catch what chapters it was covering."

"Um, seven and eight. I think."

She grabbed one of her spiral notebooks and flipped it open. Brody watched her write the chapters down, and then he saw it.

His name.

At first, he didn't believe what he was seeing, but it was there. Drawn in balloon letters, at the top of the page, sandwiched between doodles.

B R O D Y

His name, not Todd's. His heart leapt into his throat.

Joan seemed to realize Brody had seen what she'd written and slammed the notebook closed. "Okay," she said, "thanks, Jason." She abruptly gathered her books and went back to her own table. The whole time Brody watched her, hoping she'd turn and look at him.

She didn't.

When he was sure none of his friends were paying attention, Brody scribbled a quick note, tore it from his spiral notebook, folded it quickly, and put it in his back pocket. The move was dumb, maybe even childish, but what the heck. If the opportunity presented itself, and he had the courage to give it to her—

Nah, Brody decided. *She'd think I was in fifth grade or something.* He'd throw it away when he got home.

After study hall ended, Brody chose to ditch his last class of the day and head home to watch the news about Reagan. As he walked across the parking lot, he felt giddy about what he'd seen written in Joan's notebook. His seeing it, though, had embarrassed her. She didn't look at him during the rest of study hall and left quickly with the bell. Strange, but it didn't change the fact that she had taken the time to doodle his name, in big, balloon letters even. She'd been thinking about him. Maybe as much as he'd been thinking about her?

Brody dug in his pocket for his car keys as he approached his old, beat-up '63 Impala. It had been his dad's when it was new and was handed down to Brody to serve as his first car. The discount light-blue paint job from 1976 was beginning to fade, and the rust around the fender wells and rocker panels was really taking hold. The once–bright red interior upholstery was ripped in a few places (hidden by cheap seat covers) and the carpet was pink in places where the sun had taken its toll. Topped off by a dent in the left rear fender, one missing hubcap, a windshield that was too pitted to see through when driving into the sun, and a steel plate covering a hole in the driver's side floor pan, Brody's Impala was a certifiable piece of shit. It was loud. It smelled like old plastic. It smoked. It was a rust bucket. But it was *his*.

No girl would ever swoon over a car like this. The guys driving the Berlinettas and Firebirds got all the attention.

He opened the door and threw his book bag on the passenger seat, doubting Joan would ever want to be seen in a car like this. If she ever agreed to go out with him and if he ever got around to asking her, that is.

No, who was he fooling? Tomorrow, she'd continue treating him like just another face in study hall. He didn't have a chance. He remembered the note, pulled it from his pocket, read it, crumpled it up, then tossed it on the front seat. "Jesus, Brody, what are you thinking?" he said to himself.

As he stepped into the car, a voice surprised him.

"Brody?"

He turned, and there she was.

"Joan?" She stood beside the fender dent, books in her arms. She glanced down at her feet for a moment, then looked up again, smiling.

"Hey."

"Hi." *Hi? Is that the best you can do?*

"Are you leaving early?" she asked.

"Um, yeah. I was going to—"

"Ditching, huh?"

He laughed a little. "Yeah. I wanted to go home and watch the news." He regretted the words as soon as they slipped from his mouth. *Go home and watch the news? Real cool, Brody. You sound forty years old.* "And I have Martinson for last period, so I figured I could either sit there and suffer though his crap, or go home a little early." *That's better.*

Joan nodded. "Hey, do you think you could give me a ride home?"

She usually gets a ride from her boyfr—Todd. From Todd. He was really beginning to dislike that name. "Sure, hop in."

As she stepped around the rear of the Impala toward the passenger door, Brody hopped in and tossed his book bag into the backseat.

Joan grabbed the door handle and tugged.

"It doesn't work from the outside," Brody yelled, leaning over and popping the lever. As he did so, he noticed the crumpled note sitting on the seat. He quickly grabbed it and stuffed it into his front pocket.

"Thanks," she said, placing her books between them on the bench seat and slamming her door shut. "I didn't feel like walking today."

Walking? Brody wanted to ask why she wasn't getting a ride home from Todd, like she usually did (at least that's what he thought), but held his tongue. "I don't mind," he said, fastening his lap belt and cinching it tight. She was leaving early, too, he realized. Ditching, just like he was. *A couple of rebels.*

He pumped the gas pedal and turned the key, silently praying the old girl would start and save him the embarrassment. With a cough, she did. Brody winced at the cloud of blue smoke in his rearview mirror, backed out of the parking space, then suddenly realized he had no idea where to go. "Um . . . where do you live?"

"I'm only a couple of blocks away, on Lincoln," she said. "Take the first left from Michigan, and I'm the third house on the left."

"Got it." He'd noticed Joan hadn't put her seat belt on. He really wanted to say something but wasn't about to come off sounding like a dork again. He pulled out of the parking lot and headed down Central toward Michigan, suddenly self-conscious about missing a shift or grinding the gears, which would be *very* uncool.

"I like your car," she said.

"Really?"

"Yeah, I do. I love old cars like this. Impala, right? '62?"

Brody couldn't believe what he was hearing. "Close. It's a '63. It was my dad's." A girl who he'd admired from afar for most of the school year was in his car, a car she *liked*, and was actually talking to him. She could've walked home, as her house really wasn't far away, but she'd asked *him* for a ride.

BRODY

He imagined the letters again, drawn with care in her notebook.

"How fast have you had it?" she asked, grabbing the metal dash with one hand and pulling one leg up underneath her, turning her body to face him.

"Not very. Maybe 80, 85." He glanced over, took in her bright eyes, her smile. "It really starts shaking at 75, so I'm kinda nervous about going any faster." Once again, he cringed at his own words. *God, I sound like an old man!*

She laughed, and Brody immediately figured she was laughing at him, but after a second or two, realized she wasn't. "Probably a good idea," she said. "My dad had an old car when he was a kid, and one of the tie rods snapped. He swerved into a ditch and rolled a few times."

"Holy crap."

"I know. He was lucky to get out alive. Oops."

"Oops?"

"You just passed Michigan."

Sure enough, he'd driven right by. *Dork!* "Sorry. I'll take Washington. Does it go through?"

"Yeah. That'll work."

It all seemed so surreal. Joan was here, in his car, and he was driving her home. She was just inches away, too. He tried to keep his eyes on the road but couldn't help stealing a glance or two; she was wearing sandals, and her toenails were painted the same color as her fingernails, black, like a punk rocker.

He would ask her about Todd when they got to her house, he decided. That was the right thing to do. If they were still together, then this was nothing more than a ride home. But if they weren't, then maybe this was the start of something more. He also decided to ask his dad what a tie rod was.

Even though Brody had driven down this road a hundred times, he failed to notice the red light.

Chapter 5
BRODY52

Joshua, Maine
Friday, October 25, 1974

The office clock chimed for the seventh time, and Brody pushed his chair away from his desk.

His dinner was mostly untouched. Eating wasn't a priority anymore, as dining alone was a constant reminder of what was missing in his life.

How many times had he sat across the table from Reba, enjoying a meal they'd both prepared, or even takeout Chinese food? Those were the good times, the happy moments between two people who'd found the puzzle piece that made their lives complete. Sometimes they would talk about their day, sharing little bits of information that only the other could care about and understand. Or they would sit silently, with no need to speak, because they were together.

He remembered when the kids were little and the dinner table was a chaotic jumble of voices and noises, all happy things from a more joyful time.

Memories. So warm in their ability to bring past into the present, and so cold and cruel when the promise of what was to come has been ripped apart, never to be experienced again in even little ways. There would be no grandchildren, no visits from grown kids with their spouses, no family gatherings at the holidays.

When Reba passed and his children viewed him through eyes clouded with uncertainty and disdain, those warm memories became cold as steel, tiny sharpened daggers that poked and prodded Brody every moment of every day. All that could have been, what *should* have been, was gone.

Brody was nothing more than a discarded puzzle piece now, lost under a table, never to be set in place. No one would search for him. And it didn't matter, for the rest of his puzzle was gone.

Tick. She lives.

Tick-tock. She dies.

Memories of that horrid night were fragmented, random snapshots of what he could recall and what he'd been told by others. He hadn't touched another drop since that night, not that it mattered now . . .

※

The bottle had taken control of him slowly. Each day, a little more. Each week, a few too many. He'd fall asleep at his desk, passed out from the Scotch, until Reba would drag him to bed in the early morning hours.

He had no reason to turn to the bottle; there was no undue stress in his life. Financially, they were more than comfortable, and his relationship with Reba was strong. They'd continued the successful business his father had started, grown it, nurtured it, and anticipated the day when their own children would take the reins, *if* it was what the kids wanted. A decade past, he and Reba decided to take the company public, and their accounts swelled with the windfall. He'd remained as chairman of the board, holding a majority of the company's stock.

Wealth can corrupt even the cleanest soul. God knows he'd seen it happen before to other couples, but not to him and Reba. Brody had never cheated, even though the opportunities presented themselves more than he'd care to remember. Some women were attracted to men with means. But no, he'd never faltered. And neither had she.

They loved each other.

But Brody also grew to love the bottle. At first, drinking was social, but he found he enjoyed the feeling of release alcohol provided, a way to relax and escape from his responsibilities. Insidious, it was. A creeping kudzu of addiction, noticed but ignored until the growth was too substantial to cut away. On the night Reba was killed, his vice had spread its tendrils throughout his house and his family, numbing him to the point of uselessness and strangling his ability to realize how far he'd fallen.

He'd become an alcoholic. Reba knew it, and so did his kids. But Brody refused to see the truth.

Until he saw Reba's lifeless body.

A gunshot to her head and three to her chest. A violent end to an unmerciful ravaging.

They'd broken in at two in the morning. A botched robbery, the police surmised. Reba confronted them, fought back, and was raped, then killed. Brody didn't wake until it was almost over. He was drunk, in his office. Passed out.

Brody walked around the corner of his desk. The house was dark now, still and quiet. He didn't need any lights, though, as he knew the doors and hallways of their home as well as he knew his own face. He stepped down the hallway to the top of the stairs, the moonlight seeping in through the one window he *hadn't* covered, placed high in the expansive entryway foyer. The banister curved away from him, descending toward the front door.

They'd come up these same stairs, passed right by his office, and entered their bedroom. Brody turned and looked down the long hallway toward the closed door at the far end, cloaked in shadow. He hadn't slept in that room since, instead spending his nights in the guestroom or on one of the couches downstairs.

She'd died in that room. Violated and murdered, while he sat slumped in his desk chair.

The struggle had woken him. He'd sat up, still wrapped in a boozy fog, not knowing what had startled him awake. Felix was out of the house, so Brody knew it couldn't be him.

Then he heard Reba's cries, quiet but frantic, pressing through his closed office door.

Tick.

And the first gunshot. He'd been around weapons his whole life and knew exactly what he'd just heard.

Tick-tock.

At that moment, she was gone, but Brody wouldn't know that until much later. The coroner said the first shot was to the head.

He'd fumbled in his desk for the gun, cradling it in his lap while he searched the drawer for the box of cartridges. The room was spinning, his hands unsteady. He found the box, dropped it on the floor.

bang bang bang

Three more shots in quick succession.

He sat bolt upright, the room spinning. The gun slid from his lap and bounced underneath his chair. He leaned forward, tore at the cartridge box with shaking hands, ripped the cardboard packaging away.

He upended the box, dumping the shells on the carpet. He grabbed a handful. Reached for the gun.

Then he heard them. Heavy footsteps, thudding past his office door. More than one person. They were running away.

He pushed the cylinder open with his thumb, placed one, then two shells in their chambers as he rose from his chair. His legs were unsteady, the booze still wreaking havoc with his sense of balance.

The third shell dropped from his fingers. Then the fourth slipped away. He'd been trained to load a weapon by touch alone, quickly, in complete darkness. Sober. What should have been muscle memory was now a mishmash of confused, jerky motions.

He pulled the door open and ran from his office, still trying to place another shell in the chamber. It, too, dropped. All the shells in his hand fell to the wooden floor, bouncing at his feet.

He slapped the cylinder closed as he neared the top of the stairs and saw them racing down the steps, two at a time, heading for the front door.

He yelled at them to stop.

The police report said they found him at the foot of the stairs, unconscious, gun still in his hand. He'd fallen, drunken legs failing him when he needed them most.

He'd woken two days later in the hospital, confused. His children were there, but their eyes were already hooded with the knowledge of what had happened. They'd read the police report.

His blood alcohol level was off the charts when he was brought in. A pathetic man in a drunken stupor, too useless to do what a man was supposed to do: protect his home and his wife.

The killers had been in the house for nearly two hours. Two hours while he slept away, two hours while they'd violated his dear Reba, two hours while she endured the ultimate indignity, knowing her husband was passed out in his office, right down the hall. Knowing he wouldn't wake, but praying he would.

She'd been bound and gagged for most of the ordeal. The police believed the gag came loose, and that's when the killers had decided they'd had their fill of her.

His children would never forgive him.

One of them shall pass.

And neither would he.

⚔

Brody stepped down the stairs and approached the front door, his tortured soul squirming within a body that was, even now, whispering to him, driven by a jealous thirst. *Take a drink,* it said. *Just one. Make the pain go away.*

He'd told Felix to remove all the liquor from the house, or at least he thought he had. It was still there, lining the wet bar in the study, along with a half-empty bottle of eighteen-year-old Scotch still tucked in his desk drawer.

Whispering.

He stood at the door, waiting.

There would be a knock soon.

As if on cue, Brody saw the glow of headlights out front. He pulled back the side curtain, peeked outside. A patrol cruiser.

There would be two uniformed officers. They would be delivering news. Terrible news.

One of them shall pass.

A knock.

Brody took a deep breath and opened the door.

"Mr. Quail? Brody Quail?" one of the officers asked.

"Yes, officer," Brody replied, steeling himself for what he was about to hear.

"I'm sorry to have to tell you this, sir, but it's your son. Raymond."

He's dead. Died in a car accident.

"What's wrong?"

"We were notified earlier this evening that your son was severely injured in an automobile accident, sir. And I'm sorry to have to tell you this, but—"

"He's dead, isn't he."

"Yes, sir. I'm sorry."

"He was alone."

"Uh . . . yes, sir. He was the only occupant in the vehicle."

Brody nodded, surprised that the pain and shock he should be feeling simply wasn't there.

At that moment, the day ended for fifty-two-year-old Brody Quail.

Chapter 6
BRODY10

Culver, Ohio
Thursday, May 15, 1975

"Murf!" Brody screamed, watching his brother step off the curb and into the street.

Brody ran as fast as he could, weaving his way through the playground toward the side of the school building.

The car was still coming. Brody saw the driver leaning toward the passenger seat, eyes off the road, concentrating instead on whatever lay on the seat beside him instead of the distracted first grader wandering out into his path.

"Murf! Murphy! Look out!" His kid brother wasn't paying attention, wasn't listening.

Jesus don't let this happen don't let this happen don't let

Brody was going to watch his brother die, right in front of him, just feet away.

shouldn't have yelled at him shouldn't have yelled at

Others on the playground stopped what they were doing, attracted by Brody's shouting, watching the scene playing out on the street where the buses park.

Brody wouldn't be the only one forced to live with what he was about to see. They all would. A shared nightmare that would never fade completely, even years from now. Everyone would remember the day they saw six-year-old Murphy Quail disappear beneath the wheels of a tan '73 Oldsmobile. They would remember the sound. And what was left in the road.

"Murf!"

Murf stopped in the middle of the street, his feet square on the yellow line, and turned toward the approaching car. In an instant, he realized where he was, and what was about to happen. He froze.

Brody was fifteen feet away, cutting his glance from his brother, to the car, to his brother, judging the distance, calculating. The driver was sitting up now, his eyes wide, and his mouth forming a perfect O. Hitting the brakes wouldn't make a difference.

get him get him get him

The world seemed to slow down, the air thickening.

Brody was in the street, seeing the blur of the car out of the corner of his eye, hearing its engine, the whoosh of air as it drew close. His body recoiled, his mind screaming at him to stop. He hesitated, the natural instinct for self-preservation kicking in.

But, no. Brody couldn't let this happen. He had to try. Murf was his little brother, and he was supposed to protect him, keep him from danger. He could knock Murf out of the way, push him to safety. Brody could sacrifice himself. His little brother was a pain, but Brody would die for him. A thousand times over.

grab him grab

Brody willed his legs to move, his arms to grasp.

He slammed into his brother, running full speed, hugged him, and dove.

Bright sunlight glinting off chrome glared at him from the car's bumper. So close. Had he reached out, he could've touched it, felt the smooth, cold steel right before it shattered his hand, then his body, and his life.

He closed his eyes and wondered what it would feel like to fall beneath the car's tires, feel its weight rolling over him. Would he live long enough to hear his ribs splinter or his legs snap? They weren't going to make it. He should've knocked Murf out of the way. Now they would both die.

Brody waited for the impact. Waited for the pain.

There was screaming, squealing. A pain in his side.

✕

He lay still, curled into a ball, eyes clenched tightly.

People were yelling, coming closer. He heard them running, shoes scuffing against the road.

Murf wasn't in his arms. Brody experienced a flicker of hope. Maybe he'd knocked Murf clear. Maybe he'd saved him.

He heard Mrs. Carlisle scream. Brody could only imagine what she was seeing.

But he didn't feel any pain. He'd read that injured people didn't feel anything right away, even if their guts were spilling out of their bellies. It was called being in shock, if he remembered correctly.

Maybe he was in shock.

"Jesus Christ, kid! Are you okay?"

Brody slowly opened his eyes and looked up into a round face staring down at him. The driver. Same bald head and wide eyes.

There were other faces, too. Kids, surrounding him. Then Rich. Gary.

"You okay, Brody?" Rich asked.

"Murf?" Brody sat up, realizing he was unhurt. Alive. "Murf!" He heard his brother crying.

"Mrs. Carlisle's got him, dude," Rich said. "He's okay."

Brody pushed through the crowd and saw Mrs. Carlisle holding Murphy in her arms, tears streaming down her face. She was stroking his hair, saying it was all her fault.

He'd done it. Somehow, he'd done it. Murf was okay.

"They ran right out in front of me," the driver said, loud enough for everyone to hear. "Shouldn't be playing so close to the street like that."

Brody wheeled, the heat rising in his face. He wanted to scream at the man, tell him he was a stupid jerk for not paying attention. But he didn't. The man was an adult, and he couldn't talk to him like that no matter how mad he might be. Instead, he unclenched his fists and went to his brother.

He'd never seen Mrs. Carlisle cry before, and it upset him. Teachers weren't supposed to cry. She set Murf down and pulled a tissue from her pocket. "Murphy," she said, "don't you ever, *ever* go out in the street like that again."

Murphy looked down, nodded his head. "Yes, ma'am."

"Are you okay, Brody? Are you hurt?" Mrs. Carlisle asked.

Other than a dull ache in his side, which he figured came from hitting the ground, Brody felt fine. "Yes, ma'am. I'm okay."

Brody was shocked when Mrs. Carlisle wrapped her arms around him and hugged. He felt her tears on his cheek and noticed she smelled a little like his mother. Maybe they used the same shampoo.

She stood, smoothed her skirt, and turned into a teacher again. "Everyone back to the playground. Come on now, let's go," she ordered, waving her arms to get everyone moving.

Brody put his hand on Murphy's shoulder. "Murf, you okay?"

"I'm sorry, Bowdy," Murphy said, using his little-kid voice, which usually meant he was upset and scared.

Brody hugged him. "It's okay, Murf. It's okay."

"Did the car hit you?" he asked.

"No," Brody said. "It missed us both." He tousled his brother's hair. "We were lucky."

"Dude, you saved his life." Rich was speaking. "That was awesome."

"You three, back to the school. Now." Mrs. Carlisle, being a teacher again. "Go on. I'll be there in a minute."

Brody watched her fix her gaze on the driver, who was still mumbling about kids playing in the street.

"I'm going to have a few words with that gentleman first," she said, her voice a little different from what Brody was used to hearing. *She's going to rip him a new one,* as his dad liked to say.

⚹

"Really, Mom, it's okay. It wasn't that bad."

Brody's mother had received a call from the school and was frantic by the time he and Murf had returned home. She'd spent the first ten minutes after they'd walked through the door crying and hugging them both. Then, just like Mrs. Carlisle had transformed back into a teacher, his mom turned back into their mother.

"You're supposed to watch him, Brody."

I was watching him, just not enough. "I know, Mom."

"And you, Murphy Joseph Quail, are old enough to know better than to play in the street. You're not a baby anymore. You could've been hurt, or killed."

"Yes, Mommy."

She wiped her eyes with the heel of her hand and stood. "Okay, then. Now go wash up for dinner."

"Yes, ma'am," Brody said and headed upstairs to the bathroom, stopping to put his schoolbooks in his room. He noticed his mom had made his bed, like she always did, and thrown his dirty clothes in his hamper, like she always did.

Brody plopped his books on his bed and noticed something lying on the floor. It was a stupid little thing, but he'd had it for as long as he could remember: the last surviving piece of a plastic dinosaur set he'd gotten when he was little. This one was bright yellow, a Tyrannosaurus rex. (It said so on the tail, right next to "Made in Taiwan.") He picked the toy up and placed it on his shelf, right next to his 1/48-scale model of a World War II Grumman Avenger torpedo bomber. He didn't play with dinosaurs anymore (he was too old for that now), but he couldn't seem to let the little yellow T. rex go.

"Brody! Hurry up—dinner's ready," his mom called from downstairs.

"Coming," he replied, deciding to skip washing his hands. He was starving.

At that moment, the day ended for ten-year-old Brody Quail.

Chapter 7
BRODY26

Just as Brody expected, the guy behind him, Clumsy, moved first.

Brody waited, counted the man's steps, then struck to the rear with his elbow, smashing it home in the center of Clumsy's face with a satisfying crunch.

As the man collapsed to the sidewalk, a gurgling shout of pain pouring through the fingers covering his broken nose, Brody turned to meet Skinny, the second of the three thugs to lunge at him.

Brody shifted his weight, let Skinny get just close enough, then grabbed a handful of his hair and spun, causing the man to lose his balance. Brody took his legs out with a sweeping kick, then drove the man's head into the sidewalk, slamming his forehead against cement. He fought the urge to lift the man's head and continue to bash it into the sidewalk, but he didn't want to kill him. Once would be enough. He wouldn't be getting up anytime soon.

Muscles had taken a few steps but now halted his advance. "You're crazy, man! You killed him!"

"He's fine. He'll have a headache, but no, I didn't kill him." Brody took a step forward and watched Muscles's eyes grow larger. "But you, on the other hand, I might."

Muscles held his hands out, took another step back, and nearly tripped over his own feet. "It's cool, man, it's cool."

Brody lunged and laughed as Muscles *did* trip, falling on his butt and scrambling to get away. The man took off down the street, leaving his friends moaning and bloodied on the sidewalk as he disappeared into the shadows.

Yeah. That's what I thought.

Brody looked up and down the street. He was alone, and as far as he could tell, no one had seen what had happened, nor was anyone watching now. The man with the broken nose was lying on his side, still cradling his face in bloodied hands. He was bigger than Brody had figured, his gut poking out from the bottom of his shirt. Not much of a fighter, though. One shot to the nose, and he'd gone down like a little girl.

Brody stepped closer and poked the guy's belly with his boot. "Get up, fat man. Get your ass out of here." Now that he'd had a good look at him, Fat Man seemed an appropriate name.

"F-f-fuck you," Fat Man said, little droplets of blood spraying from his lips.

Brody had been in and out of jail recently, usually because he had trouble keeping his temper under control. His anger had gotten the best of him many times since he came home from Nam, but he'd been trying hard to keep it in check. He'd walked away from a few fights, swallowing his pride.

Now would not be one of those times.

These assholes had started it. He'd given them the opportunity to walk away, but they'd pressed anyway. And this guy was pissing him off.

Brody kicked the man in the face, hard enough to send him to la-la land, and added two more to his flabby midsection. He wouldn't be getting up anytime soon either.

Again, Brody checked the street. Nothing.

He checked the man's pockets, grabbed his wallet, and stuffed the cash into his jacket. There wasn't much, but every dollar helped. He did the same to Skinny, who was still facedown, motionless. He was breathing, which was a relief. Brody rolled him onto his side and made sure his mouth was clear in case he vomited.

This punk didn't deserve to die. He'd gotten the beating he deserved, though, and would lose his money because of it. Maybe he'd think twice next time before trying to jump someone who appeared to be an easy target.

Brody tossed both of the wallets into a nearby trash can and resumed his walk toward his apartment.

As he rounded the corner, though, his senses perked up once again.

He was being watched.

Brody stopped, turned slowly, and peered into the shadows. He couldn't see anyone, but the feeling remained. Someone's eyes were on him. Maybe Muscles had gotten some of his bravado back and wanted another crack at the one-armed cripple. Maybe he'd have a weapon this time.

Brody moved his eyes slowly, concentrating on his peripheral vision, where motion was easier to discern at night.

He looked left, right, stopping every ten feet or so to stare, checking the edges of his sight picture. Seeing nothing. The feeling was strong, though. Too real to ignore.

Brody decided to walk past his apartment. If it was Muscles, he definitely didn't want the man (or his friends once they recovered, for that matter) to know where he lived. That could lead to a visit in the middle of the night, when Brody wouldn't have the advantage. If they came to see him again, they wouldn't rely on their fists. They'd have bats. Knives. Guns.

Brody walked past his building without giving the place a second glance. He would take a left at the next street and double back around to catch his pursuer.

And it *was* a pursuer. He was still there, just out of sight. Brody's phantom companion must have seen him stop and look earlier, so Brody avoided the urge to do it again. Better to let the guy think Brody had decided everything was fine. The one-armed cripple was walking home, no worries now, keep following.

As Brody approached the corner, the feeling became electric, a sense of dread washing over his body. The follower was close now. Brody turned.

At first, he was surprised there wasn't someone standing directly behind him. He *was* there, though, a half block away, silhouetted in relief from the glare of a streetlight at his back.

Just standing there.

Brody could make out no details from this distance, but it wasn't Muscles. Nor was it either of his companions. This person was taller, more sturdy in build, and stood with an air of confidence the people who had attacked him earlier were lacking.

Brody squinted, trying to see his face, his clothes, but all he saw was a dark cutout of a man, a shadow in the road. Perfectly still.

Brody couldn't describe what he felt, other than an overwhelming sense that he was seeing someone—some *thing*—that didn't belong here, as if this figure had stepped through a door that was supposed to remain closed.

He felt confusion. Dread. And for the first time in a long time, fear.

"Hey," Brody yelled, his challenge echoing down the shadowy street.

He received no response. The figure remained planted in place, motionless.

"I said *hey*," Brody shouted, immediately regretting how loud he was. The last thing he wanted to do was wake someone who would peek out their windows, call the cops, and ensure he'd have another brush with the police. A description of a one-armed man in an Army field jacket would lead them directly to his door.

Brody decided to confront the man, whoever it was. Brody walked toward the figure, fighting the crackle of nervous dread he felt with each step. He hadn't been afraid to confront the three men following him—he'd faced much worse in the war—but something was wrong here. Terribly wrong. He had to find out who this person was.

Brody stopped in his tracks when the person raised his arm. Brody crouched, took a few quick steps toward a building, immediately wanting to find some sort of shelter. What he initially thought was a weapon being aimed at him, however, was not.

The man was pointing. Arm raised, index finger pointing beyond Brody, as if gesturing for him to look.

Brody did. And saw nothing. He turned back toward the figure quickly, not liking the feeling of taking his eyes off the silhouette, and gasped.

The figure was much closer now. Too close to have walked or run the distance, as if he'd simply moved in a flash of time from one point to another. But the most troubling aspect was how the figure appeared. He was directly under a streetlight now, bathed in its yellow glow, but the figure remained dark as night. No detail. Just a shadow.

It couldn't be.

Brody wondered if his eyes were playing tricks on him, until the figure moved again.

Brody wasn't about to turn away, not after the man had moved so quickly the last time.

But he wanted to. The figure wasn't just pointing; he was gesturing as if he wanted Brody to move in that direction. To keep going.

"What do you want?" Brody asked.

The figure gestured more forcefully this time, then blinked out of existence.

Seconds later, Brody spied the figure again, much farther away down the street, appearing out of nowhere. Then in a flash, he was gone once again.

Brody's heart thudded away in his chest. What he'd just seen couldn't be real. If he'd been an addict, he could blame it on a bad flashback, but he'd never taken the hard stuff.

Brody waited for the figure to return, but there was only the silent street before him, buildings partially visible in the spotty glow of streetlamps, disappearing into shadows. Nothing more.

The feeling of being watched was gone now. He was truly alone.

He started to walk back toward his apartment building, then stopped.

The figure had wanted him to go the other way, to continue down the street. He didn't know why, but Brody felt the need to do just that. He turned, took three steps—

And at that moment, the night came to a close for twenty-six-year-old Brody Quail.

Chapter 8
BRODY16

They entered the intersection, and Brody saw the other vehicle speeding toward them. In a split second, Brody took it all in, and his instincts took over.

His feet mashed the clutch and the brake pedal, and he squeezed the hard plastic steering wheel in a death grip. Every muscle in his body tensed, his bones sheathed within a weave of iron bands.

Tick.

Brody watched the smile fade from Joan's face as she realized something was wrong. She was turned away from the approaching truck and would never see the two-ton mass of motorized steel that would plow directly into her door.

Brody's last thought before impact was that he should've told Joan to put on her seat belt.

Tock.

X

Blackness.

Floating, in a place with no sound, no sensation.

Brody was aware, but unable to speak, to move. He couldn't feel anything, or even tell if he was breathing.

Flashes.

The screech of rubber against asphalt. The blare of a horn, for just a second, then abruptly silenced.

Flashes.

The impact. Violent, so loud. Metal against metal, a terrible screeching noise as steel warped and bent, failing, collapsing inward. Glass shattering.

Flashes.

Whipped around. His head striking something hard, then breaking through. A weight slamming into his side. Unbearably soft, unbearably heavy. A sickening realization: *Joan.*

Flashes.

The smell of gasoline, strong and pungent.

Flashes.

The sound of voices. Frantic. Screaming. The smell of

Flashes.

smoke. Heat against his face.

Hands gripping, pulling.

The wail of sirens.

He could feel his arms, his legs. His chest was moving, drawing breath. Pain, in his side and his head. A throbbing, piercing pain, building in intensity. He squirmed, tried to pull away from the agony, to escape.

And Joan . . .

Brody opened his eyes.

※

A bird above, motionless in the sky. The air was still, thick. Quiet, eerily so. Brody moved his head, expecting a bolt of pain, but none came.

He was lying on his back in the road. The asphalt was rough against his hands as he pushed himself up to a sitting position. There were people around him, crouching, looking down at him.

Not moving. Their eyes, wet with life, were sightless, looking straight at him, but seeing nothing. They didn't blink. Not once.

Brody looked at his hands, covered in blood. He was bathed in it, from head to toe. He felt no pain, though.

He looked up into the sky again, at the bird.

It hung there, as if suspended by unseen strings, a child's plaything.

Brody stood, and took in the scene around him. There was an ambulance, a fire truck, a cloud of black smoke coming from his—

Burning. His car, twisted and broken, engulfed in flames.

Flames that were as motionless as the bird, producing a column of smoke that filled the air. Not moving.

Brody was living within a three-dimensional snapshot, a Polaroid moment of a terrible accident. His accident.

He *felt* alive, but this couldn't be.

Then it hit him.

I'm dead.

He must've died in the crash, and now he was . . . a *spirit*?

Brody stood and took a few tentative steps toward a fireman who was midstride in the road, dragging a hose toward his car. One of his boots was off the road, and the other was barely touching the asphalt.

He's running. Was running. *Is* running.

Brody reached out, touched the rough fabric of the fireman's turnout coat.

The fabric was real, as real as the bloody smear Brody's fingers left behind on the man's shoulder.

Brody looked at his car again and could feel the heat of the fire against his face. The flames were oddly transparent, orange and white swirls suspended in midair. He stepped toward the wreck, expecting to see his body in the front seat, twisted and blackened by the flames.

And see Joan's body in there as well.

Brody spun around, looking for her. If *he'd* died in the wreck, then there was no way Joan could possibly have survived. The truck had slammed directly into the passenger door. Into her.

If she were dead, she would be here, too, right?

All around him, though, there was nothing but stillness, a diorama. Joan was nowhere to be seen. He so wanted to see her wandering around, confused and scared as he was. If he was going to be stuck here forever, then at least he could spend eternity with her.

Brody stepped closer to the car, shielding his face from the heat. Within the snapshot of a swirling inferno, Brody saw something in the front seat, pressed against the crooked steering wheel. A body. A torso. A head. Charred, and dripping, and still. Lips pulled back, revealing white teeth, grinning in a sickening death rictus.

Hands, gripping, pulling.

Only one body. Small.

They pulled me out before it started burning.

Joan was still in the car. What was left of her.

Brody fell to his knees, raised his face to the sky, and screamed.

At that moment, the day ended for sixteen-year-old Brody Quail, while a block away, a dark figure appeared, then blinked away.

PART II
BREAK

Chapter 9
BRODY52

Joshua, Maine
Friday, October 25, 1974

The sun was on its way down, right on schedule.

He couldn't recall the last time he'd actually watched the sun set. Those were moments best shared with someone else. Now the orange glow behind drawn blinds marked nothing more than the end of one more day of pain.

She'd have hated what he was becoming. A recluse. Shut off from the world, hiding behind shuttered windows, afraid to see the sun, feel the warmth against his face.

Let the outside in, Brody, she'd say.

He'd allowed the outside in once, while he was passed out in this very office. Failed to prevent the horror from slipping through their front door and into their bedroom. A creeping evil that had torn his very heart from his chest.

Brody shuddered at the memory.

He stared at his office walls, adorned with pictures and awards gathered during their life together. In another time, he would gaze upon the mementos and lose himself in the memories.

Now they stared at him through a thin layer of dust. Scorned him. Pitied him.

He opened his desk drawer, removed his revolver. Another part of a past life, cold machined steel, unfeeling.

"I'm so sorry, Reba," Brody said.

He imagined putting the barrel under his chin, squeezing the trigger. When he'd been a cop, he'd seen what happened to someone after putting a .357 round into their head. Never pretty.

But he didn't care.

He didn't care about anything now.

Let the outside in, Brody.

She'd hung the curtains in his office, and he couldn't help but think how upset she would be if he splattered his brains all over them.

He tossed the gun back in the drawer and slammed it shut, the sound unbearably loud. If he changed his mind, the gun would be there waiting for him.

He wished the fall had killed him that night, as he fumbled with the pistol at the top of the stairs, watching his wife's killers escape. Why couldn't he have broken his neck? His death would have been merciful, sparing him from the life he was forced to endure now. Without her.

Brody sat at his desk for the longest time, eyes closed, listening to the ticking of his office clock. Time marching forward, unstoppable, unforgiving.

Tick. She lives.

Tick-tock. She dies.

His wife, gone. His kids, well . . . Brody concluded he'd be lucky if he ever got to see—

one shall pass

—any of them again. They'd read the police reports from that horrible night. Seen what his blood alcohol level had been. They knew their mother had been murdered while their father sat in his office, numbed by Scotch.

Brody leaned against the cool leather of his office chair and sighed. He'd already accepted the guilt, internalized it, suffered, and managed to keep the sour bile of his drunken failure from rising up and choking him to death. But here he sat, in an office full of shadows.

He could get up. Open the blinds. Let the next day's sunlight stream in and light the path toward a new life. He could call his children, apologize for what he'd allowed to happen. At least try to make amends.

one shall pass

Something wasn't right. Brody opened his eyes and glanced at the clock, still ticking away. He'd been sitting here for . . . He wasn't sure how long it'd been. But it was after six o'clock. Felix usually came up to his office before six, bringing something to eat. Felix normally didn't deviate from his schedule and Brody wondered if something might be wrong.

Brody pushed his chair back and stood, but before he could step toward the door, he felt something else was wrong. Terribly so. Not with Felix exactly, but something closer, more dear to him. For a moment, he considered grabbing the revolver from the drawer but decided against it. He didn't sense danger, per se, but rather an unsettled feeling he couldn't quite place.

Brody left his office and walked down the hall, knowing that directly behind him, in the shadows, was the bedroom where his wife was murdered. He walked to the top of the stairs. Listened. The house was quiet.

"Felix?" he called. He waited for a few seconds. No response. *That's odd.* "Felix, are you down there?" Again, no answer.

Brody stepped down the curving staircase toward the marble-floored entryway, looking over the banister into the living room, which was lit by a small table lamp in the corner. Felix was a stickler for turning lights off when there was no one in the room but would always leave a few lights on until he retired for the evening. Everything appeared normal, but Brody still felt as if something was not quite right.

Brody walked toward the back of the house, toward the kitchen. The lights were on, he saw, and he could smell food cooking, or more likely being warmed up. *Roast again, from last night.* "Felix?"

As Brody entered the kitchen, he saw Felix standing by the stove, his back to his employer, working with something at the counter. "There you are," Brody said. "Didn't you hear me calling?" Felix didn't move a muscle, seemingly unaware of Brody's presence.

"Felix?" Louder. "Felix?"

Brody stepped closer, and Felix remained as still as a statue. Brody stood directly behind him and placed his hand on Felix's shoulder. "Felix, are you okay?"

Felix was staring down at the counter, where he was making a plate of leftover roast, the remainders of last night's dinner—

I have your evening meal, sir. I thought you might want to take it in here instead of the dining room.

—that he was probably going to carry upstairs to the office.

Felix's eyes were open, unblinking, sightless. Brody wondered if Felix was even breathing. The butler seemed to be nothing more than a mannequin, a wax figure placed in the kitchen. Brody stepped back, confused.

There was steam rising from the plate of food . . . but it *wasn't*. A small white wisp rose from the roast and, like Felix, sat motionless, suspended in midair.

I'm dreaming, Brody mused. He was surely asleep in his office right now, head down on his desk, and this was nothing more than the product of a tired mind.

A likely explanation until the steam twisted and Felix moved.

Brody watched as Felix noticed his presence from the corner of his eye. "Oh, good evening, Mr. Quail," Felix said, placing his palm over his heart. "You startled me. I didn't hear you come into the kitchen."

Not a dream.

"I was calling for you, Felix."

"Sir?"

"I called your name, more than once. From right here," Brody said, motioning at the floor with open hands.

Felix scrunched his brow. "Hmph," he said. "My apologies, sir. I must've been too preoccupied with dinner." He picked up the plate of food. "I assume you'll be taking this in your office?"

Brody didn't respond right away, still trying to comprehend what he'd witnessed.

"Unless you'd rather eat in the dining room this evening, sir?"

I knew he'd say that. "No, Felix. Thank you," Brody said. "I'm not terribly hungry."

Felix frowned ever so slightly as he placed the plate back on the counter. "If you'd like something other than the roast from last evening, I could—"

Brody shook his head. "No, Felix, this is fine." He stared into Felix's gray eyes, full of life now, normal. "Please. I'll take a few bites later. And don't worry about cleaning up," he added, knowing he wasn't going to touch the food. "I can take care of it myself."

"Very well, sir. Unless you require anything else, I will retire for the evening."

Brody nodded. After Felix wiped his hands on a dish towel, Brody watched him disappear down the hall toward the south wing of the house, where his quarters were. Brody stared after him for the longest time, wondering what had just happened. Time seemed to have stopped, and only he was aware of it.

But that's ridiculous. Things like that don't really happen.

one shall pass

Brody glanced at his watch, the unsettled feeling much worse than before. It was nearly six thirty.

Seven. Something will happen at seven.

Brody was drawn toward the front door, why, he wasn't sure, but felt as if he needed to see who was—

He jumped at the sound of knocking. Three sharp raps. Again, he looked at his watch. *No, this isn't right. Not right.*

Three more knocks at the front door. Brody could see the glow of headlights through the curtains outside. He stepped to the front door.

There would be two uniformed officers. They would be delivering news. Terrible news. Brody opened the door.

"Mr. Quail? Brody Quail?" one of the officers asked.

"Yes, officer," Brody replied.

"I'm sorry to have to tell you this, sir, but it's your son. Raymond."

"Raymond?" Brody said, knowing what he was about to hear. His son Raymond was dead.

"Um . . . Yes, sir. We were notified earlier this evening that your son was severely injured in an automobile accident, sir. And I'm sorry to have to tell you this, but—"

"He's dead."

"Yes, sir," the officer said, glancing down at his feet. "I'm sorry."

"He was alone," Brody said, a statement rather than a question. "No one else was hurt."

"Yes, sir," the officer said, seemingly not surprised that Brody had predicted what he was about to say. "He was the only occupant in the vehicle."

The pain and shock Brody should be feeling simply weren't there. His son was dead, the little boy he used to bounce on his knee, but all he felt was the same nagging churn in the pit of his stomach that he'd been feeling before he came downstairs. "Thank you, officers," Brody said. "I know this is tough. I've had to do it myself before."

"You were a cop?" the other officer asked.

"A long time ago," Brody said. He'd had to deliver similar news before (as a cop, he must've, right?) but for the life of him couldn't recall any details. "Thank you," Brody repeated, signaling to the officers that they could leave. Their duty was done.

As the officers turned and he swung the door shut, Brody heard footsteps upstairs, someone running. Then the day ended for fifty-two-year-old Brody Quail.

Chapter 10
BRODY10

Culver, Ohio
Thursday, May 15, 1975

Afternoon recess wasn't very long, but it was his favorite.

John Bullard, one of the sixth graders, was tossing a football from hand to hand, the rest of his team lining up behind.

Rich Gable was the de facto leader of Brody's team. He was bigger than any of the fifth-grade boys and the most athletic. Everyone huddled around Rich, forming a circle just like the NFL teams did on Sunday, with Rich down on one knee.

"Pass it quick and keep it away from Bullard," Rich said. "Try to get it to me, Gary, or Lance. Okay, ready, break!" Everyone clapped their hands at the last word and spread out to receive the kick.

Brody loved playing this game, but the *best* thing about it was the fact that the girls liked to watch. Brody glanced back toward the school and saw them assembled there, all the sixth-grade girls, along with the girls from his class, sitting Indian-style on the grass and trying to look disinterested. Debbie Wilson was there, too. God, she was pretty. Brody imagined himself getting the ball and crashing through the sixth graders right in front of her, heading toward the fence and scoring a touchdown. A hero for a day.

A tug on his arm. "Brody?" His little brother, Murphy. A first grader.

"Not now, Murf."

"Can I play?"

"Scram, Murf. Get off the field."

"I wanna play, too."

Brody took his brother by the arm. "Not yet, okay? You'd get squished."

squished

"Go over there and watch. Just stay out of the way," Brody said and watched the smile fade from Murf's face.

"Mom says you have to play with me."

"Not *now*, Murf."

"Ready?" Bullard called, getting ready to punt the ball to their side.

"Hey, Quail! Get your brother out of here." That was Rich, staring at him. So was everyone else. Brody felt the heat rise up the back of his neck.

"Get off the field, Murf, *now*. Go watch."

"I'm gonna tell Mom," Murf said as he turned and ran back to the playground.

Gonna tell Mom. Murf's favorite saying. Brody loved him, but the kid was a royal pain in the rear. Like now. Brody waved at Rich, embarrassed that Murf had delayed the game.

"Okay, ready!" Rich yelled, and Bullard kicked off.

As the ball arced through the sky, Brody stole a quick glance at Murf. He was walking back toward the school, head hanging down. Brody felt a pang of guilt for yelling at him, but all his friends had been waiting on him to get the game started. *Sorry, Murf.* Brody would apologize later and hopefully smooth things over before they got home so Murf wouldn't tattle to their mom.

Gary Thompson caught the kick and took off running. Brody ran beside him, staying off to his left and slightly behind, keeping his head on a swivel to stay out of the way of the bigger boys. Getting run over without having the ball always sucked. It was embarrassing, too.

getting run over

Two sixth graders draped themselves on Gary's shoulders and dragged him down. He tossed the ball to Sean Williams, who was hit immediately, tackled around the legs.

Brody was close. He held his arms out for the ball, and Sean saw him.

Sean tried to throw the ball, but it bounced across the ground, ending up at Brody's feet. Brody snatched it up and ran, weaving his way through arms grabbing at his shirt. Being small had its advantages; Brody was quick, hard to catch.

Out of the corner of his eye, he spied Lance off to his right, just as someone got ahold of Brody's shirt and pulled. Brody tossed the ball at Lance right before he was tackled, and right before his head hit the ground. Just like in the cartoons, Brody saw stars. He wanted to cry (really, really bad) but couldn't, not with the girls watching.

Brody picked himself up and cheered as Lance jinked past the last sixth grader in his way and slammed the ball against the chain link. Brody raised his arms and yelled, "Woo hoo! Way to go, Lance!" Not only had Lance just scored, but Brody had been a part of it. He turned to see if any of the girls were watching and locked eyes with Debbie Wilson. She was smiling, and those big, beautiful brown eyes of hers were looking right at him.

At least, he thought so. Brody stole a quick glance behind himself to see if she was looking at someone else, but there was no one there, not close enough anyway. The guys were all surrounding Lance, slapping him on the back.

When he turned back toward Debbie, she tilted her head slightly, still staring right at him, and Brody was completely lost. Done for. Melted. But only for a second. Beyond Debbie, he spied Murf heading off the playground and toward the road.

In a second, Brody took it all in; Mrs. Carlisle, the playground monitor who was supposed to be watching, wasn't paying attention. Murf still had his head down, and there was a car coming.

His brother was going to get hit by a car.

squished

"Hey, Murf!" Brody yelled. "Murf!" Brody ran as fast as he could, weaving his way through the playground toward the side of the school building.

The car was still coming. Brody saw the driver leaning toward the passenger seat, eyes off the road, concentrating instead on whatever lay on the seat beside him instead of the distracted first grader wandering into his path.

"Murf! Murphy! Look out!" Brody screamed. His kid brother wasn't paying attention, wasn't listening. Brody was going to watch his brother die, right in front of him, just feet away.

shouldn't have yelled at him shouldn't have yelled at

Others on the playground stopped what they were doing, attracted by Brody's shouting, watching the scene getting ready to play out on the street where the buses park. Everyone would remember the day they saw six-year-old Murphy Quail disappear beneath the wheels of a tan '73 Oldsmobile. They would remember the sound. And what was left in the road.

"Murf!" Brody screamed. Murf stopped, right in the middle of the street, his feet square on the yellow line. Turned toward the approaching car. In an instant, he realized where he was and what was about to happen. He was frozen in place.

69

Brody was fifteen feet away, cutting his glance from his brother, to the car, to his brother, judging the distance, calculating. The driver was sitting up now, his eyes wide, and his mouth forming a perfect O. Hitting the brakes wouldn't make a difference.

get him get him get him

The world seemed to slow down, the air thickening.

Brody was in the street. He could see the blur of the car out of the corner of his eye. He could hear its engine, the whoosh of air as it drew close. He could knock Murf out of the way, push him to safety, sacrifice himself.

grab him grab

Brody willed his legs to move, his arms to grasp.

He slammed into his brother running full speed, hugged him, and dove.

Brody waited for the impact. Waited for the pain.

There was screaming, squealing. A pain in his side.

)(

He lay still, curled into a ball, eyes clenched tightly.

People were yelling, coming closer. He could hear them running, shoes scuffing against the road.

Murf wasn't in his arms, and Brody experienced a flicker of hope. Maybe he'd knocked Murf clear. Maybe he'd saved him.

He heard Mrs. Carlisle scream. Brody could only imagine what she was seeing.

But he didn't feel any pain. He'd read somewhere that people really didn't feel anything right away, even if their guts were spilling out of their bellies. It was called being in shock, if he remembered correctly.

Maybe he was in shock.

"Jesus Christ, kid. Oh my God."

Brody slowly opened his eyes and looked up into a round face staring down at him. The driver. Same bald head and wide eyes.

There were other faces, too. Kids, surrounding him.

"Murf?" Brody sat up, realizing he was unhurt. "Murf!" He heard his brother crying.

"Mrs. Carlisle's got him, dude," Rich said. "He's okay." All the color had drained from Rich's face. He looked like he was going to be sick.

Brody pushed through the crowd and saw Mrs. Carlisle holding Murphy in her arms, tears streaming down her face. She was stroking his hair, saying it was all her fault.

"They ran right out in front of me," the driver said, loud enough for everyone to hear. "Shouldn't be playing so close to the street like that. Oh God. I'm so sorry. Somebody call an ambulance!"

Brody wheeled, heat rising in his face. He wanted to scream at the man, tell him he was a jerk for not paying attention. But he didn't. The man was an adult, and Brody couldn't talk to him like that no matter how mad he might be. Instead, he unclenched his fist and went to his brother. *Nobody's hurt. We don't need an ambulance.*

He'd never seen Mrs. Carlisle cry before, and it upset him. Teachers weren't supposed to cry like that. She set Murf down and pulled a tissue from her pocket. "Murphy," she said, "don't you ever, *ever* go out in the street like that again."

Murphy looked down at the ground, nodding his head. "Yes, ma'am."

Then she turned toward Brody.

"Are you okay, Brody? Are you—" Mrs. Carlisle said, stopping midsentence. She covered her mouth with her hand.

Murphy's eyes were filling with tears. "I'm sorry, Bowdy," he said, using his little-kid voice, something Brody hadn't heard in a long time.

Brody tousled his hair. "It's okay, Murf."

71

"The car hit you," Murf said.

"No," Brody replied. "It missed us both. We were lucky."

Murf shook his head. "No, Bowdy, the car hit you."

"No, Murf. It didn't," Brody said, laughing a little. "I'm okay, really."

Murf tilted his head, confused, and pointed at Brody's left side. "Then where did your left arm go?"

At that moment, the day ended for ten-year-old Brody Quail.

Chapter 11
BRODY26

Garland Trail, Nebraska
Tuesday, November 12, 1968

He slapped two bills on the bar and grabbed his field jacket from the back of the chair.

"G'night, Brody," the bartender said.

"See you tomorrow, Jimmy," Brody replied.

Brody stepped out into the night air and took a deep breath. The sky was clear, and the temps were forecast to plummet into the teens before morning. He gathered his coat closer with his right hand and began his walk to his apartment a few blocks away, his breath swirling into the darkness.

The snow crunched under his boots. He lived nearby and was halfway home, but he was going to be delayed. He was being followed. Two guys, maybe three, about twenty yards back. And getting closer. He took a deep breath to clear his thoughts, wishing he hadn't had that third Scotch. He slowed his pace slightly. He didn't want a fight, but he sure as hell wasn't going to back down from one.

Let them come.

Brody listened. One of them was crossing the street, walking fast. The other two were right behind him now, maybe fifteen feet away.

No use waiting anymore. Brody stopped and heard the two gents behind him skid to a halt. Brody didn't turn around. He wanted them to make the first move.

Five seconds ticked by. Then ten.

The guy who'd crossed the street wasn't sure what to do now, hiding in the shadows and waiting for Brody to turn around.

Talking wasn't going to do much good, but Brody gave it a shot anyway. "Walk away," he said, loud enough for all three of them to hear.

One of the guys behind him laughed. "Say what?"

Brody turned. One black guy, tall and skinny, and one white guy, a little more built than his partner, but Brody could take both of them if he had to. Even with one arm. He noticed they both had their hands in their jacket pockets, acting like they had guns.

The street-crosser slipped on the ice halfway across the street and fell. Brody heard him get up and step up behind him on the sidewalk. If this was Chicago, Brody might be a little more worried, but these guys were Garland Trail wannabes. Skinny, Muscles, and Clum—no, Fat Guy.

"I said walk away," Brody repeated. "You don't want to do this."

"And how you gonna stop us, soldier man?"

Down deep, Brody wanted to say something about being able to take all three of them with one arm tied behind his back, but he figured they wouldn't appreciate the humor. He was too tired, anyway.

Skinny pointed his finger at Brody through his pocket. "Maybe I should just shoot your white ass."

"That isn't a gun," Brody said. "Your white-ass friend doesn't have one either." The ice crunched behind him, and Brody tilted his head to the side. "And if your friend back there gets any closer, you're all going to regret it."

"All we want is your money." Muscles, this time. A little nervous.

"Then come and take it, tough guy," Brody said. These jerks had done this before but were rattled. In the next few seconds, they'd either back off or make a move.

Brody watched Skinny's eyes shift to his partner, the one at his back. Brody sighed and readied himself. They weren't going to back off, and the man behind him was making his move.

Brody waited, listening to the man's steps as he approached, then at the perfect moment, struck to the rear with his elbow.

But he'd misjudged. Brody missed.

The guy was standing there, arms outstretched, with a comically serious look on his face. Brody didn't wait for him to move and struck with an open palm to the man's nose, hard enough to break it but not hard enough to send bone splinters into the man's brain. He didn't want to kill the guy (but would if he had to), only make him regret ever trying to jump a one-armed vet in the middle of the night. He felt the crunch and quickly withdrew his hand, readying himself for whatever came next.

What he saw, though, made no sense. The man's nose was satisfyingly deformed, scrunched up like a Porky Pig mask, but he wasn't moving. Not one bit.

He didn't even blink.

He just stood there, still as a statue. Stunned maybe? Brody didn't wait to see and punched the man in the mouth.

Brody watched as the man slowly tipped backward and fell to the icy sidewalk with a thud.

Something was wrong.

Brody turned and was shocked to see the other two men standing in the exact same spots as before, not moving.

Not blinking either.

Statues.

"What the . . . ?" Brody said.

He scanned the street around him, turning left, then right. Apart from the three would-be muggers, Brody was alone. He walked slowly toward the two standing men and snapped his fingers in front of their faces. Neither of them blinked. "This is crazy," he said under his breath. He reached out and touched Muscles, noticed that his clothes felt normal, warm from his body heat. "Hey," Brody said. "Hey!"

No reaction.

Had time stopped? He shoved both of them, one after the other, and watched as they fell backward to the concrete. He almost expected them to break into a million pieces, but no, they stayed intact, the same *okay, let's kick this guy's ass* looks still etched on their faces.

"That's what you get for trying to jump me, assholes."

Brody again scanned the streets and listened. No noises. No cars, no dogs barking in the distance, just the sound of his own breathing and a cloud of white mist in front of his face.

He didn't understand what was going on but didn't particularly care. If time could stop, it could just as easily start up again, right? He turned and walked in his original direction, back to his apartment. If these guys ever came back to the land of the here and now, he didn't want to be near them. Might be fun to watch, though, seeing them come to life flat on their backs, when the last moment they would remember was rushing a one-armed vet with a smart mouth.

And the big guy. Brody laughed, thinking what that was going to be like, waking up with a busted pig-nosed face, flat on his ass.

Then Brody's senses perked up, not because of anything he'd heard, but something he felt.

He was being watched.

Brody stopped and turned slowly, peering into the shadows. He couldn't see anyone, but the feeling was still there. Someone's eyes were on him. Maybe the punks he'd left reclining on the sidewalk had snapped out of whatever trance they were in and were following him.

But, no. It wasn't them. He could still see the three bodies right where he left them.

There were eyes on him, though. Of that he was certain.

Brody moved slowly, concentrating on his peripheral vision, checking the edges of his sight picture. Seeing nothing. The feeling was strong, though. Too real to ignore.

He'd go back to his apartment. Try to figure this all out.

As he approached his block, the feeling of being watched became electric, a sense of dread washing over his body. Not only was he being watched, he was being followed. Silently. Whoever they were, they were close now. Brody stopped and turned.

At first he was surprised there wasn't someone standing directly behind him. He *was* there, though, half a block away, silhouetted by the glare of a streetlight at his back.

Just standing there.

Brody could discern no details from this distance but could tell the person was tall, sturdy in build, and standing confidently. He had to know Brody had spotted him but didn't care.

Brody squinted, trying to see his face, his clothes, but all he saw was a dark cutout of a man, a shadow in the road. Perfectly still.

Brody couldn't describe what he felt, other than an overwhelming sense that he was seeing someone—some *thing*—that didn't belong here.

He felt confusion. Dread. And for the first time in a long time, fear.

"Hello?" Brody yelled, his words echoing down the shadowy street.

He received no response. The figure remained planted in place, motionless.

"Hey, I said hello!" Brody shouted, immediately regretting how loud he was. The last thing he wanted to do was wake someone who would peek out their windows, call the cops, and ensure he'd have another brush with the police. Brody decided to confront the man and started walking toward him. Then he stopped in his tracks when the person raised his arm. Brody crouched, then took a few quick steps toward a building, immediately wanting to find some sort of shelter. To Brody, the man had appeared to be raising a weapon. But that wasn't the case.

He was pointing. Arm raised, index finger pointing beyond Brody, as if gesturing him to look.

Brody did. And saw nothing. He turned back toward the figure quickly, not liking the feeling of taking his eyes off him, and gasped.

The figure was much closer now. Too close to have walked the distance, or run it, as if he'd simply moved in a flash of time, from one point to another. He was directly under a streetlight, bathed in its glow, but still the figure remained dark as night. Just a shadow.

"What do you want?" Brody asked.

The figure gestured more forcefully this time, then blinked out of existence.

Seconds later, Brody spied the figure again, much farther away down the street, appearing out of nowhere. Then in a flash, it was gone once again.

Brody's heart thudded away. He waited for the figure to return, but there was only the silent street before him, buildings bathed in the spotty glow of streetlamps, disappearing into shadows. Nothing more.

The feeling of being watched was gone. He was truly alone.

He started to walk back toward his apartment building, then stopped.

The figure had wanted him to go the other way, to continue down the street. He didn't know why, but Brody felt the need to do just that. He turned, took three steps, and then ran, feeling a sudden urge to get past his apartment building, and go up the street to—

To where?

He couldn't remember *ever* going in that direction, but he needed to run, to go where he'd never been before.

And then he saw her. Standing in the street.

At that moment, the night came to a close for twenty-six-year-old Brody Quail.

Chapter 12
BRODY16

The president had been shot.

"Dude, are you listening?" Jason asked, slapping Brody's arm.

Brody realized he'd been staring at Joan again. It was tough not to. *God, she's pretty.* "Yeah, I was listening," he said.

"Bullshit. I saw who you were looking at," Jason said. "What did I say, then?"

"You were talking about Reagan." Safe bet, because that's all anyone was talking about.

"Okay, so do *you* think the Russkies did it?"

"I don't think they'd be stupid enough to do something like that."

"No shit," Kyle agreed. "If we found out they tried to kill him, we'd nuke the living shit out of that place. So if it wasn't them, who?"

"Your dad said it was some guy named Hinckley." Brody glanced in Joan's direction. She was looking right at him. He looked away quickly. "From Evergreen." He began to sweat a little. Every time he was around her, even just in the same room, Brody couldn't help but feel *all hot and bothered*, a saying his mom used, which Brody wished she wouldn't.

"I know that's what he said," Kyle continued, "but do you think he was working for somebody? Like Oswald was working for the CIA or Castro or some shit like that?"

"I don't know," Brody said. He shifted his glance to Joan's table and noticed she wasn't sitting there anymore. Before he could look around the room for her, though, he felt Jason scoot over, making room on the bench for someone else.

Joan. Jesus, she's going to sit right here. And she did.

Joan straddled the bench, facing Jason. All Brody could see was the back of her head, but she was only inches away. It was a strange feeling, and hard to describe, but it felt like a low-voltage current flashed through his body, as if every nerve ending screamed, *Whoa! She's right there!* Only for a second, but long enough to cause him to catch his breath. He tried to keep his eyes from wandering, but they had a mind of their own. She was so small, almost delicate in a way. She was wearing a concert T-shirt, probably the Journey one he'd seen her wear before, which ended at her button-ups, which hugged her hips like—

Jesus, Brody. Control yourself.

When she abruptly turned around toward him, though, he nearly fell off the bench.

"Hey, you've got Krichek for third period, right?" she asked, pulling her left leg up and over the bench so she could turn and face him more directly. Just that little movement caused a wave of her perfume to slap him right in the nose. It wasn't that strong or anything, but it was all he could smell at that moment.

"Yeah," Brody answered, amazed that he was able to get the word out of his mouth. "Why?"

"He said something about a test next Friday, but I didn't catch what chapters it was covering."

"Um, seven and eight. I think."

She grabbed one of her spiral notebooks and flipped it open. Brody watched her write the chapters down, and then he saw it.

His name.

At first, he didn't believe what he was seeing, but it was there. Drawn in balloon letters, at the top of the page, sandwiched between doodles.

B R O D Y

His name, not that other guy, the wrestler, Todd something-or-other. Brody felt his heart leap into his throat.

Joan slammed the notebook closed when she saw him staring at the page. Brody wasn't sure, but he could almost swear she was blushing a little. *I wasn't supposed to see that, was I?*

"Okay," Joan said, "thanks, Brody." She gathered her books and started to go back to her own table, but stopped and leaned over toward him. "Hey, can you give me a ride home?"

"Uh . . ." *Holy Mother of God she wants me to drive her home holy shit* "Sure."

"Great," Joan said, her smile nearly melting the sixteen-year-old boy sitting in front of her. "Maybe after we get out of here?" She whispered the last part.

Brody was planning on ditching his last class anyway. "Sure." *Sure? Sure? Is that all you can say?*

"Okay, I'll meet you in the parking lot."

"You know which car is mine?" Brody asked, suddenly wishing he had a better-looking car than his—

"1963 Impala, right? Light blue?"

Holy crap, she knows my car. "That's the one."

"I've never ridden in one of those. It'll be fun." With that, she turned and went back to her table.

"Jesus, Quail," Jason said. "You know she has a boyfriend, right?"

"Yeah, I know."

"Have you ever seen him? He'll kick your ass."

Brody didn't care. Joan obviously liked *him* (B R O D Y) and that's all that mattered.

※

"It doesn't work from the outside," Brody yelled, leaning over and popping the door lever. There was a crumpled ball of paper on the seat, which he tossed into the back. If he was going to start giving Joan rides home (still a big *if* at this point, but a hopeful *if*), he'd have to make sure his trash was at least picked up next time.

"Thanks," Joan said, placing her books between them on the bench seat and slamming her door shut. "Cool car."

"Thanks." Brody fastened his lap belt and cinched it tight.

seat belt

He pumped the gas pedal and turned the key.

With a cough, the Impala's engine turned over. Brody winced at the cloud of blue smoke in his rearview mirror but was glad his old heap had decided to cooperate. He backed out of the parking space, then realized he had no idea where Joan lived. "Um, where do—"

Joan giggled. "My house is on Lincoln, a couple of blocks away," she said. "Take the first left from Michigan, and I'm the third house on the left."

"Got it." Brody pulled out of the parking lot and headed down Central toward Michigan, suddenly self-conscious about missing a shift or grinding the gears, which would be *very* uncool.

"I really like your car," she said. "How fast have you had it?" She grabbed the metal dash with one hand and pulled one leg up underneath her, turning her body to face him.

"Not very fast, maybe 80, 85." He glanced over at her, took in her bright eyes, her smile. "It really starts shaking at 75, so I'm kinda nervous about going any faster." He cringed as soon as the words spilled out of his mouth. *God, I sound like an old man!*

She laughed. "My dad had an old car when he was a kid, and one of the tie rods snapped. He swerved into a ditch and rolled a few times."

"Holy crap."

"I know, right? He was lucky to get out alive."

get out alive

For a second, Brody's gut twisted, and he gasped out loud.

fire there's fire she's in it in the fire

"Are you okay?"

Brody was breathing fast. "Yeah, I'm fine, I think I—"

"Hey, you just passed Michigan."

"What?" He'd driven right by. "Sorry. I'll take Washington. It goes through, right?"

"Yeah. That'll work."

seat belt

Brody glanced at Joan and saw she wasn't wearing her seat belt. "Hey, I don't want to sound like an old man (*hurry hurry before it's*) but could you maybe (*too late*) put your belt on?" She looked at him funny. He didn't care, though. "Please?"

"Brody's rule?" she asked.

"Yeah, Brody's rule. Stupid, I know," he said, patting the steel dashboard, "but I wouldn't want you to ding your head on the—"

Suddenly, Joan's smile disappeared. "Brody! Red light!"

Brody whipped his head forward and instinctively smashed the brake pedal to the floor. The car didn't stop. The pedal was slack, no pressure whatsoever. He pressed it again and again, no response.

Out of the corner of his eye, he saw the truck entering the intersection from the right, barreling right toward them.

Tick. She lives.

Joan put her hands up, as if she could stop the truck from hitting them. She screamed.

Tick-tock. She dies.

✕

Brody opened his eyes.

The air was still, thick. And it was quiet, unnaturally so. Brody moved his head, expecting a bolt of pain, but there was nothing. He was lying on his back in the intersection. The asphalt was rough against his hands as he pushed himself up to a sitting position and looked around.

What he expected to see, he didn't.

There were no fire trucks, no ambulance. No debris from the wreck.

My car.

The Impala sat about ten yards away, right about where the truck (*where is the truck?*) had hit them. But there was no truck. There was no *anything*.

Brody stood and brushed the gravel from his hands. *Joan.* He could see her there, in the front seat of his car.

"Joan?" he yelled, running over to the car. "Are you okay?"

burning, twisted and broken, engulfed in flames

He peered through the driver's side window. She was alive, sitting with her hands

lips pulled back, revealing white teeth, grinning

in her lap.

"Joan?"

She turned and smiled. "I like your car, Brody," she said. "Impala, right? '62?"

Brody couldn't believe what he was hearing, or what he said next. "Close, it's a '63. It was my dad's."

There was a noise behind him, feet on pavement. Before he could turn around, he saw Joan's eyes focus on a point beyond.

"Who is she?" Joan asked, her eyes narrowing. "She shouldn't be here."

84

Brody turned and saw her. A girl, roughly his age, dressed in strange clothes, like what a factory worker would wear. A lock of red hair covered one eye, and in the other Brody saw his reflection. And fear.

She was terrified.

"Get out," Joan said. "You don't belong here."

The girl turned and began to run away.

"Wait!" Brody yelled after her. "Don't go!"

He watched a dark figure appear out of nowhere, directly in her path. Watched the girl drop to her knees. Heard her scream.

At that moment, the day ended for sixteen-year-old Brody Quail.

And the walls began to crack.

Chapter 13
BRODY52

Joshua, Maine
Friday, October 25, 1974

The sun was setting, right on schedule.

Brody stood by his desk, staring at the orange glow coming though his office curtains, the closest he'd come to actually watching a sunset since . . .

Reba.

Since before his wife had died.

Since you let *her die.*

He glanced at the pictures on the wall, snapshots of the two of them, of her, so vibrant once. That was all gone now.

"Excuse me, sir."

Brody turned abruptly, startled at the sound of Felix's voice. A quick look at the clock told him Felix was a little early, but no, that wasn't strange. He had no dinner tray in his hands.

"I'm sorry to interrupt, sir, but there's someone downstairs who wishes to speak to you."

"Who, Felix?"

"He didn't give me his name, sir, but he says it's imperative that he speak with you immediately."

"Regarding?" Brody asked.

"He wouldn't say."

Brody stepped around his desk, and as he passed Felix, he felt the man place his hand on his shoulder. Brody turned to look his old employee and friend in the face.

"I believe it may be something serious, sir."

one shall pass

Brody nodded and smiled at Felix's concern for his well-being. "How could it get any worse?" Brody said. Felix smiled back, but there was no joy in the expression. Only a sense of shared sorrow.

Brody left his office and turned to head downstairs but caught something out of place in the corner of his eye. He looked down the hallway toward his old bedroom, where Reba had been murdered, and saw that the door was open.

It was never open. *Never.*

"Felix, were you in the bedroom earlier?" he asked, trying hard to hide the anger that had risen so quickly in his breast. He'd ordered the door to remain shut. No one, even though only he and Felix shared the mansion now, was to enter that room. He hadn't opened that door since the police had finished their investigation and Felix had returned it to its previous appearance. The room, for all intents and purposes, appeared as it did prior to that terrible night. The bed was made, the shades were open, and one of Reba's favorite books was even sitting on her bedside table. If Reba's spirit roamed the house, she would find her room to be in order, with everything exactly as she would have wanted it.

When Brody didn't get an answer, he turned back toward the office. "Felix, I said, 'Have you been in the bedroom?'" Felix was standing behind the desk, looking at something in his hands.

But it wasn't just something. It was a gun. Brody's Smith & Wesson Model 27.

"Felix, are you all right?"

Felix looked up at him, his gray eyes uncharacteristically dull and lifeless. "A fine weapon, sir," he said, testing the heft of the gun in his right hand.

Brody wasn't sure what to think. This sort of behavior was completely out of character for Felix, and it instantly made him nervous. He switched his glance from Felix's eyes to the gun, and then back again. "It's loaded, Felix" was all he could think to say.

Felix popped out the cylinder, then snapped it back into place. "Why, yes, it is, sir." Brody had never seen Felix handle a weapon before and was surprised the man knew how to open the revolver. Felix then grabbed the gun by the barrel, moving it toward Brody, grip first. "Will you require your weapon this evening, sir?"

Will I require my weapon? "No, Felix," Brody said, immediately stepping forward and gently removing the gun from Felix's hand. His heart slowed a bit as soon as he had the gun back in his *own* hand, and he breathed a sigh of relief. "Are you feeling okay, Felix?"

"Of course, sir," Felix replied, his eyes less dull than they had been just moments before, as if he'd checked out for a minute, then returned. Brody was concerned for his old friend. Many a time he himself had sat behind that desk, holding the gun in his hand, contemplating how easy it would be to make all the pain go away. But he'd never taken his thoughts any further.

Or had he? There was a strange feeling, a momentary flash of a memory he couldn't recall clearly. There, then gone. Brody might've given the matter more thought, but he was worried about Felix.

Both he and Felix had suffered after Reba's death, of that Brody was certain. They had both loved her dearly, in their own way, but maybe Felix was having a more difficult time with this grief than Brody had realized.

"Let's keep this little gem in its proper place," Brody said, placing the revolver back in the drawer. He wondered if he should find another place for the gun, maybe lock it up. "Felix, the door to the bedroom is open. Were you in there today?"

Felix's eyes went wide, shocked that Brody would assume he'd violated the trust the closed door represented. "No, sir, I was not," Felix said, immediately stepping out into the hall and turning to face the bedroom. Brody followed.

The door was closed. Just as it should be.

Felix said nothing as he turned toward his employer, a curious look in his eyes.

"I could've sworn the door was open, Felix."

"The gentleman at the door," Felix said, apparently willing to let the moment pass without further discussion.

"Yes," Brody replied. "My mysterious caller. I'm sorry, Felix, I truly thought the door was open."

Felix nodded slightly, nothing more. He was silent for a moment longer, then added, "I assume you'll be taking your dinner in the office, sir?"

Brody stared at the bedroom door. Closed. "Yes, Felix, that'll be fine." At the mention of dinner, Brody realized how hungry he was. "After I deal with our visitor."

"Very well, sir," Felix said, and they both walked down the hall and the stairs, heading in different directions when they reached the landing, Felix toward the kitchen and Brody toward the front door.

Felix had reengaged the dead bolt after answering the door, and Brody flicked it open, hearing the *clunk* as the rod retracted into the heavy oak. He swung the door open, wondering who it could possibly be, and his breath caught in his throat. His knees suddenly buckled, and he fought to steady himself.

A woman.

"No, this can't be," he said, the words squeezing through his throat, tight with an onrush of emotion.

It was her.

His Reba.

She looked at him coldly, without the sense of wonder he was experiencing as he gazed upon the person with whom he'd spent so many years.

The woman he'd allowed to die.

But no, she was standing there, as real as day, with confusion in her eyes.

"Who are you?" she asked.

Her words cut through his heart like a dagger, and he gripped the door handle for all he was worth, trying to maintain his balance. Why hadn't Felix warned him? Why hadn't he prepared him for what he was about to see? When her name finally passed his lips, he was shocked how his voice sounded, as if he were a child again . . . small, afraid, wounded. "Reba? My God, Reba?"

She shifted her head to the right ever so slightly, her eyes locked to his face. "That's not my name," she said as she took a tentative step back.

The dress was right; she'd worn it at their company picnic a few years back, captured for eternity in one of the pictures on his office wall. Her hair, the shape of her face . . . all Reba! But the eyes, there was something wrong with her *eyes*. This woman looked like Reba, but someone else was peering at him through those eyes, someone wearing her body like a disguise. Brody watched as she pulled at her clothes, examining the fabric, then moved her attention to her hands, turning them, looking at the palms, then the backs of her hands, and a look of terror crossed her face. "Oh my God."

Behind him, from upstairs, he heard the bedroom door open, the hinges squeaking. He heard footsteps pounding down the hallway.

Brody tore his gaze from his (dead) wife and looked at the hallway railing at the top of the stairs.

There was a figure standing there, a blank nothingness with the silhouette of a man, as if someone had taken a pair of scissors and cut the shape from reality itself, leaving a shadowy hole in its place.

And it spoke.

"Get out," it hissed. "Leave this place."

At that moment, the day ended for fifty-two-year-old Brody Quail.

Chapter 14
BRODY10

"Not now, Murf."

"Can I play?"

"Scram, Murf. Get off the field."

"I wanna play, too."

Brody took his brother by the arm. "Not yet, okay? You'd get—" For some reason, Brody couldn't force the word from his mouth. He knew the word, but it just wouldn't come out.

Squished, just say it. Say it.

He shook his head, trying to clear the sudden dizziness he was feeling. "Look, just go over there and watch," Brody said instead, pointing to the edge of the playground. "You need to stay out of the way, okay?" He watched the smile fade from Murf's face. "You might get hurt out here."

"Mom says you have to play with me."

"I know, but not right now. Not this game."

"Ready?" Bullard called, getting ready to punt the ball to their side.

"Hey, Quail! Get your brother out of here." That was Rich, staring at him. So was everyone else. Brody felt the heat rise up the back of his neck, but he wasn't angry at his brother.

"Go on, Murf. Go stand by the girls or something. Maybe you can cheer me on?"

"Okay, Brody," Murf said, clearly deflated, then trotted off the field.

"Okay, Rich," Brody yelled. He didn't like the way Rich shook his head at him. *Give me a break, Rich, he's just a little kid.*

Bullard kicked the ball, and as it arced through the sky, Brody stole a quick glance at his brother. He was walking back toward the school, head hanging down. He wasn't staying on the playground like

squished

he had told him to.

Gary Thompson caught the ball, but Brody didn't care. A tiny pang of panic pierced his chest, and he ran off the field. He didn't know why, but Brody couldn't let Murf continue to walk toward the school.

the street it's the street

Brody looked but saw no cars. Maybe he was being overprotective, but something was screaming inside his head. He had to keep his brother from getting to the street.

As he passed the line of girls sitting Indian-style, he caught Debbie Wilson staring at him. She looked confused, wondering why he was leaving the game. Brody smiled, but she didn't smile back. There was a girl sitting behind Debbie, off by herself, whom he didn't recognize, but her presence wouldn't register until later, when she would be screaming at him.

"Murf!" Brody called. "Hey, Murphy!"

His brother wasn't listening. His head was down, and he was heading toward the street, where the buses parked when school was out. There was no way Murphy couldn't hear him.

"And where do you think you're going, Mr. Quail?" said Mrs. Carlisle, the playground monitor.

Brody pointed at his brother. "I'm getting Murphy, Mrs. Carlisle," Brody answered, silently adding that she should be the one to get him since it was her *job*. "Look."

She did but didn't appear overly concerned. "You need to get back to the game, Brody," she said. Her voice was flat and her eyes looked weird, like dolls' eyes. Brody wasn't sure if he'd ever seen Mrs. Carlisle look like that before. "Right now," she added forcefully.

Brody looked at his brother. He was heading right for the street, and there *was* a car

squished

coming.

He could see the blur of the car out of the corner of his eye. He could hear its engine, the whoosh of air as it drew close.

He was dizzy again and felt a sudden hunger in his gut, as if he hadn't eaten all day. He swayed slightly on his feet as Mrs. Carlisle continued to stare blankly at him, not paying any attention to Murphy, who was going to wander out into the street and into the path of the car. He pointed at his brother again, trying to get Mrs. Carlisle to look, really *look* this time, and counting the seconds until he would have to act. Murphy was getting closer to the street, and the car was

the driver was leaning toward the passenger seat, eyes off the road, concentrating instead on whatever lay on the seat beside him instead of the distracted first grader wandering out into his path

getting closer, too. Mrs. Carlisle glanced at Murphy again, clearly seeing what was going to happen, then simply repeated what she'd said earlier. "You need to get back to the game, Brody."

"I've got to get my brother," Brody said. He usually didn't disobey teachers, or any adult for that matter, but he wasn't about to let Murf get hurt. He turned away from Mrs. Carlisle and ran toward Murphy, catching up with him before he got to the street. "Murphy! Didn't you hear me? Where the heck are you going?" Brody grabbed his brother by the shoulder, but Murf easily shrugged off Brody's grip. *What the . . . ?* Murphy continued to walk in the same direction, head down, ignoring his brother.

Brody grabbed him by the shoulders, tried to pull him back, but couldn't. His hands slipped off again, unable to stop Murf. Brody glanced at the car; it was still coming, and Murf was stepping off the curb. He was going to get hit if Brody didn't tackle him, right now.

Brody wrapped his arms around Murphy's shoulders and pulled, but found himself sliding across the asphalt, his tennis shoes scraping the road. Brody kicked and pulled, but Murf (a *first* grader) motored ahead like a bulldozer, as if he were the strongest person on the planet, dragging Brody with him.

"Dammit, Murphy! Stop!" Brody yelled, but his brother wasn't listening. Brody tugged and pulled to no avail. The car was so close now, the driver looking up at the last instant. Brody could see the man's face, which had no emotion, no look of surprise or shock. Just a blank look, as if running over a couple of kids wasn't much of a big deal.

Brody's sense of self-preservation screamed at him to let go, to dive out of the way, but he wasn't about to let the car slam into his brother without trying to save him, even if it meant he would get hit, too.

But this isn't right. Not right at all.

Brody took one last look at the car, the chrome bumper reflecting both of their bodies, and yanked his brother's body as hard as he could (with no effect), gritted his teeth, and closed his eyes.

When the impact came, he—

"Hey, Quail. You okay?"

Brody could feel the hard ground under his back as he struggled to open his eyes. He didn't feel any pain, but he had to be pretty messed up. He once read that people went into shock when they were hurt badly and didn't feel anything right away. He was almost afraid to see what had happened to himself. And to Murf, who wasn't in his arms anymore. The car had smashed into them both.

"Boys, what happened?"

Mrs. Carlisle's voice again. *What do you mean,* What happened? *You were watching, and I told you! You saw what was going to happen!*

"I don't know, Mrs. Carlisle," someone said. It sounded like Rich. "He just fell over. Nobody hit him or anything."

"Brody?" Mrs. Carlisle again. Her voice was soft and concerned, no longer flat and emotionless. More *normal.* Brody opened his eyes and saw her face hovering above. She looked more like the Mrs. Carlisle he was used to. "What happened, Brody? Did you hit your head?"

He wasn't in the road, that much was clear. He was back in the field where they were playing the game. For a second, he imagined himself getting hit by the car and flying through the air and landing in the field, but that couldn't have happened. "Is my brother okay?" Brody asked, amazed at how much effort it took to talk. He still felt dizzy and weak.

He watched Mrs. Carlisle look at the crowd of kids that had gathered in a circle around him, then she motioned with her hand. "Come here, Murphy."

Then Murf was there, looking down at him, tears in his eyes. "Are you okay, Murf?" Brody asked, starting to think that the whole thing had been nothing more than a dream. He must've passed out during the game and imagined it all. *But it seemed so real, except for the part about Murf transforming into some sort of deaf-and-dumb Incredible Hulk . . .*

"I'm okay, Bowdy," Murf said, reverting to his baby voice as he usually did when he was scared or sad. "Are you sick?"

"No, I'm . . . I don't know. I think I fainted or something."

"We really didn't hit him, Mrs. Carlisle," Rich repeated. "He just fell over."

"Can you stand, Brody?" Mrs. Carlisle asked.

Brody sat up a little, resting on his elbows. Every single kid on the playground seemed to be standing there staring at him. He was still dizzy, but not as much as before. His stomach, though, was a different story. He was *starving*. Weird, because he'd eaten lunch earlier. Right?

Standing a few feet away was Debbie Wilson, who had shouldered her way toward the front of the crowd and was looking at him with concern in her eyes. *She's worried about me. How cool is that!*

"Boys," Mrs. Carlisle said, "give him a hand." Rich and Gary stepped forward and helped Brody to his feet. "Let's get you inside and get some water in you," she said. "Murphy, you can come, too. And the rest of you, go on. Everything's fine."

"You all right, man?" Gary asked.

"Yeah, I'm okay," Brody replied, stealing another glance at Debbie, who was looking over her shoulder as she walked away. Brody smiled at her, and she smiled back. He felt better already.

Murphy reached for his hand, and together they followed Mrs. Carlisle toward the school. He wasn't embarrassed to hold his little brother's hand. After what he'd imagined while he was passed out, he didn't care what anyone thought. He gave Murf's hand a squeeze. The whole dream had seemed so real, though Murf didn't actually have superhuman strength and Mrs. Carlisle didn't usually act like an uncaring robot. But the rest of it . . . sure felt real.

Mrs. Carlisle would probably call his mother, and she'd be all worried. Great.

His friends had already formed back up into teams and were getting ready to start the game again. The girls had made their way back to the edge of the field to watch. Debbie was standing close to another girl, someone Brody didn't recognize. They were having an argument. Brody stared at them as he passed. Some of the other girls were standing now, too, all facing the new girl, who looked scared. Brody was a little surprised he hadn't seen her before. She wasn't quite as pretty as Debbie, but she was still pretty in her own way. She had red hair, swept to one side and lying across one shoulder, and bright green eyes. And then he remembered.

He had seen her. *In the dream.*

Brody stopped. Murphy kept walking and yanked his arm. "Come on, Brody," Murphy said. "We have to follow Mrs. Carlisle." Brody pulled his hand away from his brother.

"You shouldn't be here," Brody heard Debbie say loudly. *Her voice.* Weird. Just like Mrs. Carlisle's. *In the dream.*

Brody felt dizzy again and swayed on his feet. Was it happening again? Had he passed out walking across the playground, and was he dreaming now?

The new girl was ignoring Debbie and looking right at him. She narrowed her eyes, as if trying to decide if she was seeing what she thought she was, then moved past Debbie, breaking through the circle of girls around her, and walked right toward him.

Brody saw Debbie turn around and saw the same blank look on her face that he'd seen on Mrs. Carlisle's. The other girls didn't move a hair and remained standing in place, looking toward the center of the circle where the new girl had been.

They all look the same, Brody noticed, and with a quick glance to his left, he saw that Mrs. Carlisle had stopped, too, and was looking at the new girl. Just as before (the dream) there was no life in her eyes, just an emotionless, glassy stare. Brody felt a twinge of uneasiness in his gut. This couldn't be another dream. He was wide awake. This was all *real*. And if it was, that meant that the episode with the car was—

"Stop," Mrs. Carlisle said, not to him, but to the new girl. "You don't belong here."

He turned back toward the girl, who was still walking toward him, but faster now, running the last few steps and stopping directly in front of Brody. She was a little shorter than he was and had to tilt her head to look into his eyes. She studied his face, looking at his eyes, his hair, and his mouth, then tentatively reached out and touched his face.

Brody shrank back at first but then relaxed and let her fingers slide down his cheek. He was scared and confused at the moment, but there was something about this girl, about her eyes, her touch, that seemed *right*.

"What's your name?" she asked.

"Brody," he said. "Brody Quail." She smiled at first, but then her eyes shifted to a point behind Brody. She grabbed his arm and pulled. Hard.

"Come on!" she yelled. "We have to go!"

Brody stumbled forward, caught off guard and off balance. "What's wrong?" he said as he tried to look over his shoulder.

She (*what's her name?*) only tugged harder, willing him to run with her. "Hurry!" she screamed.

"Wait! Who—What's wrong?" Brody said as he broke free of her grasp.

Before she could grab his arm again, Brody turned and saw a man . . . no . . . a man *shape*, as if someone had taken a knife and sliced away part of a picture revealing a blank void beyond, and it was moving toward them. "Holy *shi*—"

The girl grabbed his arm again, and this time Brody ran with her, actually passing her by and pulling her along. The other kids on the playground were all standing perfectly still, watching them (dolls' eyes) run toward the side of the school. Brody wasn't sure where he and his new friend were going, but anywhere away from that *thing* would be okay in his book.

Her hand was warm in his and he held on tight, hoping he wasn't squeezing hard enough to hurt her.

And then, he wasn't holding anything. He skidded to a stop, thinking she had fallen.

"No!" she screamed, and as Brody turned, he expected to see their pursuer holding her.

She was gone. The dark figure was gone. And the playground was nothing more than an empty nighttime street, the ground covered in snow.

At that moment, the day ended for ten-year-old Brody Quail.

But this time, he'd remember.

Chapter 15
BRODY26

Garland Trail, Nebraska
Tuesday, November 12, 1968

The snow crunched under his boots.

Brody lived nearby and was halfway home, but he was being followed. Two guys, maybe three, about twenty yards back, getting closer. He took a deep breath to clear his thoughts, wishing he hadn't had that third drink.

Or was it four? For some reason, he couldn't remember. He'd been at the bar, said good night to Jimmy (Korea), and left immediately afterward. Maybe he *did* have more than three (or four), because he honestly couldn't recall. He usually went to the bar after work, and the days seemed to blur together after a while. He didn't feel drunk, but he was a little dizzy and his stomach was growling.

Great, I'm hammered, and three guys are going to try and jump me.

But why think that? Maybe the dudes were just out for a stroll? No, not at this time of night (morning, actually), but maybe they were just some other people from the bar trying to stumble their way home, like he was.

"You're hair-triggered for this shit, Brody," he grumbled. Not everyone was looking for a fight, even at two in the morning. He always seemed to expect the worst from others, even if suspicion wasn't warranted. Problem was, most of the time it *was* warranted.

His pinned-up sleeve and Army field jacket drew attention. Got him in a lot of trouble. But Brody Quail didn't give two shits.

He slowed his pace slightly, almost hoping the guys following him were going to try something. He sure as hell wasn't going to back down from a fight.

He was tired of fighting, though. Every day, the same thing.

the same thing

Brody stopped walking. There would be three guys; one black, the other two white. Punks, all of them. Out for a quick buck. They were going to pretend they had guns, but didn't. A big guy would try to sneak up behind him and fail. He would break them, make them pay.

And I need to walk as far north as I can.

Brody had no idea where that last thought had come from, but it was strong, urgent. He glanced up the street toward his apartment, looked beyond into the shadows, and felt an overwhelming need to run as fast and as far as he could, because he didn't know what was out there. "Jesus, Brody, you've got to lay off the booze," he said to himself just as he heard his pursuers behind him.

Brody turned.

Skinny and Muscles. One black guy, tall and skinny, and one white guy, a little more built than his partner, but Brody could (would) take both of them if he had to. Even with one arm. He noticed they both had their hands in their jacket pockets, acting like they had guns. (They didn't.) The third guy (*Clumsy*) was crossing the street, taking up position behind him. (He would slip on the ice.)

Skinny and Muscles looked a little surprised that he'd turned to confront them. Good. Brody had the initiative. He walked toward them, still a little unsteady on his feet, but the adrenaline pumping through his system overpowered the grogginess.

"So, fellas, let me tell you how this is going to go down," he said, his voice cool and deadly serious. "I'm going to kick both of your scrawny asses, and then I'm going to smash the fat ass's face behind me right into the concrete." Brody relished the look on their faces. They sure didn't expect *this*.

If he was lucky, they'd turn tail and run. Brody would avoid a fight and another run-in with the police, which he certainly didn't need. Then again, he hadn't been in a good brawl in a while.

But they didn't. Turn tail and run, that is.

"Fine," Brody said, never breaking stride. "Which one of you pussies wants to be first?"

"How about me."

As soon as Brody heard the voice, he realized things weren't going to go as he expected. Clumsy had approached much more quickly than he'd expected (didn't slip on the ice, either), and shoved him in the back. As he fell toward the concrete, his breath shoved from his lungs by the hammer blow between his shoulder blades, Brody wondered why he thought this was going to be so easy. And, for that matter, why did he think (know?) Clumsy was going to slip on the ice?

Brody was able to get his arm out in front, partially breaking his fall, but not before the left side of his face scraped the frozen sidewalk. Tiny bolts of pain crisscrossed his cheek, and his hand went numb.

This has happened before.

"Who's the pussy now, *cracker?*" Skinny proceeded to kick Brody in the head before he could regain his senses. Brody saw stars. His ears hummed. He tried to protect his face, but only got his forearm in the way of another roundhouse kick, which still managed to connect with his head. This time, he cried out. And again, when Clumsy (who apparently wasn't) kicked him in the ribs. He remembered how bad it hurt to get his ass kicked.

He's going to pull a gun.

Brody rolled over onto his back, still holding his bloodied hand in front of his face, and saw what he (somehow) expected to see. Muscles was holding one of those chrome-plated .32 semiauto pistols. Cheap, tacky, but more than able to put a nice round hole in his forehead. "Okay, buddy, you win. You can have my—"

Two more kicks to the ribs from Clumsy. Another to the head from Muscles. This was getting ugly (and so was he). His ribs screamed, his head pounded. A sheen of blood appeared in his right eye, and his lower lip felt like it had been nearly ripped off.

He felt a hand reach into his back pocket and pull out his wallet. There wasn't much cash, but maybe enough to send them on their way. Brody tried to sit up but was so weak he could barely move. "Take it," he slurred, spitting blood.

"Twenty bucks, soldier boy? That all you got?"

He wasn't sure which one of them was speaking. "That's it. All of it."

One more kick to the head, and Brody slammed back to the concrete, this time unable to hold in the moan that oozed from his throat. He couldn't move, so weak. Another boot to the ribs, and this time he heard a rib (or was it two?) crack. He groaned in pain and curled into a fetal position, trying to protect both his head and midsection from further blows. His ass was kicked. If they wanted to, they could kill him where he lay and there wasn't a damned thing he could do about it. He'd survived Nam (returning with 75 percent of the limbs he'd gone there with), but might just die on a sidewalk in the middle of the night in Garland Trail, of all places.

And that's when he heard her.

"Get away from him."

What? A woman? Brody turned his head and squinted through swollen eyes. There was a woman about fifteen feet away, standing under a streetlight. She wore some sort of coveralls and had what looked like a long pipe in her hand. *Jesus, what are you doing?*

Skinny laughed. "What did you say, bitch?"

She took a step forward, slapping the end of the pipe into the palm of her other hand. "I said, leave him alone."

standing in the street

She looked familiar. Had he seen her once before? She stood with her feet shoulder-width apart, confident, unafraid. He had to admit he was glad she showed up when she did, but she was crazy to be confronting these three punks, especially since at least one of them was armed.

She had their attention, though. And that was a good thing. They weren't watching (or kicking) him anymore. He gritted his teeth and shifted his weight to his bloodied hand, fighting through the pain shooting through his body from his damaged ribs. All three of the men had stepped toward the woman.

"What are you going to do with that pipe, lady?" Muscles asked, waving his gun out in front of him like he was showing a toy to a dog. "Maybe you're gonna drop it and give us *your* money, how about that?"

"I don't have any money, asshole."

She's got some brass ones, that's for sure, Brody thought as he studied his targets. He was injured, yes, but they weren't paying attention to him. If they moved on her, he might be able to drop a couple of them, especially the guy with the gun, and possibly get his hands (hand) on the pipe.

"Come on, baby, you don't have to be like that," Skinny said. "Don't be so mean." He took a step forward, and the woman gripped the pipe like a baseball bat, holding it over her left shoulder, ready to swing.

A lefty, Brody noted as he slowly inched closer to the guy with the gun, who was now pointing it right at her. He clenched his teeth, stifling the sounds of pain bunching up in his throat. Clumsy had stepped closer to her, too, and stood with his hands on his hips, shaking his head.

"Leave, now," she commanded. Brody couldn't believe his eyes as she stepped closer, almost within swinging range. "Walk away and none of you will get hurt."

"Shut your mouth, bitch," Skinny said. Brody saw each of the men tense, obviously no longer finding any humor in the situation. They were going to attack her. Brody was closest to the guy with the gun, but he didn't think he could make it to his feet in time. And even if he did, he doubted he was in any shape to take Mr. Muscles down.

And then all three of the punks said in unison, "You shouldn't be here." Their voices were different, flat. They all relaxed a little, stood a little straighter. Were they having second thoughts? Maybe they would walk away, let the situation pass. Trouble was, Brody was past letting these guys get by without some payback.

Brody looked at the woman, caught her glance, and saw understanding in her eyes. She could see he'd moved and was going to act.

He nodded slightly.

She nodded back.

Now!

Brody drew his leg back and slammed his boot into the side of the gunman's knee, satisfied by the crunch he heard as the knee buckled in a direction it wasn't meant to move. The gunman screamed and swung the gun away from the woman as he fell. She was already swinging the pipe, connecting with the side of Clumsy's head with a loud, thudding clang.

Brody scrambled on top of Muscles, eyes fixed on the gun. He punched him in the head, one, two, three times, enough to stun him, then wrenched the small pistol from his right hand. He hoped the woman had dealt with Skinny as well, because Brody had his back turned, and apart from the sounds of a struggle, he didn't know what was going on. Not a good feeling, but he had the gun now, and that counted for something.

He turned around and quickly took it all in. Clumsy was on his side, not moving. The steel pipe to the side of the head had dropped him like a side of beef. Skinny was grappling with the girl, trying to get the pipe from her hands. Brody stood, racked the slide on the little gun (just in case the moron hadn't loaded it, or didn't have a round in the chamber), and saw a live round fall to the ground as the action slammed another round into the chamber. He figured he probably had five shots (or less) but would only need one, if it came to that. Brody quickly glanced back at the guy he'd downed; he wouldn't have to worry about Muscles, at least not right away. He was holding his knee and whimpering like a little girl. Time to deal with Skinny, who nearly had the woman's pipe in his control.

She was kicking him, holding on to the pipe as best she could.

"Back off!" Brody yelled, getting Skinny's attention. Brody didn't aim the gun at him (little pistols like this were notoriously inaccurate and he didn't want to risk shooting the girl) but held the weapon forward, clearly in view. The guy saw it and reacted immediately, releasing his grip on the pipe, raising his hands, and taking a step back from the girl.

"She doesn't belong here," he said, his voice still different from before.

He didn't get to say anything else, because the woman didn't waste any time taking advantage of the opening Brody provided. She swung the pipe, hard, and connected with the man's neck. He dropped like a marionette with severed strings.

A blow like that had probably broken the guy's neck. A dead body wasn't something Brody wanted to have connected to his name. Visions of a prison cell raced through his mind.

"Come on," the girl said, grabbing Brody's jacket and pulling.

"Jesus, I think you killed him," Brody said.

"It doesn't matter. We have to go. Now!"

He was still dizzy, worse now because of the pounding his head had taken, and his ribs began screaming at him again now that the fight was over. He was a real mess, with one eye almost swollen shut, but he could still manage to see the girl clearly. He was right about her outfit: some sort of coveralls, like a mechanic would wear. She wore work boots, and her hands were smudged from handling the pipe. She was almost his height, and maybe 110 pounds soaking wet. Red hair, long, pulled into a ponytail. Her eyes were green, big and bright, full of seriousness. But there was terror in those eyes as well. He tucked the pistol into his jacket pocket, knowing he'd have to dispose of it later. He didn't need to get caught with what was probably a stolen gun. She tugged at his jacket again.

"Okay, okay," Brody said, taking a few steps before he stumbled, nearly falling. She took his arm and put it over her shoulders, helping carry his weight. "How bad?" she asked.

"I've been better," he said, surprised at how strong she was. He tried not to lean into her, but she wasn't having any problem supporting him. "I think that fat ass you clocked back there broke a couple of ribs." *And I still feel like I'm hammered,* he didn't add.

"Stop thinking about how much it hurts. Concentrate. Tell yourself your ribs are fine."

He wasn't sure how to respond to that, so he didn't. "Where are we going?" he asked.

"Away from there," she said, tossing her head back toward where the three thugs lay. "We need to get some distance. He's coming."

"Who's coming?"

"Can we stop with the questions?" she said. "Come on, over there." She guided him toward an alley, completely dark.

"I live right up the street," Brody started to say, thinking that would definitely be a better place to end up than some dark alley, but she didn't let him finish.

"No, he knows where you live. He won't find us here," she said as she guided him into the shadows. "At least not right away."

"He knows where I live? *Who* knows?"

She stopped and helped him sit down next to a dumpster. Brody groaned as his ribs ground against each other. He could barely see her face in the darkness. "The shadow man, that's who. You've seen him, right?"

The shadow man.

a cutout of a man, a shadow in the road

Brody was confused, dizzy and weak, beat to shit, but did remember something about a *shadow man* appearing in the street after a fight with three . . . punks? But that couldn't be. It was as if he'd already been here.

"You remember something, don't you," she said, watching his face closely. She smiled, a knowing smile, as if she knew exactly what was happening inside his head.

"I do," he said, right before the woman doubled over, grunting in pain. He reached for her. "What's wrong?"

"It's—it's happening again. You have to remember, okay? Please, you have to remember."

"Remember what?" he asked.

She took his face in her hands, forced him to look into her eyes. "My face, *me*, remember me!"

Brody didn't know what she was talking about but didn't think he'd have any difficulty remembering *this* girl. "I don't even know your name," he said. She was so close, face-to-face, but then, she wasn't. Brody flinched as she once again groaned in pain and began to—*no, this can't be happening*. She was fading away right before his eyes, disappearing into the shadows. She reached for him, and he grasped for her hand, but she was nothing more than smoke as his hand passed through hers. He pulled his arm back, shocked.

Before she completely disappeared, he could still hear her voice, quiet and fearful, as if she were a spirit speaking from the other side. "My name is Connie. Remember me . . ."

As the shadow man turned the corner and ran into the ally, the day ended for twenty-six-year-old Brody Quail.

Chapter 16
BRODY16

"It doesn't work from the outside," Brody yelled, leaning over and popping the door lever.

"Thanks," Joan said, placing her books between them on the bench seat and slamming her door shut. "Cool car." She sat up a little and reached under her leg, pulling out a flattened ball of paper. "Need this?" she asked.

Brody took the paper, wondering where it had come from, and tossed it in the backseat. "Nope," he said. "Next time I'll make sure you don't have to sit on my garbage." He fastened his lap belt, cinched it tight, and realized he'd said *next time.* He glanced over at Joan, expecting some sort of reaction, but she either hadn't heard him, or *had* and let it slide (which meant there might just *be* a next time). With a quick pump of the gas pedal and turn of the key, the old Impala's engine turned over, leaving a cloud of blue smoke in his rearview mirror. *Hey, at least it runs.*

Joan giggled. "My house is on Lincoln, a couple of blocks away," she said. "Take the first left from Michigan, and I'm the third house on the left."

Brody looked at her, a little confused. "Yeah, I know where you live," he said. "And what's so funny?"

For a second, Joan's face looked *weird*. Her eyes went blank, as if she were looking right through him instead of at him. Then, just as quickly, she was back to her normal self.

She smiled and put her hand on his arm. "You've never driven me home before, so I figured you'd need directions."

Brody suddenly felt disoriented, dizzy, as if the car were tumbling forward. He slammed the brake pedal, stopping the Impala halfway out of the parking spot. He put the stick shift into neutral, let off the clutch, and grabbed his head.

never driven me home before

    never driven me home before

        never driven me home before

            never driven me home before

Brody gritted his teeth as a sharp pain crisscrossed his forehead. For a second, he thought he was having some sort of stroke.

"Brody?" He could feel Joan's hand on his shoulder. "Are you okay? What's wrong?"

The pain disappeared just as suddenly as it had come, and Brody opened his eyes. Everything was blurry as he stared through tears. "I—I don't know," he said. He was nauseous and cupped his mouth with the palm of his hand, thinking he was about to puke. He opened his door and leaned out, retching, but nothing came up.

"Jesus, Brody," Joan said. He could tell she had scooted over closer to him as she rubbed her hand across his back. "Are you okay?"

Brody straightened up and nodded. "Yeah, I think so."

"What happened?"

"I don't know. One second I was fine, and then the next I was really dizzy."

"Are you okay to drive?"

He did feel better. The dizziness had passed, quickly, but had left a slight headache. He didn't feel like he was going to puke anymore, but he was hungry, really, *really* hungry.

"Yeah, I'm fine. I don't know what the heck that was, but I feel better now." Joan was still sitting close and had real concern in her eyes. *Wow, she's worried about me! How cool is that?* "I'm fine. I promise."

"You're sure?"

He smiled at her. "I'm sure." She smiled back and moved over to her side of the seat, straightening her books, which had bunched up between them. Brody put the car back into reverse, finished backing out, and pulled away from the school, heading down Central toward Michigan.

Joan had one leg pulled up underneath her, sitting so she was facing him. "I really like your car," she said. "How fast have you had it?"

"Maybe 80, 85." He glanced over at her, took in her bright eyes, her smile, wishing she were still sitting as close as she'd been earlier. "It really starts shaking at around 75, so I'm kinda nervous about going any faster." He'd read about people experiencing déjà vu but had never felt it himself until this moment. "It's—it's an old car, and—"

"My dad had an old car when he was a kid," Joan said. "He swerved into a ditch and rolled it when one of the tie rods broke."

"He was lucky to get out alive," Brody said, wondering why he would say such a thing. His headache was getting worse, the pounding behind his eyes matching the beating of his heart.

"Yeah, that's right," Joan said. "He was lucky to get out alive."

Her voice sounded . . . *different*. Flat. Robotic. Brody turned to face Joan, and that's when a flood of visions cascaded through his mind.

A missed turn.
A red light.
A truck.
Impact.
Pain.
Fire.

Brody slammed the brakes, and the car screamed to a stop in the middle of the street. His window was open, and the smell of hot rubber wafted inside. Joan had slid from the front seat and lay in a heap on the floor under the dash.

a Brody rule put your belt on I know it's stupid

"Jesus *Christ*, Brody!" she yelled. "What are you doing?"

Brody sat still for a moment, breathing fast and heavy, his mouth hanging open. His head was really pounding now and his eyes were tearing up from the pain. "I—I don't know, I just saw—I saw—" he stammered, then realized Joan might be hurt. "Oh my God, are you all right?"

She was already crawling back onto the seat. A bright red welt appeared on her forehead where she had smacked the steel dashboard. "Why the hell did you slam on the brakes like that?"

Because I was going to drive right by Michigan and run a red light and get slammed by a truck, that's why. Brody put a hand to his head, trying to soothe the throbbing thunder behind his eyes. Something was terribly wrong with him.

"No," Joan said. "You don't belong here."

What? Brody looked at Joan and saw her looking past him, out the driver's side window. Her face was blank, all the anger that was there seconds before completely gone. The hinges creaked. He felt the driver's door open. A hand gripped his shirt and pulled.

shadow man
it's the shadow man

114

Brody recoiled, pulling away from the hand gripping his shirt. When he turned, he expected to see something horrid and empty in the shape of a man.

But it was a girl.

She was roughly his age, maybe a little younger, or at least the splash of freckles across her cheeks made her seem so, with red hair and large green eyes. Brody's first thought was that she looked much too young to be working at a gas station, as she was dressed in work coveralls, like a mechanic, and then he remembered.

He'd seen her before. Somewhere.

"Come on, get out of the car," she said. "We have to go!"

Brody fumbled with his seat belt buckle, never once taking his eyes off her. He didn't know her name, but she looked so damned *familiar*. He unlatched the buckle and tossed the loose belt toward the center of the bench seat.

"Brody, no," Joan said, grabbing his arm. "You have to stay here."

Joan was back to normal and looked so incredibly beautiful. The same girl whom he'd crushed on during study hall. The girl he wasn't ever going to have a chance to be with but who was letting him drive her home.

she'd written B R O D Y balloon letters in the notebook

"I need you to take me home, Brody," she said, gently caressing his arm. "You're supposed to drive me home."

"Come *on*!" the other girl shouted, yanking Brody from the car. He tumbled out the door and ended up on all fours in the road.

"What are you doing?" he shouted.

The other girl was looking around, nervous, jumpy, and motioned to Brody to get up and follow her. "We need to get out of the street before he shows up," she said. "Come on, *come on*!"

Brody was about to ask who, but somehow, he knew.

shadow man

it's the shadow man

Brody scrambled to his feet, fighting the pain in his head. He was weak and had trouble standing. The other girl put her arm around his shoulder and prodded him along, heading toward a gas station on the corner. *Maybe that's where she works,* he thought. Funny how her helping him walk like this seemed awfully familiar.

"We need to get inside. Hurry." She opened the glass door and stepped inside, immediately heading toward a back room, maybe an office. The place smelled like gasoline, oil, and axle grease. Papers were spread across a small desk—invoices, Brody guessed—that was flanked by a small swivel chair. A pinup calendar hung on the wall above a grubby phone, the handset blackened by the greasy hands that used it. Brody plopped down in the chair and put his head between his knees, wishing the pain would go away.

"You're going to be fine," the girl said. "It'll pass." She was looking out the office door, toward the gas station's front windows.

She's looking for him, Brody thought, then wondered how in the hell he would know anything about some *shadow man.* This was all crazy. So wrong. But the girl was right. His head was feeling better already. "Who are you?" Brody asked.

She smiled at him, and for the first time, Brody noticed how pretty she was. "You don't remember me, do you?" she said.

"I know you?"

"Not really. But you've seen me before."

Brody couldn't recall ever stopping for gas at this station, but it was so close to school he figured he must have at some point. Maybe he'd seen her working here. But why did she remember him? "Um, here?"

"Yes. Out there. On the street."

"On the street? But—"

She crouched down, balancing on the balls of her feet, her hands on her knees so she could look at him directly. "Look at me. Really *look* at me." She had an urgency to her voice that made Brody a little nervous.

Brody stared into her eyes, studied the curve of her brows, the shape of her nose, the way her lips looked a little too small for her face, a face he felt he knew, but no more than any other face he might've glanced at in passing. She was pretty, so maybe that's why he thought he'd remember her, but he couldn't recall when.

"Dammit," she said. She shook her head and stood. "You don't remember me."

But he did, in a way. "You do look familiar," he said. "I just don't remember ever—"

"It's okay," she said, turning away, a touch of sadness in her voice.

"What's your name?"

She turned, and Brody could see a tear in her eye. "I'm Connie. Not that you'll remember, anyway."

Before he could respond, Brody heard Joan calling his name from outside the station. "Brody? You have to drive me home. You have to drive me home now."

Both he and Connie peered out the office door and saw Joan standing in the middle of the street, hands at her sides, staring inside the station. The cars had stopped in the road. "Dammit," Connie said, reaching for Brody's hand. "Come on, we have to find someplace else. He'll know we're here!"

"Who?" Brody asked, wanting to hear her say what was already in his mind.

"Not a who, a *what*," Connie replied, pulling Brody to his feet. Together, they made their way to the front door.

"It's empty, isn't it," Brody said. "Like a hole."

Connie stopped and turned to face him. "You've seen it."

"No, I—I haven't. But I know what you're—oh *crap*, I don't know what to think."

Connie shook her head. "Look, it's okay. I know this is confusing, and you don't have a clue about what's going on, but if you know about that shadow thing, believe me, you've seen it before."

"But I don't—"

"You've *seen* it, okay? You have. Somewhere, you *have*." She turned and tugged at his hand. "And if we don't find another place to hide, it's going to find us, thanks to your girlfriend out there."

"She's not my girlfriend," Brody said, amazed at how quickly the words had popped out of his mouth.

"Oh yeah?" Connie laughed as they stepped outside. "She's awfully pretty. Are you sure?"

"Maybe she would be, if I—"

"Brody, you need to drive me home, okay?" Joan again, still standing in the street staring at them as the duo turned left and headed down the sidewalk, walking quickly. "You need to drive me home." And then, as if switching personalities, she said, "She doesn't belong here." Flat, deadened voice.

"Come on, Romeo," Connie said, "we need to find another place where what's-her-name won't be able to find us."

"Her name's Joan."

"Okay, Joan, then. She's going to get us killed."

"Killed?"

Joan tugged harder. "The *shadow man*, genius. Now come *on!*"

Shadow man. He didn't like the sound of that. Brody took a quick glance back at Joan and saw her standing in the same spot, still staring into the station. Like a statue.

"Look, there's a theater up ahead. We'll hide inside there."

"Connie, wait." She didn't. "Wait," Brody said loudly, pulling his hand free.

"What the hell are you doing?" she said, her eyes flashing.

"I need to know what's going on."

"Look, it can wait, okay? I'll tell you what I know when we get inside the—"

Brody watched the blood drain from her face and her eyes widen as she stared past him down the street.

Brody turned, knowing what he was going to see.

He (it) was there. A shadow in the shape of a man, running down the street toward them. "Oh crap."

"Come on! Hurry!" Connie screamed, breaking into a run.

Brody sprinted after her, amazed at how fast Connie was running, especially in work boots. "Where are we going?" Brody asked through ragged breaths.

"Just run!"

Brody looked over his shoulder and saw it. Closer, gaining on them. It was moving so fast, too fast. "It's going to catch us!" he yelled.

"In here!" Connie yelled, darting into an alleyway between two buildings. Brody followed, knowing there was no way they were going to get away from the shadow man. He watched as Connie pulled open a side door to the building on their right, motioning him to follow as she ran inside. He grabbed its handle before the door swung shut, just as he heard Connie make a noise he couldn't quite place: not a scream, not a moan, but a combination of the two?

"Connie!" he yelled, standing in the open doorway. The inside was impossibly black. He looked back outside and saw it, the shadow man, walking down the alley. Not running, but walking quickly, as if it knew there would be no escape and there was no need to hurry.

As Brody moved into the open doorway, he heard the shadow speak.

"Nooo," it said, more of a hiss than an actual voice. Brody looked back, and it waved an arm at him as if waving him off. *It doesn't want me to go in here.* Brody stepped inside and slammed the door.

He was encased in darkness, unable to see his hand in front of his face. He fumbled with the door handle but could find no lock. And then he couldn't even find the door handle. He backed away a few steps, waiting for the door to slam open, but nothing happened. Five seconds . . . ten . . . fifteen.

Nothing but silence, apart from his own breathing. He turned around, still unable to see a thing, and called out, "Connie? Connie, are you okay?" His voice echoed in the darkened space. He listened, trying to hear movement. If Connie had tripped and fallen, maybe she had hit her head and was hurt. Still, he could hear only his breathing and the thudding of his heart.

"Connie? Where are you?" He took a few tentative steps forward, baby steps. "Connie!" Louder this time. "Connie! Answer me! Are you okay?"

Again nothing.

But then, he saw something up ahead. A pinpoint of light. Small, barely visible, but it was there. "Connie? Is that you?" Brody started walking toward the light, taking small steps, tapping his foot where he intended to step, just in case there was a hole in the floor or a stairway going down or something else he couldn't see that would cause him to fall and break his neck.

The light grew brighter as Brody crept ahead. As his eyes adjusted to the dark, he could see the floor in front of him, barely enough to tell if he was going to step into some sort of bottomless chasm. *Jeez, don't be such a pussy. How many buildings have bottomless chasms in them, right?* "Connie? Are you there?"

Still nothing.

As he neared the light, Brody could tell it was a keyhole. There was a door, and it had an old-fashioned doorknob, the kind that took a large, old-timey key. The kind of keyhole someone could peer through.

Which is exactly what he did.

The light on the other side of the door wasn't very bright, but it was still much brighter than the room he was in now. He reached out and turned the knob, thankful that it wasn't locked. The latch opened with a loud click. Brody slowly opened the door.

He found himself in a long hallway, shadowy and dark, but still lit enough to have guided him here through the keyhole. As he stepped inside, his mind grappled with what he was seeing. He wasn't too sure, but he didn't remember the outside of the building looking so fancy.

"Connie?" he whispered. "Are you here?" He stepped down the hallway, trying to tread as lightly as he could, the floorboards creaking slightly with each step. He was intruding, creeping through someplace he shouldn't be.

But was that true?

⋇

This place. So foreign and yet so familiar. "Connie?" he whispered again. "Where are you?" He stood perfectly still, listening. There were no voices, no sound, no movement. Nothing. Maybe she hadn't come through the door and was still inside the darkened room. Maybe she really had fallen and hurt herself, and he had passed right by her in the dark.

He had to check.

Brody turned around and stepped to the door. Beyond, there was no darkened room. Not anymore.

He saw a bedroom.

He was suddenly overcome with a feeling of sadness so great, so painful, that he had to close his eyes. And when he did, he knew what had happened here, in this very room. Not something he had witnessed, but something he had been *told*.

A person died here. A person whom he had loved.

And her death had been his fault.

Brody opened his eyes, hoping the room was gone, but it was still there. Every corner of the room, every crease in the sheets, every fold of the blankets was as it should be, *because she would want it this way*.

He felt something in his hand, heavy and cold. A revolver, blued steel and wood. Familiar. He raised the weapon and popped the cylinder, spun it, and slammed it shut. He'd never handled a gun before, but this, this was his.

Then from behind, footsteps.

He wheeled around and saw an older man standing in the hallway, staring at him. He was tall, thin, balding with gray hair at the temples. In his hands he held a tray of food. "Good evening, sir," the man said. "A fine weapon."

Brody's head began to pound again, throbbing hammer blows behind his eyes. He dropped the gun. The pistol thudded loudly against the wooden hallway floor, then he fell to his knees and gripped his skull.

The man stood there, expressionless, watching. Then he spoke again. "I assume you'll be taking dinner in your office again, sir?"

Brody felt a trickle of blood run from his nose and heard the stream splatter against the floor. He heard himself begin to scream.

At that moment, the day ended for sixteen-year-old Brody Quail.

Chapter 17
CONNIE

Darkness.

A place without feeling, without perception. Silent and cold. A simple nothingness, smothering and all-encompassing, an endless unseen landscape. A place where time doesn't seem to exist, for if it did, insanity would creep and creep, building in intensity until the fire it fueled would blossom into a white-hot explosion of despair, of hopelessness, until the flame would flicker out and die.

But even then, she believed, there would be no death. No release. Only the dark.

She was aware of every single moment. Unable to speak, to see, to move. Shackled to the shadows by invisible chains.

Her name was Connie. Her name was all that was left.

Just a name.

What she had been, no more. Her existence, what she could remember of it, came in flashes, glimpses of places and people, but they were short lived, convoluted, broken.

And they were beginning to disappear.

When this nightmare began, no one would listen to her. No one believed. The people she loved and trusted would laugh, explain it away, or simply ignore her pleas for help. She would slip away into this dark place, and there was nothing she could do. Time and time again she could feel a painful cold in her arms and legs and a twisting certainty in her gut that the darkness was calling her, that it would not be denied.

And it never was.

The darkness would envelop her, shroud her senses, and there she would stay until she emerged somewhere familiar once again. Those moments were becoming less and less frequent now, sometimes only lasting minutes at a time. Her time as Connie, her life with the people she knew, was fading.

No one seemed to care.

She initially thought she was ill, passing out. When she mentioned her blackouts, her friends and family, even her father and mother, changed the subject, ignored her, laughed it off. She was stuck in some sort of cyclic torment and had only herself to rely on. So she did.

When the blackness would come, she fought it, struggled to stay where she was, in *her* world, until she finally slipped away. With each episode, she watched, learned, and remembered.

Things were not as they seemed.

Yet something followed her from the darkness. A shadow man, a figure cut from the very reality around her, as if someone had taken a knife and sliced away the world, leaving a blank shape of a person, black and empty.

He—*it*—was always there now, chasing her, coming for her. To drag her back to *this* place. Forever.

She wouldn't let that happen. She would run and hide, and all the while the people she knew around her were oblivious to his presence, as if she were the only person who could see him. She'd watched. Learned.

Explored her boundaries. And remembered. She wasn't sick. She was Connie, just a name. And that's all she was.

Until she'd seen the other. In *his* world, not hers.

She wasn't alone, after all. There was someone else out there, fighting against the darkness. He didn't understand what was going on yet. But he would, with her help.

His name was Brody.

Brody Quail.

PART III
MERGE

Chapter 18
BRODY52

Joshua, Maine
Friday, October 25, 1974

He found himself standing in his office doorway. Just standing there, leaning against the doorjamb, with no idea why, or when, he'd gotten up from his desk. The house was dark. None of the lights was on in his office or the hallway, so he was bathed in shadows.

He could hear the steady ticking of his office clock, time inexorably moving forward, further and further away from what used to be his life.

Tick.

Tock.

Tick.

He used to have moments like this before: periods of time that were nothing but a blank, a lost chunk of life never to be remembered. But he was a drunk then, a worthless, pathetic human being (and maybe still was). He hadn't touched a bottle since the last time he'd passed out. *That* night.

He carefully walked to his desk and flipped the switch on the small lamp sitting on the left corner. He was surprised to see the bottle. Scotch. Half-empty. Resting on his desktop in exactly the spot where he would have placed it.

He'd ordered Felix to remove all the alcohol from the house, could remember the moment clearly, but for some reason, it was all still here. Even downstairs in the study. In the kitchen. Everywhere he looked, there it was. His old demon, mocking him from within the glass.

I'll have to have a word with Felix, he thought sternly, but then again, how many times had he had that exact conversation with the man? Was Felix doing it on purpose? Maybe as a way to punish him for allowing the woman they both loved to be taken from them?

No. That wasn't Felix. The man didn't have a spiteful bone in him. *But.*

The amber liquid called to him, gently, so tranquil and still in the muted lamplight. Brody could feel the pull, the need, growing stronger by the second. He looked away, rubbing the stubble around his mouth with his palm.

He'd blacked out apparently, waking to find himself standing in the doorway. He didn't feel drunk, but then again, most alcoholics don't recognize when the alcohol has taken control.

"Felix!" he yelled, stepping once again to the office door. "Felix!" No answer. He walked down the hall a few steps toward the stairs and reached for the hallway light switch, then paused. Unseen eyes swept across his back. He turned abruptly, startled by the eerie feeling that he wasn't alone upstairs, as he'd thought.

But there was no one there.

Just an open door.

He stood and stared at the entrance to his wife's bedroom (he had ceased seeing it as his bedroom, by choice), expecting to see Felix walk out. But there was no one. Just the darkness inside.

"Felix, are you in there?" Brody called, knowing deep down that there would be no answer. And there wasn't.

He slowly walked down the hall, the wooden floor creaking slightly with each step and sounding unnaturally loud in the silent house. He passed by his office door, resisting the urge to glance at the bottle on his desk and thus admit he'd somehow returned to a dark place he'd sworn never to enter again. For now, he'd pretend the bottle wasn't there. He'd pretend he hadn't experienced another blackout. He'd deal with the demon later. Or have Felix do it, properly supervised this time. If he'd actually touched the bottle again and couldn't remember doing so, then he would personally ensure that every ounce of liquor in the house went down the drain and command Felix to never again allow another drop through the front door.

As he approached the bedroom door, he wondered if he would be able to glance inside. Thankfully, it was dark, and he wouldn't see much anyway, but he knew exactly what was in the room and how everything was arranged.

He couldn't look inside.

Brody turned his head and fumbled for the doorknob, wishing he'd held his breath, too. He caught a tiny bit of her scent, a memory floating through the air. He paused, breathed deeply, and caught the sob that was building in his throat.

He gently shut the door, dropped his hand from the knob, and wiped a tear from his cheek. Her scent lingered as he stood outside the door, awash in a flood of memories that soothed and cut.

The hand on his shoulder startled him.

He turned, and it was her.

The shock of seeing her again, so close, caused his knees to buckle. His back thudded against the closed bedroom door. The tears came, so sudden and free-flowing, as the joy of seeing his beloved Reba again overpowered self-control. "Reba," he breathed, fighting to say her name, because even though the sight of her brought him more happiness than he'd felt in—*Months? How long had it been?*—she was nothing more than a vision, a trick of the mind prompted by the scent of her perfume.

He was dreaming.

Still passed out on his desk.

"You know me, don't you," she said.

Brody looked into her eyes and saw someone else. She looked so much like Reba, but something was wrong, as if an entirely different person were staring through his wife's eyes directly into his. Brody was frightened, and he pressed his back harder against the door.

"I look like someone you knew, don't I?" she said, nodding slightly. "Reba. Was that her name?"

Brody nodded involuntarily, then caught himself. He wiped the tears from his cheeks and stood straighter. If this were only a dream, then he had nothing to fear. "You're not her," he said, surprised at the despair and disappointment in his own voice.

"No. I'm not her," she said. "I'm sorry." She looked down at her dress, as if noticing it for the first time. "I'm sorry it has to be this way, but I can't control—" She stopped, then said, "I can tell you loved her very much."

They both jumped at the sound of a knock on the front door.

Brody knew he had to go downstairs.

one shall pass

He moved to go around the woman, feeling a little odd stepping away at the moment, but he had to *answer the door.*

"Wait," the woman said, placing her hand on his arm. "You don't have to go down there."

Her touch was warm, so real, so unlike a dream. Brody wanted to pull away from her touch, but let her hand linger.

"Think, okay?" she said. "I want you to tell me who is at the door."

The police.

Brody didn't have to think. He knew what they were going to tell him.

"One shall pass," he said quietly, his voice strangely level, even to his own ears. Then, to the woman he said, "It's my son. He's dead."

"Your son?"

Brody nodded, surprised at how nonchalantly he'd accepted the fact that one of his children, Raymond, had died. At least he *thought* Raymond had died, or *knew* he had, or . . .

"This isn't right." Brody began to shake, felt his hands trembling and his knees growing weak. The woman reached out to steady him, and as before, he didn't shrink away from her touch.

Her hands were warm, her grip firm yet gentle as she helped him regain his balance. She was dressed like Reba and at first glance had looked so much like the Reba in his pictures, but she definitely wasn't her. What was going on? Where did she come from, and why was she here? None of it made any sense, unless . . .

"No, this is a dream," he said, shaking his head and shrugging her hands away from his body. "It's not real, *you're* not real." *I'm in my office, asleep in my chair. I'm not drunk, just asleep. Just asleep.*

The woman took a step back, then turned toward the top of the stairs as the knocking on the door resumed. "Go answer it," she said, motioning down the hallway with an outstretched hand. "I won't stop you."

"Why should I? If this is a dream, what difference does it make?"

The woman's face brightened for a second, then she smiled. "Tell me about your dreams, then."

"What?"

"Tell me. All about them. What do you dream about?"

More knocking at the door, louder this time.

Answer the door. You have to answer the door!

Brody moved, but the woman blocked his path. "If this is a dream, why do you want to answer the door so badly?" she asked him. "You just told me it didn't matter."

answer the door answer the door answer

"It—It doesn't," Brody replied, trying desperately to stifle the growing urge he felt to run down the stairs and throw open the front door.

"Then tell me about your *other* dreams!" the woman said. "Tell me!"

"Get out of my way!" Brody pushed her aside and strode forcefully down the hall. He would answer his goddamned front door, dream or no dream. There would be two uniformed officers there waiting for him. They would tell him his son Raymond had been killed in a car accident, and he would fight the urge to take another drink.

Another drink.

Brody stopped at the top of the stairs, dumbstruck.

He knew exactly what was going to happen. Every detail, including what the officers were going to say.

"I'm sorry to have to tell you this, sir, but it's your son. Raymond."

one shall pass

one shall pass

"We were notified earlier this evening that your son was severely injured in an automobile accident, sir. Again, I'm sorry to have to tell you this."

And how he was going to feel. What he would do.

He would sit at his desk, open the bottle.

He would sit at his desk, fight the urge.

He would take out the gun from the drawer, then put it back.

He would put it in his mouth. Pull the trigger.

Brody gripped his head as the visions tumbled through his mind, each so real and detailed; each one a separate memory, each one different from the next, all swirling around a single event.

He heard more pounding on the door, much louder now.

He would always answer the door. His son would always be dead.

He turned toward the woman, half expecting her to be gone. If he were losing his mind then she was nothing more than another fragment of his twisted consciousness, not real.

But she was still there. Standing, staring at him. He saw compassion in her eyes, a knowing look tinged with pity.

"I know what you're going through," she said, stepping toward him. "You're confused and scared, and you have no idea what's happening."

"I don't understand what—who—" Brody fell to his knees, a sudden sharp pain shooting through his skull. He grimaced and through squinting eyes saw the woman kneel down beside him. She gripped his shoulders, turned his body to face her.

"I know what you're feeling," she said. "It happens to me, too."

The world around Brody swirled, and he felt he was losing consciousness. He struggled to speak, to ask the woman what was happening to him, but the words wouldn't come. He stared into her eyes, so green and deep (and so much like his Reba's, but still, she wasn't there), and struggled to stay awake. But his vision grew dark and her face began to fade away.

Before the day ended for fifty-two-year-old Brody Quail, he heard the woman speak again.

"My name is Connie. *Connie*. Please, remember me."

Blackness then.

Chapter 19
BRODY10

Culver, Ohio
Thursday, May 15, 1975

The sky is wrong.

Brody opened his eyes, staring straight up. He was outside, lying on his back. He blinked, trying to focus. Maybe he'd bonked his head pretty hard playing Smear the Queer (*Annihilation* when Mrs. Carlisle was around, don't forget), but he felt okay. His head didn't hurt. He raised one hand, held it in front of his face: four fingers and a thumb, clear as a bell. His eyes were fine, so why did the sky look so funny?

Brody sat up, looked around. Like he thought, he was in the field, but he was alone. There was no one else anywhere on the playground, as a matter of fact. "God, I missed the bell," he said, but why would everyone just leave him lying out in the middle of the field like this?

He stood, brushed the grass from his sleeves.

Not only did the sky look weird, but it was a darker, slate-blue color, as if some of the brighter hues had been sucked away, but everything looked wrong, the shadows deep and dark, and the colors lifeless.

The grass was green but didn't look *real*. Brody looked up at the sky again. There were no clouds, either, just a slate-blue dome stretching across the sky.

And no sun.

He wheeled around, searching the sky for the sun—he couldn't see it. Anywhere. But if the sun had set, it would be pitch-black, right? And why would he be out here at night? Chills suddenly snaked up Brody's arms and legs, and he felt a twinge of pain at the back of his head.

Maybe he *had* hit his head. He couldn't feel any bumps or lumps and wasn't bleeding or anything, so that was good.

Maybe the impact had given him super night-vision. It really was pitch-black outside, and he was seeing things like a cat would, or something like that. Maybe he was invisible, too. No one brought him inside because they couldn't see him anymore. He'd just disappeared from the playground—*poof!* And if he was invisible, boy, could he have a lot of fun, sneaking around all over the place (even places where he wasn't supposed to be), and no one would ever know!

His mother was probably worried sick. Maybe Debbie Wilson was worried, too. It would be *awesome* if Debbie was worried about him. Maybe they'd put his picture on a milk carton or something.

No, this is wrong.

He didn't have super cat-vision. He wasn't invisible. He was alone, completely alone, and nothing looked right. Brody started walking toward the school, as it seemed like the most logical place to go. He suddenly didn't like being out in the middle of the field all by himself. He glanced around, looking into the shadows behind the trees on the far end of the little-kid playground equipment, and imagined something there, watching him. Eyes, following his every move as he walked toward the school building, out in the open, defenseless.

Brody ran.

The feeling of being watched suddenly seemed very real, not a figment of his imagination. He sensed eyes on him, from the shadows.

Something was there, getting ready to burst from the trees and chase him down.

Something black, empty.

Brody sprinted the last few yards to the school entrance and grabbed the door handle, hoping it was unlocked.

It was.

He slipped inside and watched the door swing close, the latch engaging with an unnaturally loud click. He stood still for a second, peering through the door's rectangular glass panels, expecting to see something running across the playground, following him. Wanting to come inside. He stepped closer to the door, closer to the glass, and searched the parts of the playground he could still see for any movement. Each breath fogged the glass.

He was scared. Really scared. The feeling of being watched had been so strong when he was in the field that he was certain he wouldn't make it to the building without getting chased by—

black, empty, in the shape of a man

Brody jumped back from the door, taking three, four, five steps back. He had no way to lock the door. He felt the urge to hide, get away from the door, because if it (the shadow man) wanted in, it could open the door, just as he had done.

Brody turned, looked down the main hall. The overhead fluorescents were on, but just like outside, the light was somehow *wrong*, dim and muted. The end of the hallway stretched into shadow. The gym was down there, but it was dark. His classroom was nearby, down the first hall to the left. He walked slowly and steadily, trying to be as quiet as possible, listening, hoping to hear someone talking . . . his classmates, teachers, *anyone*.

The building was silent, with only the buzz from the overhead lights keeping Brody company.

Alone.

As he walked toward the hallway that would lead to his classroom, he kept his eyes fixed on the gym, staring into the darkness at the end of the hallway. His eyes played tricks on him, and his heart jumped into his throat when he thought he saw something move, but there was nothing.

Brody turned the corner, relieved to be away from the main hallway and the open maw of the gym, and heard the playground door open. He heard the catch release, heard the door's hinges squeak.

Someone, some *thing*, was coming inside.

black, empty, in the shape of a man the shadow man

Brody ran, covering the distance to his classroom as quickly as he could, his eyes bright with fear. He skidded to a stop by the door, his tennis shoes squeaking against the tile floor. *Too loud!* He gently turned the handle, slipped inside, and closed the door, wincing as it clicked shut. He wheeled around and looked for a place to hide. The rows of little desks wouldn't do him any good, but maybe he could crawl under the teacher's desk. Nobody could see him under there, as the front was solid. He walked down the nearest row of desks, passing his own.

He pulled the teacher's chair back from the desk and crawled into the foot well, pulling the chair back into place. There wasn't much room, but he was completely hidden. Unless whatever had entered the school walked around the back of the desk and pulled the chair out. But it wouldn't have any reason to do that, right? It (shadow man) would look through the classroom door, see the room was empty, and move on. He hoped.

Brody listened carefully. He couldn't hear any footsteps outside in the hallway, but maybe the shadow man was being quiet, too, moving slowly and listening for *him*.

The minutes slowly ticked by. He wasn't sure how many. Five, ten, fifteen? His legs were starting to cramp, and he wanted nothing more than to be able to stand up and stretch his—

He nearly screamed when he heard the classroom door open. He clamped his hand over his mouth as the hinges squealed, and he tried to control his breathing. His heart pounded away in his chest, and he slunk back against the front of the desk as far as he could go, pulling his feet and knees up close to his body. He wrapped his arm around his legs to keep them in place, knowing he wouldn't be able to hold the position for a long time.

There's nobody in here, he chanted to himself. *It's empty, no one is here, go on to the next room.*

"Brody?"

He couldn't believe his ears. It was a *girl's* voice? He wasn't about to answer, no way. Not yet. Maybe the shadow man was trying to trick him, get him to show himself.

"Brody, are you in here?"

He'd heard that voice before. Was it Debbie? How cool would *that* be if Debbie was searching for him! But, no, it didn't sound like Debbie. He couldn't place the voice, but it was so familiar. He dropped his hand from his mouth, was almost ready to say something (what do you say when you're hiding from a shadow monster under a desk?), then heard the hinges squeak again. Whoever it was, she was leaving. Or *it* was leaving.

He let out a huge breath when the door clicked shut. He didn't think he'd been holding his breath, but apparently he was, and now he could breathe again. He slowly pushed the teacher's chair out with his feet.

"Brody? Are you here?"

He heard her voice again, in the hallway. The stranger was definitely searching for him. Before he gave himself up, though, he needed to be sure who it was. Brody stepped around the desks and grabbed the door handle. He turned it slowly, hoping it wouldn't make any noise, and when he felt (more than heard, thankfully) the catch release, he pulled the door open, gently, to keep the hinges quiet.

Opening it just enough to stick his head out, Brody looked down the hallway and saw a figure enter another classroom, two rooms down. It didn't *look* like a shadow man. As soon as that door swung shut, Brody moved.

He closed the door behind him, making sure it didn't swing shut on its own. He walked as softly as he could down the hall toward the other door; he would peer inside the rectangular window to see who (or what) was following him and calling his name. Three feet away, two feet, one.

He readied himself, and on the count of three leaned over and looked inside.

Dammit. He couldn't see anyone. She, or it, was out of view.

"Brody, if you're in here, would you please answer me? We don't have much time. We have to hurry."

Hurry.

That one little word, spoken by a girl whose face he couldn't place, unleashed a flood of memories through Brody's mind, coming so fast that he grabbed his head with his hands.

"Hurry!" she screamed.

"Wait! Who—What's wrong?" Brody said, as he broke free of her grasp. Before she could grab his arm again, Brody turned, and saw.

A man—no, a man shape—as if someone had taken a knife and sliced away part of a picture revealing a blank void beyond, and it was moving toward them. "Holy shi—"

The girl grabbed his arm again, and this time Brody ran with her, actually passing her by and pulling her along. He reached down and grabbed her hand. The other kids on the playground were all standing perfectly still, watching them (dolls' eyes) run toward the side of the school. Brody wasn't sure where they were going, but anywhere away from that thing would be okay.

Her hand was warm in his, and he held on tight, hoping he wasn't squeezing hard enough to hurt her.

And then, he wasn't holding anything.

She'd disappeared.

Brody slumped against the wall with a thud and struggled to keep himself from sliding to the floor. He heard the classroom door open, and there she was again—the same girl from the playground, he realized, who had vanished right into thin air—with the shadow man close behind.

She grabbed his arms to steady him. "Are you okay?" she asked. Brody couldn't look away. This was all so unreal. The strange sky with no sun, the empty playground, the empty school building, *all* of it, and now, her, a girl he didn't know (but *did* know) searching for him. He was scared, more frightened than he'd been when he was running toward the school, knowing he was being watched. No, this was worse, because he didn't understand *any* of it.

"I don't have very much time, Brody," she said. "I can feel it coming."

"It?" Brody said, thinking she meant the shadow man, but when she grimaced in pain, he wondered if she meant something else.

"We don't have much time. Come on, we have to find a safe place to talk." She pulled his arm, trying to get him to follow. Brody resisted at first but remembered he'd gone with her once before. She'd touched his cheek and it had felt so right, not in a Debbie-Wilson-dream-that-he'd-never-tell-anyone-about sort of way, but in a way he couldn't explain. He trusted her.

"What's going on?" Brody asked.

She spoke as she led him away farther down the hall. "You remember me, don't you."

"I think so," Brody replied, noticing she was smiling as she said it, but wishing they weren't going into the part of the building that was so dark.

"The last time I saw you," she said, "we were outside, in that playground, running away from that *shadow*, right? Come on, this way."

He remembered the moment, especially what they were running from. "What happened? I was holding your hand, then you screamed and—"

"And then I wasn't there anymore. I know. And it's going to happen again, and quick." She led him into, of all things, the janitor's closet and shut the door. The space was completely dark. They were standing face-to-face, just inches apart, but Brody couldn't see a thing.

"We'll be safe here, for now," she said.

"From the shadow man?"

"Yes. The shadow man."

"What is it? Why was it chasing you?" He had a million questions, but she shushed him.

"Look, Brody, I don't know what it is, okay? I don't." She groaned, almost like she had a bad stomachache.

"What's wrong? Are you okay?"

"Grab my hands, grab my hands," she said. Brody felt her fingers touch his arms, and he grasped her hands. "Listen to me, okay?" she continued. "That whatever-it-is, the shadow man, wants me. It wants you, too. I don't know why, but we can't let it get to us, okay?"

Brody didn't care a bit about Debbie Wilson anymore. He cared about this girl and wanted to protect her, keep her safe. "I won't let it."

She groaned again, louder this time, and was having trouble standing. Brody held her hands tighter. "What's happening?" he said.

"Hold on to me, Brody. I don't want to go back!"

"To where? Where are you going?"

Her breathing was heavy now, as if she were in pain. "If you don't see me again, you need to go to a place you've never been before, okay? Promise me you'll go to a place you've never been. Run there as fast as you can! Oh God, I don't want to go!"

Brody wrapped his arms around her and held her tight. Her whole body was trembling.

"Remember me again, Brody, okay? Don't forget me!"

"I don't even know your name!"

"I'm Connie!"

Connie. Of course her name is Connie.

And his arms were empty.

⋊⋉

Brody didn't know how long he stayed in the closet. He refused to venture out until he was sure he didn't hear the shadow man searching for him. He listened for classroom doors opening and shutting, but there was nothing. Only silence.

Connie had disappeared again, just as she had on the playground the last time he saw her, except this time it happened while he was holding her in his arms, holding her tight.

She said she didn't want to go back, but to where?

Saying her name felt as if a small curtain had been raised, revealing a part of his mind where he could see her more clearly.

Connie.

She was *real.* He'd convinced himself of that as soon as he felt her body trembling in his arms. Brody had never held a girl like that, and the feeling was much more amazing than anything he could've ever imagined in a dream. She was warm. He could feel her breathing, feel her heart pounding away against his chest. And she was soft.

He didn't know what was happening, or why, and was about as scared as he'd ever been, but at that moment, right before her body vanished, he realized this wasn't some sort of strange dream. Connie was real. And she was scared, too, scared of the shadow man, and scared that he'd forget her name.

"I won't forget you, Connie," he whispered to himself. "And I'll hold on tighter next time, I promise."

Brody stayed in the closet a bit longer, until he was as certain as he could be that the shadow man wasn't going to be standing right outside the door as soon as he opened it. He'd heard nothing since Connie vanished.

He opened the door, peered outside. Opened it wider, stepped into the hall. He was still alone.

She said to go to someplace I've never been before, to run there fast, but what did she mean? Now that he was back in the hallway, though, all Brody wanted to do was go home. If home was like this, though . . . What if the sky was still wrong, and the house was empty?

No, it wouldn't be. His mom would be there, in the kitchen like she always was. Murf would be there, too. It would be okay. It would have to be okay.

Brody trotted down the hall toward the side exit. He stopped at the door and looked outside; nothing had changed. The world was just as it was when he'd awakened in the field, a slate-blue sky, no sun, and the colors all wrong. He took a deep breath, stepped outside the door, and from the corner of his eye saw the shadow man come around the corner of the building.

He didn't even spare the extra second it would take to look directly at him (it). Brody ran. He ran as fast as his legs would take him, across the street (*Murf almost got hit by a car here*) and down the sidewalk, heading for Grant Avenue, where his house was. The street was more than a mile away, but he'd run all the way there if he had to.

He glanced over his shoulder, and the shadow man was still there but not right on his heels like he expected. It was standing by the edge of the school, seemingly staring in his direction. Watching. Not coming after him, just watching. Brody slowed to a walk, wondering why the shadow man wasn't coming after him. Wait, was it pointing?

Brody stopped. Part of him wanted to keep running home, but his curiosity was getting the better of him. *Curiosity killed the cat. Don't be a cat, Brody. If it moves, run like hell.* The shadow man had one arm outstretched, as if pointing down the street, in the opposite direction he was running. Pointing at what? There was nothing there, as far as Brody could see.

For what seemed like a full minute, Brody stood on the sidewalk, staring back at the shadow man. It never moved, not once, just kept its arm pointed down the street. When it *did* move, Brody took a few steps back, ready to run away, but ignored his own advice and watched it slip through the side entrance to the school and disappear from view.

"What the heck?" Brody said, wondering why it hadn't come after him, as it had Connie. She was super frightened of the shadow man (and so was he, who was he kidding!), but it didn't chase him.

Did it want me to go down the street? Brody was torn between wanting to continue home (and maybe get something to eat), or head down the street where it was pointing. For some reason, he didn't feel any danger from it, the shadow man. He didn't want to walk right up to it and ask if it knew whether or not the Browns would ever win a Super Bowl or something (which would be silly, in a lot of ways), but it didn't seem as dangerous as it had before.

It didn't try to catch him.

Maybe it was trying to show him something.

Brody turned and looked up the street, to the intersection with Grant Avenue—not too far away. Home was less than a mile from where he was standing. But if it was like this (*empty, no people, no mom, no Murf*), then was there really any reason to go back there?

Connie said she wanted him to go someplace where he'd never been before. She didn't say why, but she was insistent.

Brody couldn't ever remember going very far down the street in the direction the shadow man was pointing. He recognized all the houses down there (the ones he could see), but what was beyond? Had his mom ever driven down that street with him? Had he ever walked with friends that far?

The answer was no.

"Okay, I'll go," he said, both to the shadow man and to Connie, neither of whom were anywhere near enough to hear him. Wherever Connie had disappeared to probably wasn't a nice place, either. She was terrified about going back. Scared to death. Brody hoped the same thing wouldn't end up happening to him.

Brody Quail walked down the street, past the school (keeping a close eye on the side door, just because), and headed toward a place he'd never been.

He didn't get far.

The day ended for ten-year-old Brody Quail, but the memory of this empty place, and of Connie, would remain.

Chapter 20
BRODY26

Elephant grass.

The heat, the stink. His mouth was dry, his hands bloody. Not all his own blood. Bullets whistled through the tall grass, buzzing right over his head. The *bap-bap-bap-bap* of AK-47s filled the air, along with the higher-pitched *pop-pop-pop* of their own M16s. They'd been under constant fire from the moment they'd stepped off their Hueys into a hot LZ.

The enemy was everywhere. The brass had dropped them in a goddamned valley, and the North Vietnamese Army held all the high ground. Not Viet Cong, either. These were regular army, the NVA. Their briefings hadn't said anything about this. What the holy hell were the generals in Saigon thinking?

He and his buddies were sitting ducks. His first sight once he set foot on solid ground was guys to his left, right, even *behind* him dropping to the ground, screaming or grabbing their throats to stanch the blood that poured from open wounds, or simply spinning around and falling, dead before they had a chance to fight back. Guys he'd trained with, guys he knew. Brothers.

Through the thunderous gunfire, he heard the goddamned trumpets, the NVA blowing their horns, urging their men forward into the grass. He heard the scream of artillery—incoming and friendly—and the ground shook beneath him as the shells hit. One after another, *boom-boom-boom*, throwing columns of dirt, and bodies (enemy bodies, he hoped), into the air. And most weren't whole.

The NVA blew their damned horns, pushing forward, advancing. *Bam-bam-bam-bam.* More screams from his right. A man calling for his mother, over and over and over. There was a *whap-whap-whap* sound in the distance as the Hueys circled, the pilots trying to decide whether it was worth it to risk flying into a hot LZ. They could see the field was turning into a goddamned Air Cav abattoir.

He sensed something flash overhead and heard, as well as felt, the thunder as the rumble rolled across the ground around him. A jet fighter pulled up into the blue sky, and the napalm tanks it dropped slammed into the trees to his front. Even from a distance, he felt the overpressure from the explosion and the searing heat. As the flames leapt into the sky, he heard a horrid wailing, the sound of men being eaten alive by flame.

There was a body to his left, faceup, or what was left of his face. He'd taken a few rounds to the chest and one to the jaw that had torn it clean off, leaving a permanent, silent scream. He didn't recognize the man. Brody may have known him, even been his friend, but not anymore. He grabbed the man's rifle and pulled the magazine from it, then emptied the magazine pouches. Ammunition was precious in a firefight, and dead men pulled no triggers.

Bap-bap-bap-bap. Someone called for a medic, his voice high-pitched, screaming like a little girl. A horrible sound. *Bap-bap-bap-bap.* Then silence, from him at least.

Pop-pop-pop, return fire. The *whump* of mortar fire, nearby. The crash of incoming rounds, so close.

Brody flattened himself to the ground as bullets sliced through the grass overhead, angry bees whose sting could kill him or tear him apart, just like the poor sap next to him. They weren't ready for this, none of them were. This was their first taste of combat, and it was nothing like they were told it would be. They were being massacred.

Another scream to his left, more AK-47 fire.

He could hear enemy voices, too. Chattering away in a tongue he didn't understand. Getting closer. He checked his selector, made sure it was set to full-auto fire, and slowly raised his head. They were there, only ten meters away. Five of the little bastards. If he was going to die in this place, he would go down fighting and take as many of them with him as he could.

Brody crouched, aimed, and pulled the trigger. The first man went down with a head shot. Brody was shocked at how the man's head exploded out the other side in a blossom of red mist, a memory he later hoped to suppress, though he would never forget the sight. He swept his rifle back and forth, watching his rounds cut into the NVA soldiers as they began to react, swinging their AKs in his direction. *Pop-pop-pop-pop-pop-pop-pop.* But he didn't give them a chance.

He flattened his body to the ground and rolled to his right, knowing others would be firing at his position. And they did. The ground erupted as Soviet 7.62 mm shells rocketed through the grass and slammed into the dirt right where he had been hiding, raising a dust cloud into the hot, stinking air. *Bap-bap-bap-bap.*

Jesus Christ I'm not going to get out of this not going to get out of this God please help me

He felt a stinging sensation in his left calf and instinctively pulled his leg toward his body. There was blood pouring from a hole in his uniform, right above his boot. He'd been shot. It didn't hurt as much as he thought it would, but the pain would come soon enough. He grabbed his leg with both hands and—

Both hands.

Brody stared at his hands. Bloody, grimy, but they were both there.

He held his left hand in front of his face, turned it, looking at the back, then at the palm. His left hand. His left *arm*. For a split second, Brody was overjoyed to have a missing part of himself back in place, but that was impossible. *This* was impossible. It was 1968, and he hadn't been in a firefight since 1965. And battle had *never* been like this, even when he'd lost his left arm.

I'm dreaming, that's all this is. I'm only dreaming. This isn't real.

The ground exploded about thirty meters to his left, and a shower of dirt and debris rained down on him, the dust choking and thick. He coughed and spat the dirt from his mouth. He was so thirsty.

Dream or not, he couldn't help but make himself as small as possible as the bullets crisscrossed above him. The stench of blood-soaked ground was strong. *That* was just as he'd remembered. It was a smell no man could ever forget.

Brody grabbed for his rifle as another man appeared through the thin shafts of elephant grass and dropped down beside him. He was wearing sergeant stripes and had lost his helmet. His face was bloody— a long crease across his left cheek. A bullet had grazed him. Another fraction of an inch and his head would've—

"Are you hit, Corporal?" he yelled.

"In the leg, but I'm okay," Brody yelled back. The sergeant (Brody saw his name was Collins) motioned off to their rear. "We need to get to those trees! Can you move?"

Brody put some weight on his leg. It didn't feel broken, which meant the bullet had probably passed right through. The wound was starting to hurt now, really *hurt*, but he could still use the leg. *It shouldn't hurt this bad, because this isn't real. It isn't real.*

The sergeant grabbed him by the uniform, shook him. "Can you move?"

Brody nodded without thinking.

"Follow me!" the sergeant yelled and started weaving through the grass at a crouch, bullets whipping right over his head.

Brody moved quickly, out of instinct more than anything else. He gripped his rifle (with *both hands*) as he followed the sergeant through the grass. He skidded to a stop as the shells impacted the sergeant's body a fraction of a second before he heard the clanging *bap-bap-bap* of an AK-47 to his right. The sergeant stood straight up, arms wide, his rifle tumbling through the air. There was blood. So much blood. He fell facedown into the grass, dead before he even hit the dirt.

Brody brought his rifle to his shoulder, swung right, and squeezed the trigger before he had a target. *Pop-pop-pop-pop-pop.* His spent shells spun away from his M16, and he saw his target. Saw the man . . . No, not a man, more like a boy. He had a surprised look on his face and knew what was about to happen. Brody watched him close his eyes. Then he watched his own bullets stitch across the soldier's shoulders, left to right, the boy's body twitching violently with each impact. Then the body fell backward, disappearing into the grass.

Brody crouched, dropped his empty magazine, dug another one out of a pouch, inserted it, and slammed the bolt release with the palm of his hand. He swung around, searching for another target—*there!* He took aim, began to squeeze the trigger, then relaxed his pull. It wasn't another NVA, and it wasn't one of his own. It was something so out of place, so bold and unafraid, that he couldn't quite believe his eyes.

A man, dressed in all black, stood about fifteen meters away. But no, it was no man. It was a hole. A chasm. A shadow, in the shape of a man.

Brody had seen it before. His let his rifle drop off target. He was confused, not only by what he was seeing, but by the silence that surrounded him.

The firing had stopped. All at once, the war decided to take a time-out.

All Brody heard was the wind snaking through the elephant grass, the thin blades whispering in the breeze.

He was alone now. There were no other soldiers around him, no cries for help, no screams of artillery or sharp reports from rifle muzzles. They were all gone. Only he remained, and the

shadow man

shadow man

"He knows where I live? Who knows?"

"The shadow man, that's who."

Brody lined up his iron sights, flicked his selector switch to SEMI, and pulled the trigger. The M16 bucked against his shoulder, just once, sending a 55-grain full metal jacketed projectile right at its head at over 3,100 feet per second. If it were a man, a physical being, it would be dead, but the bullet only disappeared into the blackness where its head *should* be. The experience was like shooting through a doorway into a dark shroud beyond.

Not real, Brody said to himself. He tossed his rifle to the ground. "I'm dreaming," he said loudly. "You're not real." The thing—the shadow man—didn't move toward him. Rather, it pointed *at* him. Directly at Brody's chest.

"What do you want?" Brody screamed, wishing he could wake up and leave this crazy nightmare behind. The figure continued to point at his chest, and Brody could now actually discern a finger, as if the shadow man were taking shape.

Brody looked down. His uniform was caked in dirt and blood, the lower part of his pant leg stained blackish-red from his bullet wound. He wasn't sure what he was supposed to be seeing.

The shadow man brought its hand to its face—it *was* a hand, and there was a face now, too, hidden behind some sort of black helmet visor. It held two fingers to the visor, each finger pointing to where its eyes should be, then it pointed to the right side of its chest. Brody watched as it repeated the motion, then pointed at *his* chest. Brody looked down again, and then he saw what the shadow man was pointing at.

The name tape.

J O H N S O N

Not Q U A I L.

"Brody! Get away from it!"

Brody wheeled to his right and saw a girl running through the elephant grass toward him. She had red hair.

You have to remember, okay? Please, you have to remember.

His head throbbed murderously, and he dropped to his knees. The pain shot from the back of his head down across his shoulders and rocketed down his spine, like he'd been struck by lightning. When he opened his eyes again, he wasn't in South Vietnam. The bloody battlefield was no more. He was on a street.

The air was cold. Icy. Nighttime.

He was home again.

The shadow man was still there, but he was no longer a shadow. He was newly visible, clad in black from his helmet to his boots. His head was turned to Brody's right. Brody looked in the same direction and saw her.

The girl. Red hair, coveralls. *Connie. Her name is Connie.* Brody heard the man's boots pounding across the street as he watched Connie skid to a halt.

She looked at Brody, her eyes wide and full of fright. "Brody, run!" she screamed, turning around and heading for one of the buildings nearby.

Brody stood up and spied his rifle lying in the street. Wherever he'd come from (a battlefield dream, a *something*), the weapon had tagged along. He grabbed the M16 by the pistol grip and brought it to his shoulder, or at least he tried to. His left arm wasn't there, only a stump, pointing to where a long-gone hand would've grabbed the rifle's forestock.

He didn't need the hand.

He brought the rifle up, jammed the butt stock into his armpit, and aimed as best he could, tracking the shadow man as he ran across the street. "Come on, slow and steady," he told himself, trying to keep the muzzle pointed at his target. The last thing he wanted to do was shoot Connie by mistake. He'd shot the M16 one-handed like this before, but it had been so long ago. (1965 was a long time ago, wasn't it?) He took a deep breath, concentrated on the black shape in the street, and pulled the trigger.

The rifle barked once, the report incredibly loud in the darkened street.

But there was no shadow man in the street. Brody had hit him, he *knew* he had, but there was no body.

The shadow man was gone. Disappeared, just like Connie, he remembered. *Just like Connie did. The last time I saw her.*

Disjointed memories flooded through his mind, each one similar, yet so different. He'd been on this street, walking home, when he was jumped by three men—

who walked away

who pretended to have a gun

who pulled a gun

who he managed to ward off

who kicked his ass

who shot him

who he killed

But how could that be?

"Brody?" Connie's voice. She was walking toward him, tentatively, her eyes fixed on the black rifle tucked under his arm. Brody swung the barrel away from her.

"I remember you," he said. "From this place. Before."

She smiled and actually looked relieved.

"Thank God, oh thank God," she said. "You're the only one."

The only one? "I don't understand what's going on," Brody said. "What just happened? You saw it, right? I was in Vietnam again, and then there you were."

She cocked her head slightly. "Vietnam?"

"The valley, the firefight, *where we just were!*"

"A valley? I don't understand."

"You were there with me, and then we were back *here*." *Oh, come on. I didn't imagine the whole thing, did I?* Then he remembered the rifle in his hand. "Where I brought *this thing* from."

She stared at him, silent.

"Brody," she said softly, "I never saw a valley. The first thing I remember was seeing you in the street and the shadow man close to you. I screamed at you to get away from it, then you shot it."

"You didn't see the valley? The soldiers? Any of that?"

She shook her head.

"Jesus Christ," Brody said, "what's wrong with me?"

Connie put her hand on his shoulder, quickly cutting her eyes to the rifle and then back to his face. "Nothing. There's nothing wrong with you. It's just starting with you. And it's going to get worse."

"What's starting?"

"The same thing that happened to me. *Is* happening."

"Lady, I'd really appreciate it if you would give me some goddamned answers here." From the look that spread across her face, Brody immediately regretted his tone. He sighed, then said, "I need to understand what's going on. That's all."

"Come on," Connie said, her voice a little colder than before. "We need to move before it comes back."

"I shot it," Brody said, knowing she was referring to the shadow man. "I don't think it's coming back."

"It doesn't matter. It'll be back." She started walking down the street and motioned for him to follow. Brody began to drop his rifle, but she said, "No, keep it."

"If it didn't work, then—"

"It made him go away. Bought us some time. It might work again."

Brody thumbed the selector switch to SAFE and clutched the rifle by the carry handle. He followed her, still numbed by everything that had just happened. Nothing was making any sense, and this girl, Connie, had answers. Or at least more than *he* had at the moment, which would have to suffice. "Where are we going?" he asked.

"Anywhere but here. He appears where things are familiar, the places that are whole. We need to find a boundary."

"A boundary?"

"You'll see," she said. "But we have to hurry. I don't know how much time I have."

Before she disappears. Brody walked behind her, his eyes cutting to the shadows that filled the empty spaces between the buildings and houses on the street, the places where the shadow man could be watching them, unseen, then emerge before they had a chance to react. He wondered if there were three thugs lying in the street behind them, or if they were following him and Connie right now. He looked over his shoulder, but there was only a cold, dark street. One streetlight was flickering.

"You said you don't know how much time you have."

"It's never the same," she replied. "Sometimes, it's only a few seconds, and other times it's hours."

"Before you disappear."

"Yes. Before I leave whatever place I'm in, and go back to—" They both jumped at a crashing sound behind them, far down the street and out of view. Connie cut into an alley. "Come on!"

Brody followed, keeping his eyes on the street, looking for the shadow man to emerge into the streetlights.

When they were almost all the way through the alley to the other side, Connie slowed. "Brody, have you ever been here before?"

He felt a slight pang of pain in the back of his head.

He needed to run, to go where he'd never been before.

The pain passed quickly. "In this alley?" he replied. "No, I don't think so."

"Come here," she said.

Brody stood beside her and looked out of the alley into the street beyond. He squinted, trying to comprehend what he was seeing.

The scene before him was nothing more than a swirling black mass, as if an army of shadows were coalescing, turning, spinning; black ghosts without form or being chasing one another, becoming one, then splitting into two, three, four clouds of darkness, then back again. A black canvas of nothingness where other buildings and houses should be.

"What in God's name is *that*?" Brody said, dropping his rifle to the asphalt.

"You never asked me where I go when I disappear," Connie said, her voice trembling. "Now you know."

At that moment, the day ended for twenty-six-year-old Brody Quail.

And Connie disappeared into the nothingness.

Chapter 21

BRODY16

Brody found himself standing in a completely unfamiliar place, the middle of a bleak expanse, barren and flat, stretching away as far as he could see. Mountains stood in the distance to the west, low and brown, while buildings appeared to the north, but they weren't shaped like any cityscape he'd seen before.

They're wrecked. Even at this distance, Brody could see the structures had been destroyed. Blackened and burnt, ruined high-rises stretching into a grayish sky. Brody was confused, scared. None of this felt right. The ground below him was covered by a fine, gray dust, the hot wind swirling it around his feet. He tasted the dust in his mouth. Gritty and bitter, like ash.

He remembered being in school, talking to his friends. Seeing Joan.

He was driving her home.

He felt a sharp pain in the back of his head and winced at the ferocity of it. The sensation passed quickly, but tears had started to form. He wiped them away but only managed to get ash in his eyes. It stung, making his eyes water even more.

"I'm dreaming," he said to himself. "None of this is real." He'd wake up soon. He was still in bed, and when his alarm clock went off, he'd get up and get ready for school.

No. This was all too real. He spat some of the gritty ash onto the ground, the thick glob of saliva causing a puff of ash to float into the air.

Everything was burnt. The ground, the mountains, even the buildings in the distance were charred. The sky was as gray as the soil upon which he stood.

This place was dead, with only the moaning of the hot wind to keep him company.

He stood where he was for quite a while, waiting patiently for the dream to end (the dream that sure didn't feel like one). Minutes passed, and Brody had a more and more difficult time breathing. And he was starving. Sweat trickled down his back. Even though the sun was hidden, he still felt the heat beating down on him.

What are you going to do, Brody? Stand here and melt? He decided to walk toward the buildings in the distance. He was unable to judge exactly how far away they were, but he had to find some sort of shelter from the heat and wind, dream or no dream. The buildings would provide at least some relief from the elements, and anyway, he wanted to take a closer look.

As he walked, he thought about what he and his friends had talked about (was it yesterday, the day before?) after the news of Reagan's assassination attempt had swept through school.

Had the Russians been behind it?

If we found out they tried to kill him, we'd nuke the living shit out of that place, Kyle had said.

That's what this place looked like. The aftermath of a nuclear war. It all made sense; the ruined, blackened buildings, the ash (fallout?) covering the ground . . . It looked like the entire landscape had been nuked. Fallout was radioactive, and he was covered with it. With every step, swirls of the ash rose into the air, sticking to his clothes, getting into his mouth, his nose, his lungs. If this was fallout, he was a goner.

But wait a minute. This wasn't real. Couldn't be. Why would he suddenly find himself in the middle of a radioactive wasteland with no memory of how he got there? No, he was dreaming. Had to be.

His eyes were drawn to a reflection in the distance, a quick flash, nothing more, as if the sunlight (what little of it there was) had glinted off something metallic. Then he saw the dust plume, rising into the air. A vehicle was heading his way, throwing up a long tail of ash and dust as it drove across the landscape.

Brody wanted to run, to hide, but instead dropped to the ground, trying not to inhale too much (radioactive) dust. Where could he go? At first, he thought they might just drive by without seeing him, but they were coming directly at him. He could run, but they'd surely spotted him. The vehicle was a large truck, like the army used. Maybe they'd take him back to the city (what was left of it) and help him. He was incredibly thirsty, and his stomach was growling like crazy. He noticed how weak he felt, too, and hoped it wasn't because of the amount of radioactive crap he'd already gotten all over (and inside) his body. He wasn't sure, but he thought he'd read somewhere how slow and painful death from radiation poisoning could be.

But it doesn't matter, because none of this is real, he tried to convince himself.

The truck drew closer, the front grille big and square, with muted sunlight reflecting off its flat windshield. The dust it kicked up rose into the sky like a jet contrail, drifting away with the wind. He heard the engine now, too, low and growling, the pitch changing as it down-shifted, slowing.

Brody fought to control the dread squirming in his chest.

The truck came to a halt fifty feet or so in front of him, the dust cloud from behind enveloping the vehicle for a moment until it blew away. The doors opened, and one, then two, three, four people emerged from the truck, all wearing what looked like hazmat suits, dirty gray with visors and gas masks. They all carried rifles.

And aimed them right at him.

Brody raised his hands, surprised at the effort it took to lift his arms. He was so tired all of a sudden, so weak.

The four men approached slowly, their rifles trained on him. Brody stared at the barrels, a twisting knot of fear vibrating in his belly. He'd never had a gun (let alone four) pointed at him before, and it produced an awful feeling. He could barely see their faces through their faceplates. When one of them finally spoke, the sound was electronic, as if the man's voice was coming through a speaker.

"Identify yourself," the man said.

Brody tried to speak but only coughed. His throat was dry, the gritty ash covering his tongue.

"Identify yourself," the man repeated, adding, "Name and district."

Brody made a croaking sound, trying to clear his throat. All he wanted to do was close his eyes and go to sleep. His arms felt heavy, as if every bit of energy he had was being drained from his body. *The radioactivity, it's already starting to take effect.*

All four men suddenly lowered their rifles. Their leader (at least Brody assumed it was the guy in charge) took a few steps closer. "You don't belong here," he said.

No shit, Brody wanted to say but thought better of it, his eyes fixed on the rifle barrels. They weren't pointing at him anymore, but it didn't make them any less threatening.

"You don't belong here," the leader repeated. "You have to leave."

As Brody stared at the man, wanting nothing more than to agree with him, everything around him changed.

He was in school, study hall. Jason was looking at him, smiling.

He was in the parking lot, standing by his car.

He saw Joan's face.

He saw another girl—Connie?—urging him to come with her.

He was in a house, dark and familiar.

He was on a playground, surrounded by little kids.

He was in a street.

He was in the black.

Chapter 22
BRODY52

Joshua, Maine
Friday, October 25, 1974

"Mr. Quail? Brody Quail?" one of the officers asked.

"Yes, officer," Brody replied, knowing in his gut what he was about to hear.

"I'm sorry to have to tell you this, sir, but it's your son. Raymond."

Brody said nothing. He turned around and looked at the top of the stairs, expecting to see someone (Reba?) standing at the railing. But that would be impossible, because she was dead. A memory was there, though, struggling to make its way to the surface. A woman, here in this house. Reba, but *not* Reba. His head throbbed slightly, and he blinked away the pain, turning back to the officers at his front door.

"I'm sorry, gentlemen, but you'll have to leave," Brody said, the pull from upstairs growing stronger. *She's here, right now. Upstairs.* Her name was pirouetting on the tip of his tongue, so close but still out of reach. *Reba, but not Reba.*

The officers looked at each other, then one spoke. "Sir, we have some bad news we have to deliver, then we'll be on our way."

Brody sighed. "Go ahead, then."

"We were notified earlier this evening that your son was severely injured in an automobile accident, Mr. Quail. I'm sorry to have to tell you this, but—"

"He's dead."

"Yes, sir. He was killed."

"And he was alone, the only occupant in the vehicle, yes?"

"Yes, sir."

"Thank you, gentlemen." Brody slammed the door in their faces and flicked the dead bolt shut. He felt no gut punch from the news that his son had died, no feeling whatsoever. Because he'd heard the news before. He'd stood at this door more times than he wanted to admit, receiving the same information over and over again. He didn't want to run upstairs to the office and grab a bottle. He had no desire to remove his old service revolver from the drawer and blow his brains out. He'd done both things before.

Impossible, but real. As real as the pull he felt from the upper floor, where someone would be waiting for him, someone who looked so much like Reba, the same dress, the same hairstyle, but who was nothing more than a fakery designed to—

To what? Torture him?

Little by little, other memories surfaced, bits and pieces quickly coalescing into coherent thought. *I know what you're feeling,* she'd said. *It happens to me, too.* No, she wasn't there to make things worse for him; this woman (Connie was her name, he suddenly remembered) had experienced (or was *experiencing*) this as well. And she'd asked him about his dreams. Brody was full of questions, and Connie hopefully had some answers.

Brody looked back up at the stair railing, hoping she'd be there. When he saw that she wasn't, he headed upstairs. She was up there, or soon would be. He was halfway up the flight when Felix interrupted him.

"Sir? Will you be eating in the dining room this evening, or in your office?"

Brody turned to his old employee. He looked Felix in the eye, trying to discern if anything was obviously different about him, but saw only the man he'd grown to know and call a friend over their many years together. "Felix," Brody asked, "where do I usually take my evening meal?"

Felix answered without missing a beat. "In your office, sir."

"And why is that, Felix?"

This time Felix paused, as if he wasn't sure how to respond. Brody saw a strange glassiness flash across Felix's eyes, like he'd checked out for a split second, then returned. "I don't believe it's my place to ask, Mr. Quail."

Brody expected Felix to give such an answer. "You've known me for a number of years, correct?" Brody asked, leaning against the banister halfway up the stairs.

"Yes, sir," Felix replied, smiling broadly. "A very long time."

"We trust each other, don't we, Felix?"

"Yes, sir. Implicitly."

"I can always count on you to give me the truth, no matter what. Isn't that correct?"

"Yes, sir."

"Then tell me the truth now. What is going on in this house?"

Just as Brody expected, Felix paused again, and Brody saw the same glassy look in Felix's eyes.

"I'm not sure I understand, sir," Felix finally replied.

"There were just two gentlemen at the front door. Did you hear them knocking?"

"I'm sorry, Mr. Quail, but I must have been busy in the kitchen at the time and didn't hear them at the door. My apologies."

"It was two policemen, Felix. They came to deliver some bad news."

"Oh, not too terrible, I hope."

"Very terrible. Very terrible, indeed."

"May I inquire as to what news the two men delivered?"

As each second of their conversation ticked by, Brody understood more of what had happened (was happening?) to him. He felt like a player in a stage play, acting out the same scene over and over with script variations being written by someone unknown. Felix was playing his part.

Before he answered Felix, Brody felt a presence at the top of the stairs—Connie, just as he'd expected, and she was emerging from the hallway. She was dressed the same as she had been yesterday (or was it *today?*), looking like his dear wife. Brody held his hand up, gesturing at her to stop. He turned back to Felix, who couldn't see Connie because of the curve of the stairs, and watched him look up at the top railing, an inquisitive glint in his eyes.

"Sir, is there someone else upstairs?" Felix asked.

Brody ignored the question. "You asked me what news the two officers delivered."

"Yes, sir." Felix's gaze shifted from Brody to the top railing and back again.

"And you don't have any idea what they said."

"No, Mr. Quail. How could I?"

"I believe you're lying to me, Felix." Brody had never accused Felix of lying to him, and even though the accusation had to be true, the statement left a bad taste in his mouth.

Felix's face, however, didn't show the indignation that Brody expected. That in itself confirmed Brody's suspicions, made even more sinister by the strange pain he was experiencing. A dull ache spread from the back of Brody's head down into his shoulders. He tried to ignore the growing discomfort.

Felix spoke. "I would never do such a thing, Mr. Quail."

"But you did, just a few seconds ago. You know exactly what the two officers told me, Felix. Admit it."

"No, sir, I do not. And I must say, I'm very concerned with your well-being at the present moment."

"My well-being?"

"You seem confused, sir. Not your normal self. May I bring you a—"

"Drink, Felix? Do you think I need a drink?"

"If that's what you wish, sir."

"Felix, did I or did I not instruct you to remove every ounce of liquor from this house after Miss Rebecca passed?"

Felix paused. "You did, sir."

"Then why, pray tell, are there bottles of whiskey in this house? In my office, in the kitchen? Where else are they, Felix?" Brody's head was throbbing.

"I must apologize for being so lax in my duties, sir," Felix replied. "I will dispose of the bottles immediately."

"You're never *lax in your duties*, Felix. Never."

This time, Felix didn't reply. He began to walk to the foot of the stairs, his eyes fixed on the top.

"What are you doing, Felix?" Brody asked.

"She doesn't belong here." Glassy eyes, emotionless voice.

Brody looked up at Connie, who stepped from the hallway into view. "Brody," she said, "you're beginning to understand now, aren't you."

He nodded and was surprised to feel Felix brush against him as the man ascended the stairs. Brody grabbed his arm, and when Felix turned to look at him, Brody saw nothing in the butler's eyes. Felix's face was intact, but the person he knew, or thought he knew, wasn't looking back at him. "Stop," Brody said. "Stay right where you are."

"She doesn't belong here," Felix said. "And neither does he."

Brody looked up to see an empty black shape emerge from the hallway behind Connie and wrap its arm around her neck. For a moment, he wasn't sure what he was seeing. The darkness in the hallway appeared to have suddenly taken form and enveloped her.

Connie's eyes went wide with fear as the shadow man dragged her back into the hallway, snatching her from view.

Brody shoved Felix out of the way and ran up the stairs, reaching the top just as the bedroom door slammed shut. He ran down the hall, then skidded to a halt by his office door. He quickly stepped to his desk and retrieved his pistol from the drawer. He flipped open the cylinder and saw that it was loaded (*just as it should be*). He slammed it shut and ran to the bedroom door. He grabbed the handle and turned. *Locked.* He banged on the door. "Connie!"

No answer.

"Connie!"

He smashed into the door with his shoulder. Twice. Three times. The door didn't budge. He kicked at it, again and again, the throbbing in his head growing worse by the second. Still, the door held fast.

He imagined Reba in that room . . .

He took a step back, gripped the .357 with both hands, and shot a round into the door handle. The boom was incredibly loud, and wood splinters flew into his face. His ears rang from the gunshot as he kicked at the door again. And again.

Not this time. I won't let something bad happen again.

He aimed and fired three more rounds into the door handle. *Bangbangbang!* The knob hung loosely in the frame, and Brody kicked again for all he was worth.

The door flew open, and Brody stared into the blackness.

The bedroom wasn't there anymore. Only a swirling, shifting black cloud, as if he were looking into the heart of a storm in the dark of night.

"Connie!" he screamed, wanting nothing more than to hear her voice again, to see her face.

"She didn't belong here."

Brody wheeled and saw Felix standing in the hallway. With shaking hands, he pointed the pistol at Felix's head. The pain in his head was nearly unbearable, his vision fading. "Tell me what the hell is going on!"

"Please move away from the doorway, sir."

"Answer my question!" Brody yelled, each word making him wince in pain. "What is this all about! Who are you?"

"Step away from the doorway, Mr. Quail. Everything is going to be all right." Felix approached, a gun pointing at his face seemingly unimportant.

"Nothing is all right, goddamn you. Nothing!" Brody began to squeeze the trigger.

He heard something behind him: a whimper, maybe a muffled scream. Brody turned and stared into the blackness. "Connie?"

Felix's hand was suddenly on the gun, trying to wrench it away. The man had moved incredibly fast, as Brody hadn't even registered his footsteps. Brody tightened his grip on the weapon and shoved Felix as hard as he could, but the man wouldn't let go.

"Please, Mr. Quail, you have to stop this insanity!"

The pain was terrible now, so hot and thick that Brody could barely breathe. And he was so weak, so tired. Felix tore the pistol from Brody's hand, stepped back, and held it at his side.

Brody slumped to the floor, his back against the door frame, his skull feeling like it might explode. "Please," he said, "tell me what's going on. I don't understand."

"Everything is going to be fine now, Mr. Quail," Felix said as he raised the pistol, aiming it at Brody's head. "Everything is going to be fine."

As Felix pulled the trigger, Brody used every ounce of strength he had left to roll to his left. He heard the boom of the gun, heard the zing of the bullet, and felt a stinging sensation in his right ear as he tumbled into the blackness beyond the bedroom door.

X

There was only the darkness. No feeling, no perception, just nothingness.

At first he was sure he was falling, tumbling through the air into an unseen chasm, but the sensation trickled away until there was nothing to feel at all.

Only the darkness.

The day had ended for fifty-two-year-old Brody Quail.

And he was one with the shadows.

Chapter 23
BRODY10

Culver, Ohio
Thursday, May 15, 1975

He opened his eyes to the sound of screaming. His own.

Brody was on his knees, his arms wrapped tightly around his chest. He was cold, shaking, disoriented. The scene around him gradually registered. Brody was in the middle of the playground. He was at school, during recess, with all his friends standing around staring at him.

At least he thought it must be recess. His friends were getting ready to play the game. Bullard had the ball, and he was tossing it up in the air and catching it again. Rich was there. So was Gary. All the girls were sitting in a row off to the side of the field (where they always were?), including Debbie Wilson. She was looking right at him, along with everyone else.

"Brody? Can I play, too?"

Murphy was standing right beside him. "Murf?" Brody said, finding it difficult to speak. His mouth was dry, like he'd chomped down on a dirt clod or something. The taste was gritty, bitter. He tried to spit, but couldn't.

"I want to play, too. Mom says you have to play with me."

Brody stared at his brother. How many times had he heard that same line, right here on *this* playground, before *this* game, on *this* day? He remembered. The game. Wanting to be a hero. Debbie smiling at him. His brother wandering into the road. The car. Over and over again, each time a little different from the other.

The sky is wrong.

The last time, the sky wasn't right. *Nothing* was. And there weren't any other people.

Except for one.

Brody took another look at the girls . . . No, she wasn't there. He felt a strange longing, a pain dead center in his chest. She'd disappeared while he was holding her in his arms.

"Hey, Quail! Get your brother out of here," Rich yelled.

Brody stood, his legs unsteady. He was weak, tired. He felt a dull ache in the back of his head, a subtle throbbing. He'd felt it before.

"Hey, Quail! Get your brother out of here," Rich yelled again.

"Start without me," Brody replied. He grabbed Murf's hand and led him off the field.

"Where are we going, Brody?"

"I'm taking you home."

Murf yanked away from Brody, unwilling to follow. "We have to stay here, Brody. You have to play the game."

"I'm not playing the game anymore, Murf."

"Hey, Quail! Get your brother out of here," Rich yelled.

Brody looked at him. Rich was standing in the same place he'd been when Brody stood up. He'd said the same thing three times. In the exact same tone of voice. "Start without me, Rich. All of you. I'm not playing."

"Hey, Quail! Get your brother out of here."

Brody felt a chill descend through his body; that wasn't the Rich he knew. He tugged at Murf's hand, but the kid wouldn't move, like he was cemented in place.

"If you don't play the game, I'm going to tell Mom."

Brody dropped Murf's hand. The Murphy standing in front of him was no longer his little brother. He was one of *them*. Brody opened his mouth to speak but couldn't think of anything to say. He was sad, looking down into the face of a little boy he loved more than he loved himself. How many times had he run into the street to keep his brother from getting hit by a car? How many times had he been too late (it had happened) and watched his brother's body disappear below the car, rolling around between the steel and the asphalt, bones snapping, and listened to Murf's screams? How many times had he pushed Murf away just in time (that had happened, too), only to get crushed under the wheels himself? How many times had he gone home, faced his mother, endured the heartache of letting his brother die or explained how he had saved him at the last moment? And how many times had he simply not gone home at all?

The pain in his head worsened, pulsing with a white-hotness directly behind his eyes. His teeth ached. His vision blurred.

He had to get away from this place. As far away as he could.

Promise me you'll go to a place you've never been.

Connie. One of the last things she'd said before she'd disappeared.

Run there as fast as you can!

And that was exactly what he was going to do. He turned, but Debbie Wilson was standing right in front of him.

"Don't you want to play the game for me, Brody?" she said. Her eyes were so bright and beautiful, and her voice was appealing, soft. Brody was taken aback, but only for a second. The other kids were gathering, too. Forming a circle around him. Blocking his path.

Brody looked at each of them, kids he'd known for years, friends, most of them, like Rich and Gary, and others who were familiar even if he didn't know their names.

The other kids, even the little ones, were coming onto the field as well. They were converging on him, surrounding him. Brody was scared.

Debbie reached out, touched his arm. Brody pulled his arm back, but she only smiled at him, her beautiful, perfect smile. "I want you to play the game for me, Brody. For me. I want to watch you."

Brody closed his eyes tight, trying to wish himself away from this place, maybe go to the place Connie had gone—

Oh God, I don't want to go!

—but it was a bad place, a place Connie didn't want to ever go back to again, but did. Brody couldn't stop her, couldn't hold on to her tightly enough to prevent her from disappearing. She wasn't here now, which meant maybe she was gone for good and he'd never see her again.

Brody opened his eyes. They were *all* there. Inching closer. Mrs. Carlisle was towering above the group near the back of the crowd. "You have to play the game," she said.

"You have to play the game," Bullard said.

"You have to play the game," Rich said.

"You have to play the game," Gary said.

"You have to play the game," they chanted, again and again, their voices all the same. Debbie's smile had disappeared, and her eyes were . . . lifeless. All of them stared at him with little colored orbs of glass in their heads, chanting, chanting.

Brody tried to run, to shove his way through, but they were a solid wall of bodies, immovable, just as Murf had been. Brody shoved his shoulder into Rich, and that's when they grabbed at him, gripped his clothes, pushed him and punched him, their bodies pressing against his.

Brody fell to the ground, curled his body into a fetal position, and wrapped his arms around his head to protect his face. And still they chanted, "You have to play the game! You have to play the game!"

An angry mob of kids who were supposed to be his classmates was going to kill him.

Brody was too weak to fight back and wouldn't have had a chance against so many even if he wasn't so tired, so full of pain arcing from his head to the rest of his body.

There was no escape.

He had to do something.

"Okay!" Brody screamed. "I'll play! I'll play!"

It stopped.

Just like that.

Brody lay writhing on the ground, his body racked by the pain from their blows, but the pulsing heat in his skull was gone. He opened his eyes and saw his schoolmates walking away, going back to where they were when he'd first . . . appeared? The chanting had stopped.

He sat up and continued to watch them spread out across the playground. The little kids went back to the playground right by the school building, and the bigger kids formed their teams again.

"I want to play, Brody."

Murphy, still standing by his side.

Brody had to run. He stood, looked across the field to the chainlink fence at the far end. He was weak, and he was hurt, but he had to try. He looked down at Murf (or whatever was supposed to look like his little brother) and said, "Okay, Murf. You can play."

"Really?"

"Really. You're on Bullard's team, okay?"

"Cool!" Murf said as he turned and ran toward the group of kids on the other team. For a split second, things were normal again. The kid was his brother. *And stay out of the road, kid.*

Brody took off running, as fast as he could.

"Hey, Quail? What are you doing?" Lance's voice. He was the fast one. Brody didn't have to look behind to know that they would be running after him. And they were. He could hear their feet, a muted thunder, across the grassy field. Lance would catch him.

Brody kept his eyes locked on the fence, closer and closer, as the sounds behind him grew louder.

"Quail! Get back here!" Lance again, so close.

Fifteen feet. Ten.

He could feel Lance right behind him, could hear him breathing.

Five feet. Three. Brody leapt, grabbed the chain link, and kicked with his feet, climbing. He felt Lance grab at his shirt, fingers scratching his back. Brody climbed the six-foot fence and threw himself over the top. He tumbled to the ground, rolling in the grass. All he wanted to do was stay down and close his eyes.

He heard the clang of the fence. They were all there, slamming against the fence, shaking the chain-link panels. "You have to play the game!" the kids screamed. Brody stood, turned to run away, and stared into an endless void, so black and empty. In the shape of a man.

The shadow man was here again, and right in front of him.

He remembered the last time, how it had stopped chasing him and pointed down the street. He hadn't been afraid of it then. Brody took a step back, careful not to get too close to the fence, where little-kid hands were sticking through, grasping for his body. The crowd of kids were all saying the same thing, a symphony of emotionless voices. "He doesn't belong here . . ."

Brody stared at the shadow man and could see a person where the open hole had been. It *was* a man, dressed all in black, his face hidden behind a helmet and visor. Brody could see his own reflection in the faceplate, and the wall of kids behind him, a couple of them starting to climb the fence. "He has to leave," they said. "He doesn't belong here."

The man reached out a hand.

Brody was still afraid of the shadow man but felt like he wanted to help in some way. Brody reached out to take his hand when he heard something change behind him.

"She doesn't belong here! She has to leave!"

She?

Brody felt her hand on his arm, pulling. *Connie!*

"No, Brody! It's a trick!" Connie yelled, pulling him out of the way just as the shadow man leapt at both of them. Brody felt the gloved hands brush against his back as Connie dragged him away. "Run! Come on, Brody, run!"

He kept up with her as they ran along the length of the fence, the kids on the other side running with them, screaming at Connie to leave this place, chanting that she didn't belong here. Brody's legs were like lead, and the pain in his head had returned. He could barely walk, much less run, and he fell.

He looked up at Connie—

He was lying in a street, the asphalt freezing cold. A woman was standing before him, dressed in coveralls and work boots. *Connie.*

He was in a darkened hallway, an older woman standing in front of him, wearing a flowered dress. *Connie.*

He was in an intersection, a teenage girl reaching for him. *Connie.*

He was in the grass, the kids pounding against the chain link just a few feet away. He felt the blood gush from his nose and run down his lip and into his mouth as he saw a bright flash of stars, and his skull felt like it split open. He opened his mouth to scream, then felt Connie's hand on his arm. "It's okay, Brody, it's okay, oh God, please don't go!"

Darkness then.

Cold and numbing.

The pain was gone.

Then he opened his eyes.

Chapter 24
BRODY26

Garland Trail, Nebraska
Tuesday, November 12, 1968

Brody was in the bar, with two dollar bills clutched in his (right) hand and his field jacket draped over the back of his chair.

Jimmy, the bartender, was wiping the bar with a rag. Smiling at him.

Brody knew what was going to happen from this point on. He'd pay for his drinks, which he never really remembered having in the first place, then walk outside into a chilly night. He'd walk home (in the *direction* of home, anyway), but he wouldn't make it there.

He never did.

There would be three goons out there waiting for him; one black, two white. They'd follow him, then approach and confront him.

"G'night, Brody," the bartender said.

Brody stared back at him, wondering how this would play out when he didn't leave. "You know, Jimmy my man, I think I'll have one more for the road," Brody said, stuffing the dollar bills back into his pocket.

Jimmy paused, only for a moment, but long enough for Brody to notice. Then he said, "Are you sure?"

"My money not good enough for you, Jimmy?" Brody asked, hoping the bartender would buy his fake smile. His senses were heightened, as if he were walking point again, watching and listening for anything out of the ordinary along the trail: trip wires, movement in the brush to either side, noises from the trees above.

Jimmy laughed (genuinely enough), and said, "Of course it is. You usually have your three doubles on the rocks, and that's all. A good bartender notices his customers' habits, you know?"

Brody leaned back in his chair, then slapped the bar with his palm. "How 'bout one more, Jimmy."

"Sure. Another double?"

"Nope. I'm feeling like a beer this time."

The bartender grabbed a bottle from under the bar, popped the top, and handed it to Brody. "Want a glass?"

"Are you kidding?" Brody said. He took a swig, then said, "Hey, I've been meaning to ask you a question."

"Shoot, kid," Jimmy said, leaning against the bar with the rag still in his hand.

"You were in Korea, right?"

"You bet. First of the Seventh Marines."

"Part of the Chosin Few, huh?"

"Damn right."

"Pretty bad, wasn't it."

Jimmy nodded, then sighed. "Proud to have been there, but not something I like to talk about to too many people. Especially these days, know what I mean? Why are you asking, kid?"

"Do you ever have flashbacks? I don't know, dreams that you're still there?" Brody asked.

"It never goes away, Brody," Jimmy said. "It's always there. You just have to learn how to deal with it." He glanced at Brody's pinned-up left sleeve. "Are you having any trouble, kid?"

Brody took a long pull on the bottle. This wasn't going exactly as he'd expected. The 1/7 Marines *were* at Chosin Reservoir, and the battles against the Chinese were bloody and brutal enough that he wasn't surprised Jimmy wouldn't want to talk about his experiences there. Brody wasn't sure how he knew that, but he did.

"I might be," Brody finally said.

Jimmy nodded slightly. He grabbed another bottle of beer from under the bar, opened it, and held it toward Brody. "To those who know, Brody."

They clinked bottles and each took a drink. A toast from one warrior to another. Jimmy put his bottle down, then said, "There aren't any answers in this stuff, though. It'll dull it for a while, but like I said, it's always there. If you want to talk sometime, then we'll talk. I don't know what you went through, but I can guess it wasn't exactly nice. Right?"

"Yeah. It wasn't very nice." This seemed all very real to Brody. He almost expected Jimmy to stumble as soon as Brody changed the sequence of things (assuming there really *was* a sequence). He had been back in Vietnam (flashback?), but the fight wasn't his, nor was the name on his uniform.

J O H N S O N
Not Q U A I L.

Maybe this was all connected somehow. He'd read about other vets who had gone off the deep end after returning home. Seeing things. Hearing things. Going crazy. Slowly. Could the shadow man and the girl all be part of his imagination? If so, he was going to need to see someone. A professional. Talking it over with a bartender was probably better than nothing, but there was only so much an old vet offering drinks could do to help.

Brody wanted to go home. Get some sleep. He dug the bills from his pocket and put them on the bar, then reached for his wallet to get a couple more to cover the beer.

"On the house, kid," Jimmy said.

"Are you sure?"

"I'm sure. But just this once," he added with a smile. "I gotta make a living, you know?"

"Yeah," Brody replied. "Thanks, Jimmy."

"Take care, kid. See you tomorrow."

Brody was slipping on his field jacket when he saw Jimmy's eyes glaze over. Brody turned, and he saw her, across the room.

Connie.

All at once, the second he saw the girl, the sliver of certainty he'd been holding on to, the hope that everything was fine and he was only having some sort of flashback problem (which wasn't fine exactly, but he might be able to fix it), disappeared.

He turned back to Jimmy, who was reaching under the bar again. "She doesn't belong here," Jimmy said, his voice different from just before.

"Brody, we need to get out of here," Connie said. "Now." She was standing by the door, and Brody noticed the bar had grown deathly silent, with every patron staring right at Connie. One by one, they all said the same thing: "She doesn't belong here."

Brody's senses were screaming. There was danger here. Behind him.

He turned and saw the shotgun in Jimmy's hands. He was aiming it at Connie.

Brody struck at the barrel with his right hand just as it fired, the boom incredibly loud in the confined space. *Jesus Christ, he's trying to kill her!* He looked back quickly to where Connie had been standing and saw a number of people on the floor. The shotgun blast had taken out at least five people and injured about as many more who were standing in place, buckshot wounds peppering their faces and arms. But they didn't seem to *feel* their injuries. Brody glimpsed a flash of red hair among the heap of bodies. Connie, her eyes wide with shock, had dived out of the way of the blast and was getting to her feet. "Goddammit, Brody! Move!"

He would, but not before he took care of the immediate threat. He vaulted on top of the bar, grabbed the shotgun by the barrel (warm to the touch after the blast), and tried to wrestle it away from Jimmy. *Who wasn't really Jimmy.*

"She—doesn't—belong—here!" Jimmy grunted as he pulled the gun back, dragging Brody across the bar with it. Brody slid off the bar, to the other side now, and tried to keep the barrel away from his body in case Jimmy—

Boom!

The shelves behind the bar exploded in a shower of wood and glass, and Brody's ears hummed. At first he thought he'd been shot, as the back of his head erupted in a fiery burst of pain that nearly took the breath from his lungs. But no, he was still able to move and fight. He kicked at Jimmy's knees, and the man buckled over, dropping the shotgun. Brody reached for the weapon, then decided he needed to get away from this place more than he needed to get in a wrestling match over a shotgun with a hulking ex-Marine.

The others would be moving, too. At Connie. At him. He wasn't sure why he felt they would be coming after them, but somehow he just *knew*. Brody ran around the bar right as he saw Connie run out the door. Two of the patrons were walking toward her.

"She doesn't belong here."

Brody shouldered past them, hoping he'd done enough damage to Jimmy's knees to keep him on the floor and away from the shotgun. If he hadn't, the pain in the back of his head would probably get much, much worse. Like *where did my head go* worse.

Once outside, grateful he hadn't heard another boom from the shotgun, Brody saw Connie running down the street. He sprinted to follow. She was heading to the same spot they'd been . . . yesterday? Today?

We need to find a boundary, she'd said then, whenever *then* was. He remembered running into an alley with her, then seeing

a black canvas of nothingness, where other buildings and houses should be the boundary. Where Connie went when she disappeared.

He remembered all of it.

Out of the corner of his eye, he saw the three goons standing together on the sidewalk across the street. "Hey, cracker!" the black guy called. "She don't belong here, fool!" Brody didn't slow his pace, even though he really wanted to stop and confront the three of them.

who walked away

    who pretended to have a gun

       who pulled a gun

          who he managed to ward off

           who kicked his ass

              who shot him

                who he killed

"Not tonight, asshole!" Brody yelled over his shoulder. Some type of game was being played here, and he was a big part of it. He wasn't going to play anymore.

Connie darted into the same alley as before. Brody followed. This time she stopped halfway down the alley, then turned to face him.

"Are you okay?" Brody asked, trying to see if any of the buckshot had hit her.

"I'm fine," Connie replied, breathing heavily. "But barely. If you hadn't grabbed for the gun, I don't know what would've happened."

"Did you see the other people in there?"

"I was kinda busy trying to get my ass out the door, so no."

"They were shot. Some of them went down, but others were just standing there. Bleeding. Not reacting."

"Welcome to your new world, Brody Quail."

My new world. What did she mean by that? "I need some answers, Connie. That is your name, isn't it?"

"Yes, it's my name. That much I know. As for the rest, all I can do is tell you what's happened to me. I don't have very many answers."

"Then we need to find a safe place to talk. You said before the shadow man could only go where things were stable, right?" That memory had returned, too. How he'd seen the thing during his firefight flashback (or whatever the living hell it was), how he'd shot at the silhouette, the bullet disappearing into what seemed to be an empty black chasm in the shape of a man. He'd seen it other times, too, but those memories were out of reach.

"That's right. I've only seen him where things are put together, away from the boundaries."

"Like the one at the end of the alley?"

They both looked down the alley, Brody remembering the swirling black clouds.

"Yes, like that," Connie replied. "But they're hard to find. Once you've been to a place, they're gone. They're only where you haven't been before."

"So you're saying the one at the end of the alley is gone?"

"It might be, or it might still be there. I don't *know*, Brody. It might be different with you. I'm only telling you what I've seen."

Brody could tell Connie was frustrated and scared. "Okay. We'll go take a look. If it's not there, we'll find another one."

"Okay, but we have to hurry."

Brody remembered. "Sometimes, you have hours, sometimes, minutes."

"Yeah." She smiled at him. "You're remembering a lot of it now, aren't you."

"I'm remembering things, but I can't say *a lot*, because I don't know what that means."

"It'll come, believe me." She took his hand, and they walked to the end of the alley.

The boundary was gone. Beyond the alley was another street lined by buildings. Just as it should be. "You were right," Brody said. "It's back to normal."

"Yeah, normal." Connie moaned a little, and Brody steadied her.

"It's happening again, isn't it."

Connie took a deep breath, then let it out slowly. "Like I said, could be hours, could be minutes. We have to make use of the time we have. We need to find a place you've never been before, okay?"

Brody remembered the shadow man pointing up the street, as if he were urging him to go in that direction. "Before," Brody began, finding it difficult to find the word to describe time—*Today? Yesterday?*—"the shadow man was there on the street, pointing past my apartment. It was like he wanted me to go there."

"Then we shouldn't," Connie replied quickly.

"Why?"

"It wants us, Brody. Can't you feel it?"

He did, but for some reason he wasn't as fearful of the shadow man. "I do, but—"

"Then quick, someplace else."

Brody didn't want to retrace their path, not with the bar patrons (wounded ones, at that) and the three thugs lying in wait. Or maybe they were following him and Connie right now. He looked at the other end of the alley, half expecting to see them there, led by Jimmy himself, shotgun in hand. But no one was there. "Before yesterday, or whenever it was, I'd never been *here* before. I don't think I've ever been to any place on this street. Would one of the buildings work?"

"Let's find out," Connie said.

Brody took a step and kicked something. When he looked down, he saw his rifle lying at his feet. "I dropped this," he said, not bothering to qualify his statement with any frame of reference (yesterday, today) simply because his grasp on time was eroding.

"Bring it," Connie said. "It might come in handy."

"Ever shot one of these before?" Brody asked.

Connie shook her head.

"Too bad. I used to be pretty good with a rifle, when I had both arms."

"You seemed to shoot well enough last time."

"Well, let's hope I don't have to do it again."

✕

They quickly walked down the street (the one that wasn't there previously) and ducked inside another alley. They crouched behind a dumpster.

"We should be okay here for a while," Connie said, hugging her knees to her chest, her back against brick.

Brody leaned his rifle against the wall. "How are you feeling?" he asked. She hadn't shown any additional signs that her time was running out, no moaning or grimacing from pain as before.

"I'm fine," she replied. "*You're* looking better than the last time we were in an alley hiding behind a dumpster."

Brody remembered his ribs, how badly they'd hurt after the beating he'd taken. Probably broken. But now perfectly fine. "Okay, Connie. Tell me what the heck is going on here."

"Do you dream, Brody?"

That was an odd question, not what he wanted to hear from her. He wanted an explanation. "What does that have to do with anything?"

"Just answer my question," Connie said forcefully. "Do you have any dreams?"

Brody wanted to say yes, but honestly, he couldn't. He didn't even remember the last time he'd made it back to his apartment and crawled into his bed. (Had he ever?) "I'm—I'm not sure."

"*Exactly.* I wasn't sure either." Connie had said that she knew what was happening to him because she'd gone through it, too. Whatever *it* was.

"And you do now? Have dreams?" he asked.

"Yes. And you will, too."

Brody swallowed, hard, at the tone of her voice, feeling trapped in an unavoidable downward spiral. "You've got to tell me what's happening, Connie."

"I wish I could. All I know is, I'm here, and then I'm not."

"And when you're not—here, that is—you're in the . . . whatever the hell that black crap was that used to be where we are right now." Even as he said it, he had a hard time grasping the meaning of the words that were coming from his mouth.

"Yeah, I'm in *that* place."

Brody saw her shudder and placed his hand on her shoulder. "You okay?"

"I don't even know who I am anymore," she said, on the verge of sobbing, her voice tight. "This place is all wrong. All wrong."

"What do you mean?"

"You've heard them yourself, Brody. *She doesn't belong here.* And they're right. I don't belong here. Everything I know—*knew*—is gone. *I'm* gone."

"I don't understand."

"I was a worker in an underground facility, fifteen miles outside of Las Vegas, Nevada. After the war. My job was to keep the purification machinery running."

That explains the coveralls, Brody thought. *After the war* didn't make any sense, though. There were half a million US troops over there still.

"I had a family there, people I knew," she continued. "Then it all changed. I thought I was blacking out at first, but then I started to remember things, just like you are." She wiped a tear—only one—from her cheek. "Like those three clowns on the street that beat the crap out of you the last time we were here. You've seen them before, right? More times than you can remember?"

Brody nodded, dumbstruck.

"And I'll bet you remember them doing things differently, sometimes big things, sometimes not, every time you saw them?"

Her words ran true. He remembered the same general sequence of events: leaving the bar, knowing he was being followed, then being confronted by three thugs, but each time led to a different outcome. More than he could remember. He nodded again.

"The same thing started happening to me, Brody. The *same thing.* Then everything began to get shorter. I'd only remember being at my job for a few minutes at a time before I'd black out. And other times, everyone else would just be standing there, still as statues, and then when they started moving again, it was as if nothing had happened. But I *knew.* And I *remembered.* God, I thought I was going crazy!"

Brody was overcome by dread. He remembered the three thugs, still as statues like she said. He *was* experiencing the same things that Connie had, which meant she was probably right. Everything that was happening to her would happen to him, too. In time.

His time would get shorter. He would go to the black place.

Brody glanced at the rifle leaning against the wall. It was real, so the firefight had to have been real, too, right? Impossible; that was a battle he had *not* been a part of while he was over there. Not to mention he had been wearing someone else's uniform (J O H N S O N) and had both of his arms.

"Now it's all gone," Connie said. "All I know is *this* place." She paused, then added, "And you."

"What about your dreams?"

"Once I started having them, I realized that I'd never dreamt before. Never. Not once. But now, I'm having them all the time. When I'm in the other place."

"What do you dream about?"

She shook her head, as if trying to clear the visions from her mind. "Mostly they're nightmares. Horrible things. I'm little and . . . it's weird, and I'm not sure I can explain it," she said, staring at the wall on the other side of the alley. "I'm me, but it doesn't seem like me, if that makes any sense."

Brody didn't say anything, wanting her to continue. If this was going to happen to him, too, then he wanted to know what to expect.

Connie took a deep breath. "They're visions, mostly, snapshots of me as a little girl, but I'm someplace completely different, aboveground, in a house with people who are acting like my parents, but they're not my mom and dad."

Aboveground. "How long have you lived underground?" Brody asked. "I mean, before all this started happening to you."

"My whole life. I was born in Nevada Six."

She said it matter-of-factly and stared at him like he should know what she meant. He didn't. Maybe Nevada Six was some sort of government project that they kept hidden from the public or something. "What's Nevada Six?" he asked.

"One of the Arks." She was searching his face for any sort of recognition, but she couldn't find any. "There were fifteen Arks built right after the war," she said. "Most of them in Nevada, Utah, and Arizona. We lived in the sixth of the eight Nevada Arks." She paused, staring at him closely. "You don't know what I'm talking about, do you?"

Brody shook his head. A week ago (or was it even a week? A day?), he would've called her delusional. But she was telling the truth. He could see it in her eyes, hear it in the tone of her voice. "What war, Connie?"

"The China War." She raised her arms toward the buildings and said, "None of this should be here, Brody. It was all gone before I was born!"

Brody felt a dull ache at the back of his head, and he remembered.

There was a desert. Sand, like ash. A dead sky. He'd walked across that ground, but that hadn't been *him*, just like Connie had said about her dreams; it was her, but *not* her. Maybe he was dreaming now.

"You're remembering something, aren't you," Connie said.

"I think so." Brody rubbed the back of his head as the throbbing subsided. "What year was the China War?"

"2027," she answered. "I was born five years after it ended."

"Connie, it's 1968. Right here, right now, it's *1968*."

"That can't be possible," she said, shaking her head.

"It's 1968, and we're in Garland Trail, Nebraska."

"What, so I'm from the *future*? Is that what you're saying?" Her voice was cracking. Brody moved closer and put his arm around her shoulders. He could feel

her body trembling

Again the ache pounded at the back of his head, this time a little stronger. He winced but managed to hide the pain from Connie. He'd experienced a quick flash (him, but *not* him) of hiding in a dark place, with a girl in his arms. Small. Trembling. *Connie?*

"I don't think either of us knows exactly what's going on," Brody said. "But right now, we have this." He pulled his arm back and grabbed her hand, squeezing it tightly.

A tiny smile crossed her lips as she looked up at him.

"We'll stick together," he said, "and figure this out, okay?"

She nodded with little conviction. "Until I disappear again."

"When I saw you last—one of the other times before this—you said I was the only one who remembered your name," Brody said.

She smiled. "Yeah, Brody Quail. You're the only other person I've run into here that's remembered me. The rest of them yell at me to leave, say that I don't belong there. God, if I knew how to get back home, I would."

"And the shadow man?" Brody asked.

"And the shadow man," Connie said with a sigh. "I used to see him, too. Before I started coming here."

"In that underground place? Nevada Six?"

She nodded. "At first, I couldn't see him, but I knew someone was there, watching me. Know what I mean? Then I started to actually *see* him. An empty hole shaped like a person."

"And it's the same perso—*thing* that's chasing us here?"

"It's the same. It's evil, Brody. It wants us both."

Brody remembered how the shadow man had pointed down the street, trying to get him to go in a particular direction. In that instance, he hadn't felt any danger but instead thought it was trying to help. "Why does it want us?" he asked.

"It wants to kill us, Brody. Just like it killed my family."

Connie suddenly threw her head back, hitting the brick wall, and she let out a tiny scream of pain. She squeezed his hand so tightly it hurt.

She was going to disappear. "No no no, not yet!" Brody said.

"Oh God, Brody!"

"Hold on, Connie! Hold on!" He pulled her closer, wishing he could wrap another arm around her to hold her tight.

The effort would be futile.

The other girl, in the dark place, had vanished right from his (but *not* his) arms.

Her breaths were coming quick and furious. "Come back here! We'll find each other here!" She screamed—and then wasn't there, her voice echoing through the alley and into the night.

Brody scrambled to his feet. He ran from the alley and turned left, his boots thudding against the asphalt as he ran to a place he'd never been before. The buildings flashed by in the corner of his eye, one after the other, until the street ended in a swirling black cloud.

A boundary.

Connie was in there somewhere. In the blackness.

Brody held his breath, closed his eyes, and ran into the shadows.

Chapter 25
BRODY16

West Glenn, Colorado
Monday, March 30, 1981

"It doesn't work from the outside," Brody yelled, leaning over and popping the door lever.

"Thanks," Joan said, placing her books between them on the bench seat and slamming her door shut. "Ouch! What the heck?" She sat up a little and reached under her leg, pulling out whatever she'd sat on. She held it up for Brody to see. "Brody Quail, are you still playing with little-kid toys?"

Where in the heck did that come from? "That's not mine," he said, suddenly embarrassed. He took the toy from Joan's hand and tossed it in the backseat. He really had no idea how it had gotten in his car; no one else had ridden with him for . . . well, he wasn't sure, but he was certain no one had sat in the passenger seat for a long time, maybe even since his dad taught him how to drive. Brody wondered why his memory was so fuzzy all of a sudden. Remembering when someone was in your car should be easy, right?

"Little brother, maybe?" Joan asked. From the twinkle in her eyes, she was obviously enjoying this.

Brody smiled but only to hide the onset of confusion he was feeling. "Nah, I don't have a little—"

Brother.

He saw a face in his mind, a small boy's. A face he felt he knew.

And then a sledgehammer hit him. He grabbed the back of his head as a fiery pain rocketed down his neck and through his spine. His vision swirled, tiny points of light shooting across his closed eyelids. He could hear himself screaming, but even that faded away as blackness overtook him.

He felt himself tumbling, head over heels, as if he'd been pulled from the car and tossed into the air by a giant unseen hand.

And then it stopped.

There was no impact, no thud against the ground as he came to rest, as he half expected.

It just *stopped.*

The pain was gone, and the horrible vertigo had ceased along with it. He wasn't hurt, as far as he could tell, but was afraid to open his eyes.

But, no, that wasn't right.

His eyes weren't closed. He was blinking. His eyes were open, but there was nothing to see. *My God, I'm blind,* he thought, his heart thudding away. He tried to bring his hand to his face, but he couldn't. He tried to move his legs. *Why aren't they moving?*

He was fixed in place. Brody was confused, shocked. He could feel the panic building in his body. He wanted to scream but couldn't produce a sound.

The space was silent and cold, wherever he was. Brody was alone in the darkness, unable to move, speak, or see. There was no sound, no scent, and no way to judge the passage of time.

Had he been here for minutes? Hours? How did he get here? He tried to move again but couldn't shift any of his extremities. A terrible, frustrating feeling, made worse by the burning in his gut. He ached from *hunger*.

But that meant he wasn't dead, right? If this was death, and he was trapped in some dark place (as opposed to going where angels sing and everyone you've ever known is there waiting), then he wouldn't feel anything, right? No, he wasn't dead. He could sense the rise and fall of his chest, feel himself blinking, moving his eyes. If he were really dead, none of that should be possible.

He *was* alive.

Slowly, the faces came. Brody saw his friends Kyle, Jason, and Tim. He saw Joan, looking as beautiful as always. He was in his car with her, getting ready to drive her home, when she sat on something (a yellow plastic dinosaur, of all things) and he threw it in the backseat. She asked if it belonged to his little brother.

That was it! Brody remembered the pain, the feeling of falling headlong into a dark abyss right after she asked him that question.

The face. The little boy's face!

He struggled to remember what he'd seen: a kid, maybe five, six years old, staring up at him.

He's a pain in the ass, but I'd die for him.

But that couldn't be. Brody didn't have a brother. The feelings he had for the little boy, though, were impossible to ignore. He'd glimpsed another life, one where he *did*, in fact, have a little brother named—

His name is Murphy. Murf.

The name came through as clear as a bell. And then so did other things. Remembering his brother's name released memories, images of people and places so familiar, and yet so *un*familiar, that the entire experience was hard to fathom.

But there remained a constant: his life.

My name is Brody Quail. I'm sixteen years old, living in West Glenn, Colorado, a sophomore at Forrest J. Gerber Senior High. I drive a beat-up 1963 Chevy Impala.

His life.

But there was more.

He saw a house where love had been broken apart by a terrible tragedy. He saw a bottle of booze and a gun in a drawer, both of which seemed to call to him, to pull his strings.

He saw an icy street where people wanted to hurt him.

He saw a playground where kids played a game with a football, and Murf wanted nothing more than to join in.

As each wave of memories washed over him, he explored them, watched, listened, noted every detail that he could. Even the little things, like the yellow toy dinosaur Joan had sat on, a T. rex, became more and more real to him. Because they *were* real.

All these strange memories seemed just as real as his own life.

And then he remembered something—some*one*—else.

The other constant.

Her name was Connie.

There was a sudden flash of brightness.

※

"It doesn't work from the outside," Brody yelled, leaning over and popping the door lever.

"Thanks," Joan said, placing her books between them on the bench seat and slamming her door shut. "Ouch! What the heck?" She sat up a little and reached under her leg, pulling out whatever she'd sat on. She held it up for Brody to see. "Brody Quail, are you still playing with little-kid toys?"

Brody took the dinosaur from her. He stared at it, turned it over in his hands, and knew it was his. But it belonged somewhere else.

"Is it your little brother's?" Joan asked.

Brody expected to feel the familiar pain, but it didn't come, at least not as violently as before. His head throbbed a little, but the pain was manageable.

"Nah," he said, placing the T. rex back down on the front seat. "Not mine. And I don't have a brother." In a way, he felt like he was lying to her. "I don't know where it came from." Another lie, because he knew exactly where the toy belonged: in a bedroom, on a shelf right next to a model of a World War II Grumman Avenger torpedo bomber.

His room. His *other* room.

"My house is on Lincoln," Joan said, "a couple of blocks away. Take the first left from Michigan and—"

"You're the third house on the left," Brody said, finishing her statement for her.

"Um, that's right," Joan said, a little surprised. "How do you know where I live?"

"I guess Jason must've mentioned it," he lied. "Want to put your seat belt on?"

She smiled at him. "A Brody rule, huh?"

"Yep. You never know when some moron will run a red light and smash into you." He watched her face as he said it but saw no reaction.

"Yeah, I guess so." Joan shoved her lap belt into the buckle and settled back in the seat.

Brody started the car and backed out of the parking space. He would probably never make it to Joan's house if he did everything the same way he'd done it before. And he *had* done it before, more times than he could remember. This time would be different, though; he would stop at the red light and avoid the accident. He'd get Joan safely home, and then he'd look for Connie. But as soon as he'd formulated the plan in his mind, he knew he'd never get the chance, at least not this time.

He felt the sensation come on quickly. He gripped the wheel tightly, clenching his teeth, trying to keep it together. Pointless. He would go away, to the dark place, just like Connie. The place where he couldn't move, couldn't feel. The place where he would wait and remember. The pain built in intensity until it felt as if someone were pouring molten lead through a hole in the back of his skull, where it burned its way down through his neck and into his chest. He began to scream.

"Cool car," he heard Joan say. "How fast have you had it?"

Brody stopped fighting the pain. Darkness swallowed him.

Chapter 26
BRODY52

Joshua, Maine
Friday, October 25, 1974

Brody found himself standing outside the bedroom door.

He wasn't sure, at first, exactly how long he'd been standing there. All he knew was that he *was* there, with no recollection of what he'd been doing hours or even minutes before. As he stared at the closed door, he slowly became aware that things weren't as they seemed. Bits and pieces of memory began to slip into his consciousness, like tiny wisps of steam from a cup of coffee, there for a moment, glimpsed, then disappearing into thin air.

Something had happened in that room. Something bad. And for the first time, he was certain it had nothing to do with his Reba.

At least, not exactly. She looked like Reba but wasn't really her. She had a different name, too, although it remained just out of reach in his mind. Another wisp of steam.

She had been in the bedroom . . . No . . . she had been *dragged* into the room by something dark, ominous.

Brody raised his hand to his ear, felt the curve, expected to find a piece missing. No, his ear was intact, and there was no pain, no blood. But why did he think a part of his ear was gone? He closed his eyes, searched his thoughts, peeking into the shadows in his mind.

He'd been shot at, the bullet missing his head but clipping his ear, and then he'd fallen into—

Connie. That was her name. The woman dressed like his Reba but not really her. The wisps of steam were remaining visible longer. "Everything is going to be fine now, Mr. Quail," Brody whispered to himself. "Everything is going to be fine."

Felix. With the gun, shooting at him.

He'd stared down the barrel of his old service weapon, heard the hammer click, seen the flash, and heard the boom. Heard the zing of the bullet as it passed. Felt the sting as it clipped his ear.

Brody felt a sharp pain in the back of his head, which quickly subsided, leaving a dull throb. He was remembering, and it hurt. Just like before.

Brody turned away from the door and stepped down the hall to his office, keeping an eye on the top of the stairs, expecting Felix to appear at any moment.

His old friend. But not anymore.

Something was terribly wrong in this house. After all the pain he'd endured, all the suffering, another layer of darkness had descended upon his home.

Brody opened his desk drawer and found his Smith & Wesson Model 27 sitting right where it always was. He opened the cylinder and saw six .357 Magnum cartridge primers staring back at him. He reached toward the back of the drawer and found the box of ammo. He emptied it into his hand and put the cartridges into his pockets. He didn't have a holster for the weapon anymore, so he tucked the loaded revolver into the back of his pants, the cold steel pressing against his lower back. Not the smartest way to carry a loaded weapon, but it would have to do.

Please, Mr. Quail, you have to stop this insanity! Felix had said.

I will stop it, Felix, Brody said to himself. *I'll stop it right now.*

Brody walked from his office and turned toward the bedroom just as he heard the first knock at the front door.

Two police officers. Telling him his son had been killed in a car accident earlier in the day. Then he would stare at his pistol, think about blowing his own head off, or grab a bottle and wrestle with all the old demons.

Because it was what he was supposed to do.

"No more," Brody said out loud. "I'm done playing your game." He turned, his eyes searching the hallway but finding nothing. "Do you hear me?" he said louder. "I'm not playing your game anymore. I'm done!"

He stepped to the bedroom door and grasped the handle. He paused, the memories of his life in this house tumbling before his eyes.

More knocks from downstairs, the officers at the front door.

The office. It was always the office. He had the pictures of his life with Reba, all the fun times as they raised their family, hanging on the wall, but he couldn't remember anything else. What had they done *in between* those pictures? Had they ever fought? Spent time together in the mountains? Traveled to any foreign countries?

Nothing was there. Not a goddamned thing.

Only the office. Only the pictures.

As clarity descended, another sharp pain sliced through his head behind his eyes, causing his legs to buckle and turning his stomach. He clenched his teeth, fighting through the ordeal. Tears filled his eyes. The pain grew worse. "No!" he screamed. "I'm not going to play—your—game—anymore!" His hand shook, the doorknob rattling in his grip.

Then the torment in his skull began to subside once again, the dull throbbing settling into a rhythm with the beat of his heart. He could *do* this, he could manage the pain. He had to, in order to discover exactly what was going on. He took some deep breaths and let them out slowly. He turned the knob and opened the door.

"Connie?" Brody said into the shadows. No answer. He flicked on the light switch, squinting against the sudden brightness. The bedroom was exactly as he had ordered it to be, as his Reba would have wanted it.

Brody stepped inside, opened the closet, looked under the bed, even looked out the window. He felt a little foolish looking for someone who obviously wasn't there.

Connie had been dragged into the room by some dark figure, of that he was certain. The memory was fresh—and *new*—so unlike all his other memories. No, Connie wasn't here. At least not this time. Not right now.

Something had happened to him following Reba's death, but *when* and *how* were questions he couldn't answer. Brody Quail felt as if everything had been constructed for him, and his only memories hung on his office wall. Felix and the two officers at the front door were only playing their parts.

But if that were true, everything he was would be a lie. Brody Quail, the fifty-two-year-old widower living in a big, empty house in Joshua, Maine, would be an ugly falsehood, a living tapestry of fabrications and deceit, forced to relive the news of his son's death time and time again, while someone, somewhere, enjoyed watching his struggles with the gun and the booze.

It would stop now. Brody would never again step dutifully down the stairs to answer the door and listen to the officers give their scripted speech about his son. Never again would he go back upstairs to his office and hold a bottle in his hand, fighting the urge to take a drink. Never again would he reach into his drawer, place the gun into his mouth, and send a bullet into his skull.

Whoever had done this to him would pay, starting now.

Brody took the pistol from his pants and walked out of the bedroom and down the hallway to the stairs.

He could still picture Connie standing in the hallway and remember how he thought he was seeing his Reba again. He frowned, wondering if there even was a Reba in the first place. He didn't want to consider the possibility, and he decided that, for now, he wouldn't. His feelings for his deceased wife were strong, so very strong and real that he couldn't believe she was nothing more than another fabrication.

He heard the officers knocking on the door again, patiently waiting for him to greet them so they could play their part. He would greet them, all right. For the last time.

Brody strode confidently to the front door, his pistol hanging at his side. He thumbed the hammer back as he approached. He grabbed the handle and opened the door.

They were standing side by side, their faces grim, actors ready to deliver their lines. He watched their eyes as he brought the pistol to bear, aiming it at the man closest to the door. There was no reaction from the first man as the gun boomed, the bullet striking him directly in the forehead a little above his left eye. The pistol bucked in Brody's hand, and he controlled the recoil, bringing the weapon back down toward the other officer, who was standing completely still, his face gone slack.

Empty and emotionless.

Brody pulled the trigger again, and the bullet struck the other man just to the right of the bridge of his nose.

The gun wavered in Brody's hand, and he took a step back.

This wasn't right.

Both men were still standing, dead eyes staring past him, looking at nothing. Both had holes in their heads, clean entry wounds, nearly perfect circles where the bullets had hit their marks, but the aftermath of the shots wasn't spread all over his front walk.

Both men, who had looked so normal just seconds before, now appeared as wax mannequins standing on wooden legs.

The fury Brody had felt when he opened the door rapidly vanished, replaced with a cold certainty that all he'd assumed was, in fact, correct.

He raised the gun again and fired into their chests, two in the first man, one in the other. The gun bucked in his hand, again and again, until the hammer clicked on an empty cylinder. He opened the cylinder and reached into his pocket for another handful of cartridges. He loaded the gun again by feel alone, keeping his eyes locked on the two false-hoods standing silently before him, holes in their heads and chests. He snapped the cylinder closed again, pulled the hammer back, and aimed.

Behind the two men, though, the landscape had changed—it was no longer the early evening in Joshua. The terrain had become nothing more than a deep, dark expanse with no beginning or end, a swirling mass of shadows, spinning and cavorting like cloaked spirits.

"Why did you do that, sir?"

Felix stood close behind him.

Brody spun, placing the front sight post directly between Felix's eyes. "I'm not playing your sick game anymore, Felix, or whatever your name is. Do you understand me? I'm done."

"My name *is* Felix, sir. I've been your employee for years."

"You and I both know that's not true," Brody said, his voice shaky as the throbbing in his head built in intensity.

"Sir, please. You're tired. You need to rest. Please give me the gun," Felix said, taking a step forward.

"Stay right where you are," Brody commanded, tightening his pull on the trigger. "We're going to have a little talk."

"No, sir, we are not," Felix said. "You're going to give me the gun, then I'm going to bring you some dinner. Would you like to take it in your office, sir?"

dinner

With that one little word, Brody's stomach clenched tightly, and every bit of energy seemed to drain away. He was lightheaded, weak, and insatiably hungry. Brody fought through it, along with the dull throbbing at the back of his skull.

"Last time, you tried to kill me, Felix," Brody said. "I'm not giving you this gun."

Brody expected a fight but instead watched as Felix dropped his arms to his side, the life disappearing from his eyes. All at once Felix was just as much a wax mannequin as the two officers standing at the front door.

Apparently, the game was over. There would be no fight for the gun as before.

Brody lowered his revolver and gently thumbed the hammer back down. He shoved the gun into the back of his pants again and stepped closer. Felix was standing absolutely still, not breathing, his eyes dead and still. *Not real.*

Brody sensed motion at the top of the stairs, and he saw her.

"Brody?"

"Connie," Brody replied, running up the stairs two at a time with all the strength he could muster. He was relieved to see her, as she was the only person he knew to be real in this crazy place, and he had thought he'd never see her again after she'd been dragged into the bedroom. As he reached the top of the stairs, he could see that she was in pain, tears streaming down her face. *It hurts,* he remembered. *Before she disappears, it hurts.* He had to talk to her, explain what he'd concluded was going on in this house, how they were both nothing more than players in someone's sick, twisted game. She couldn't go already, not now! "Is it happening?"

"Yes," she said, her voice tight. "I don't have much time."

He helped her to the floor, held her in his arms, felt her body trembling.

trembling

Visions of a closet, a dark, confined space, flashed through his mind. A place where he had held her just like this, but she had been different then, much younger, smaller.

And so had he.

"Hold on, Connie. Please, don't go yet."

"Do you dream, Brody?" she asked, and he remembered her asking that question before.

"Dream?"

"Of other places, where you are you, but *not* you," she said, her voice cracking with the effort.

He thought about the closet and nodded his head. "Yes, I think so. With you. You were there, too."

"No, Brody," she said, her body tightening against his, a slight moan escaping her lips. "Oh God, it's happening!"

"Stay with me," Brody said, holding on to her body as tightly as he could, even though it wouldn't do any good.

"Do you dream of another place, where *you* are *you*, but everything else is different?"

"What have you seen, Connie?" Brody asked. "Please, tell me. Quickly."

"I've seen it, Brody. I've seen how it all started." She began to shake and struggled to speak. "Remember this moment, Brody. Remember, and I'll—"

Brody's arms collapsed against his chest.

She was gone.

Find a boundary, he heard in his head. A voice, so familiar.

A boundary

A boundary

The darkness

Brody ran down the stairs toward the front door. The officers were gone, and the shifting, swirling shadows licked the door frame, tiny wisps spreading inside and crawling along the walls. The outside was coming in.

Brody recoiled, but it was in the darkness where he would find his answers.

He closed his eyes and let the blackness take him.

✕

Brody floats in the darkness, seeing nothing, feeling nothing. It is silent here, and cold. He is aware of the rise and fall of his chest, but the sensation of breathing is wrong. He cannot speak, nor make any other sound. His limbs are fixed in place. He tries to flex his fingers, then his toes, but can't tell if he's actually moving them.

Time passes without meaning, seconds ticking by with nothing awaiting them and leaving nothing behind. Here and now is all that matters, for there is nothing else.

The searing pain in the back of his head is gone now, but the hunger remains. Brody knows this place. He has been here many times before.

The house in Joshua is an escape, a door through which he will pass, to live a life that isn't real. Felix, the police officers, and all he knows on the other side of the shadows are false people and places designed to test him, push and prod him, while someone watches.

The shadow man.

But Brody knows he isn't alone. He isn't the only player. Connie is part of this game, too. She disappears into this dark place, just as he does, and emerges in the house in Joshua—

And other places.

Brody sees her dressed as his dearest Reba.

He sees her as a young girl on a playground, chased by the shadow man. Feels her body trembling against his in a pitch-black closet.

He sees her on an icy street, swinging a pipe, fighting off people trying to hurt her, and he sees her as a teenager, running down a sunlit street, trying to escape the shadow man. In each place Connie is there with him, different in appearance and age, but inside she is the same.

Just as he is the same, in Joshua; Culver, Ohio; Garland Trail, Nebraska; and West Glenn, Colorado.

Brody slowly retreats deeper into himself, falling down a long tunnel of his mind, to a place where he simply exists, waits, and survives. He wonders if he will dream.

He sees himself as a ten-year-old boy, trying to keep his little brother from getting hit by a car. He sees a yellow dinosaur.

and

A twentysomething war vet fighting for survival in the early morning hours.

and

A high school kid with an old car, sweet on a pretty girl named Joan, whom he would watch die in a fiery car wreck. A note, crumpled on the car seat.

No, he isn't dreaming. This is the game. *His* game.

Brody relaxes his mind, confident in the knowledge he has finally unlocked. Here in the shadows he will wait until he emerges into one of his four worlds.

He would find Connie. She would be there. Why, he wasn't certain, but she would appear wherever he was; they were both playing the same game. *I've seen it, Brody. I've seen how it all started,* she'd said. Connie was the key. She *knew*, and she would be his partner in the coming struggle.

Together they would fight the shadow man.

And end this insane game.

He feels himself rise from the depths, ascending from the shadowy place into another place. This is how it happens, the strings being pulled by the puppeteer, dragging him to another existence where he will dance and sing to the amusement of the shadow man.

Bright flashes cross his vision, and—

Chapter 27
BRODY10

Culver, Ohio
Thursday, May 15, 1975

Brody opened his eyes. He was in his bedroom, lying on his bed. He was ten years old, but for the first time ever in this place, he was much more than just a little kid.

He swung his legs off the side of the bed and stood, looking around his room. *There it is.* He spied something he'd seen while suspended in the dark place and quickly stuck it in his pocket.

"Brody, dinner's ready," his mom called from downstairs.

"Okay, Mom," he replied. This was all part of the shadow man's sick game. This house, his mother, everything—all lies put here for some twisted purpose. But he would play along. For now.

Brody hadn't been here for the longest time. Usually, his memories stopped at the playground, after he'd tried to save, or *had* saved, his brother from the car. The mention of dinner sent a pang of hunger through his body so urgent and overpowering it was difficult not to run downstairs and stuff whatever food he could find into his mouth. He would eat, then he would leave. He had to find Connie.

"Tell Murphy, too," his mother added.

Brody opened his door and stepped into the hallway. Brody smelled the food from downstairs, and his stomach growled. He was weak, as if he hadn't eaten for days, but there was no more pain in the back of his head, which was a blessing. Murf's room was right next to his, and the door was open. He peered inside and saw Murf sitting on the side of his bed.

Brody had a hard time looking into Murf's eyes and thinking anything was wrong. Deep inside, he loved that kid, and thinking about Murf being anything other than a real, live little boy made Brody angry. He recalled all the times he'd run after Murf as he wandered out into the street, and all the times the car had hit him, or had hit both of them, or had barely missed them both. The memories were nearly too hard to fathom.

"What's wrong, Bowdy?" Murphy said, using his little-boy voice again.

"Nothing's wrong, Murf," Brody replied. He walked into his brother's room and tousled the kid's hair. "Dinner's ready. Have you washed your hands?"

Murf held his hands out in front of him, palms up, so Brody could see.

The events all seemed so real and so right. He felt content knowing he was at home with his little brother, going downstairs to eat dinner with their mother. A normal day with his normal family. He sighed and shook his head.

"I washed them, really I did," Murf said.

"It's not that, Murf."

"Are you okay, Bowdy?"

"Come on, kiddo," Brody said. His heart was breaking because if he deviated from the script he was supposed to play, his brother (or whatever he was) would no longer act like the Murf he had grown to love. He would be like Felix, or the kids at the playground, a glassy-eyed mannequin, angry that Brody wasn't doing what he was supposed to. For now, he would play along, then he would try to find Connie at the first opportunity. "Let's go eat."

⋊

Brody couldn't help himself when he sat down at the table, shoving forkful after forkful into his mouth. He was starving.

"Slow down, Brody," his mother said. "You'll make yourself sick!"

Brody looked at the woman he'd known as his mom for as long as he could remember (at least in this place) and was sickened by the knowledge that she was really no different from the others. She had blond hair, brown eyes, and a nose that looked just like his. But she was a falsehood, a fake. "Sorry, Mom. This is really good." Which was true. The food tasted great, but the hunger was still there even after he'd cleared half his plate and downed a whole glass of milk.

"I'm glad you like it, but don't eat so fast. You ate lunch at school today, right?"

He nodded but couldn't remember whether or not he'd eaten.

No, you don't remember because you were never at school today. You were in the darkness, then you were in your room, he reminded himself. *Play the game. Just play the game.*

"I called your father a little while ago, Brody," his mom said. "And I told him what you did today. He's very proud of you."

The car. It had to be the car again, right? "It was nothing," Brody replied.

"Nothing? You saved your brother's life today!" She looked at Murf. "And you, young man, are very, very lucky your brother was there."

"Yes, ma'am," Murf said quietly. "I won't do it again."

Brody decided to chime in. "Yeah, Murf. You know better than to walk out into the street without looking." As soon as he said it, Brody noticed a change in the room. Both his mother and Murf were staring at him.

"Street?" his mother asked. "What are you talking about, Brody?"

"The car, at school," Brody said. "I saw Murf walking out into the street, and I grabbed him right before he got hit by the car."

"No, Brody," Murf said, his voice oddly flat. "I was choking, and you hit me on the back."

"There was no car today, Brody," his mother said, her voice also lacking emotion and her eyes quickly losing life. "You shouldn't be talking about the car."

Brody pushed his chair back from the table and stood as a sharp pain rocketed down his spine from the back of his head. He groaned and grabbed the chair to keep his balance. His mother and brother sat there, staring at him.

Brody remembered what had happened at school when the other kids had chased him and Connie, when they had beaten him. It was time to leave.

He turned and ran from the house, slamming the front door closed behind him and taking off down the street toward the school. If Connie was going to appear, it would be there. At least he hoped so. The sun was out, white, puffy clouds floated across the blue dome of the sky, and birds were chirping. He felt a breeze, saw people walking around and cars driving up and down the streets. Culver, Ohio, in mid-May. Completely normal.

But it wasn't. His mother's and brother's faces at the dining room table confirmed that much. He'd said something that had thrown them off script, and he had already experienced what happened after *that*.

In the darkness, he had learned the truth: this was one of four places where he was Brody Quail. And it couldn't be real.

He had to find Connie, talk to her, let her know what he'd realized was happening. She would know what to do next because she knew how it had all started. She'd seen it in one of her dreams. He had to know, too.

Brody ran, pumping his arms and legs, hoping the fierce flash of pain he'd felt at the table wouldn't return. His head was throbbing slightly, but it wasn't too bad. He half expected the people along the streets to stop and stare as his brother and mother had, and take off after him (*he's not doing what he's supposed to do*), but thankfully, they didn't seem to care. So far.

As Brody approached the school, he saw it was abandoned, which made sense because he'd started this day (Day? What was it, really? A session?) in his room, well after school had ended. The playground was empty, no kids lining the fence screaming at him as before, no hive-minded mob wanting to pummel him for not staying on script. He'd hoped to see Connie there, waiting for him, but there was no sign of her.

He remembered a moment from before, in another place, a big, empty house where the shadow man dragged Connie into a room, into the darkness. His heart sank, thinking maybe he'd never see Connie again.

He stopped running.

The shadow man had gotten her.

Brody didn't want to consider having to go through this alone, without the only other person who seemed to know what was going on. He would look for her, find her. He would step into the darkness wherever he found it.

it's a boundary

a boundary

go to a place you've never been before

First, he would search the school. Just in case.

Brody ran to the school's front door and pulled it. It was locked. He tried two, then three of the side doors and found them locked as well. He searched the ground until he found a rock big enough to do the trick and walked to the back of the school, where the trees would hide him from prying eyes. If the school had an alarm, so be it. He would be in and out quickly enough to avoid the police (if there even were police in this place). If she wasn't there, then he would find a boundary.

He remembered the darkness, how it had felt, and he shuddered. It was an awful place, so empty and constricting, but it was where he had learned the truth about himself, and the only place where he thought he could find Connie.

If she was even alive.

Brody threw the rock at a small window. The glass spiderwebbed but didn't break. He picked the rock up and threw it again, and again, until the glass finally gave way. He grabbed a stick from the ground and poked at the shards of glass around the edges. Luckily there were no sirens or bells, but maybe they had a silent alarm, like a bank.

He squirmed through the window and dropped to the floor, careful not to cut his hands on the shards of glass. He opened his mouth to call out Connie's name, then stopped himself. He assumed the building was empty, but there could still be a janitor inside, a possibility he forgot to consider before he broke the window. If anyone was inside, he or she would probably have heard the glass breaking. He'd have to be careful. He walked quickly down the hall, searching each classroom as he went. Down the main hall toward the office, he found nothing. The gym, empty. There was no one here. No janitor, thankfully. But no Connie either.

He made his way down the last hall, past his own classroom, where he'd hidden behind his teacher's desk one of the last times he'd been here, when *the sky was wrong*

      the shadows deep and dark

            the colors flat and lifeless

and stood before the janitor's closet where he and Connie had hidden. Where he'd held her in his arms and she had vanished into thin air. "Please be here," he whispered and opened the door.

For a second, Brody wasn't sure what he was seeing. The inside of the closet was dark, too dark. Swirling shadows, an emptiness stretching away far beyond the back of the closet.

In the shape of a man.

Brody stumbled back, falling on his butt, kicking with his feet to get away as the thing slowly emerged from the closet.

The shadow man, an outline of a person cut from the air, reaching for him.

Brody scrambled to his feet and ran for all he was worth, back toward the window. He didn't look back, but it was there, so close, following him.

It's evil, Brody. It wants us both.

It killed my family.

Brody slipped as he turned the corner and slid into the wall. He fell to the floor and risked a glance behind him. The shadow man was there, walking quickly. He was once again whole, a man in black clothing, boots, and a visored helmet. He was close enough that Brody could see his own reflection in the shiny faceplate and the terror etched across his face.

He crawled down the hall, scrambling to his feet. He stopped, grabbed his window-breaking rock from the floor, and turned. He held it up, ready to throw. "Stop!" he screamed as the shadow man turned the corner. "Leave me alone!"

The shadow man didn't stop but slowed his pace. Still, he came closer. Closer.

Brody threw the rock, and it struck the shadow man in the shoulder, bouncing off harmlessly. Brody turned and ran, slipping on the glass shards on the floor and nearly losing his footing.

The glass!

He quickly looked around, searching for a piece large enough to use as a weapon. *There!* He grabbed a long shard of windowpane, triangular with a sharpened end, the wide portion almost too big to fit in his hand. The edges were sharp, and he could feel them digging into his fingers.

This time, the shadow man stopped. He held up his hand, motioning at Brody to stop.

"Get back," Brody commanded. "Leave me alone."

The shadow man raised his other hand, brought it to his face. He seemed to flick some sort of switch by his mouthpiece.

"What did you do with Connie?" Brody screamed. "Where is she?"

For the first time, he heard the shadow man speak.

"Forget about the girl."

His voice was electronic, as if he were speaking through a microphone.

"What did you do to her?" Brody screamed, slowly backing up toward the window.

The shadow man took another step forward. "You need to forget about her, Brody."

It—he knows my name.

"You killed her family," Brody said coldly. "And you killed her, too, didn't you."

"The girl isn't here, Brody. Put the glass down."

"No!" Brody had been gripping the shard so tightly that it had cut into his fingers, and he could feel a trickle of blood running down his wrist. He didn't care, though. He wasn't going to play this game anymore.

Brody was backed against the wall now, the window's bottom edge pressing against his shoulders. He'd have to turn and lift himself up before the shadow man could cover the distance and grab him. He wasn't sure he could get out in time. "I'm through playing your game. I'm *done*, do you understand? I'm not going to play this anymore. None of this is real!"

"It's not a game, Brody," the shadow man said. "Look at your hand . . . You're bleeding. Put the glass down, and come with me."

"Where is Connie?"

"You have to forget about her."

Brody decided. He turned and lifted himself up, the glass still clutched in his hand. He heard the shadow man move toward him, felt him grab his leg. He was halfway out the window, being dragged back. He tried to hold on to the edge of the window with his empty hand, gripping it as tightly as he could, but his fingers slipped, and he fell back inside.

And that's when Brody Quail fought back.

Brody swung his weapon with all the strength he could muster and shoved the pointed shard of broken glass into the shadow man's shoulder.

He let out a tinny, electronic scream and tumbled back, the glass sticking out of his shoulder, covered in blood.

Brody's blood.

Brody watched as the shadow man vanished, leaving the glass shard suspended in midair for a moment before it fell to the floor, bouncing once and breaking in half.

Then the pain hit him like a sledgehammer. He screamed as the darkness flooded the halls, devouring the scene around him.

Only blackness remained.

Chapter 28

THE SHADOW MAN

He ripped the visor from his face and gripped his shoulder. He could feel the blood seeping through his clothing, running between his fingers.

"He cut me!"

"How bad?" The man standing close by, Lead, motioned another man over as he took a closer look at his diver's wound.

"Bad enough. Jesus, this hurts like a bitch."

"Get him to medical," Lead ordered. He turned to another man standing in the shadows, the next diver in the queue. "Suit up."

"Roger, sir."

"And hurry up. We're running out of time."

Chapter 29
BRODY26

He was in his apartment, standing in the middle of the darkened room, with no idea when or where he had come from. His head was throbbing, and he was so famished that he immediately went to his small fridge and yanked the door open.

There were a couple of cans of cheap beer, some cold cuts, a jug of orange juice, and a bottle of vodka. He grabbed the lunch meat, ripped open the package with his teeth (having just one hand made opening things an adventure sometimes), and started stuffing the thin-sliced salami into his mouth, one piece after another, savoring the flavor. His stomach growled as he made quick work of the entire package. He washed it down with the orange juice, drinking almost the entire half-gallon carton.

Still, though, he was ravenous, and weak, as if he hadn't eaten for days.

He went to a small cupboard that served as his pantry and grabbed a box of breakfast cereal. Frosted Flakes. After eating five or six handfuls, he took another gulp of orange juice, emptying the carton.

He felt as if he were eating air. He was still hungry, but not quite as much as before.

During the minutes he'd been here, the awareness of where he was and who he was began to seep into his consciousness. He was twenty-six years old, a disabled (he hated that word) veteran living in Garland Trail, Nebraska.

Another memory flashed before him, and he instinctively glanced at his palm, expecting to find his fingers bloody and shredded by a piece of broken glass. He remembered the school, looking for Connie, then being chased by the shadow man. He'd cut him, with the glass. Shoved it into his shoulder as far as it would go, then the shadow man had vanished, and the darkness had enveloped him.

He had to find Connie, right now, before he disappeared into the black again, or the shadow man found him.

But where should he go?

The alley, where you saw her last.

His rifle was (or might be) there, too. Brody stepped outside his apartment, taking one last look in case he'd never see the place again. He'd lived in this crappy little spot for a few years and couldn't help but feel a connection. But if what he'd realized in the darkness was true, the apartment was nothing more than another stage prop, part of the elaborate farce constructed for the shadow man's entertainment.

The truth seemed so hard to believe, that everything he knew and remembered wasn't real. All his time in Vietnam, the stinking mud during the rains, the insects biting without relief, and the dark, dangerous Viet Cong tunnels.

Brody glanced down at the pinned-up sleeve of his field jacket, and doubt tumbled through his mind. His arm *was* gone. He remembered the day clearly and how the pain nearly drove him insane. He'd never forget the sound of the grenade blast, the feel of the shock wave hammering his body, and the realization that he was terribly hurt. And then the horror of seeing what remained of his left arm twitching in the mud.

How could that possibly *not* be real?

Brody slammed the door shut and went downstairs. He would head back to the alley, hopefully find his weapon there (where he left it today? Yesterday? When?), and try to find Connie. But there was one thing he had to check first.

A newspaper vending machine was outside the building, and luckily, it still had a paper at the bottom. He fished in his pocket for a dime and felt something else. He pulled it out and stared. Yellow, plastic. A toy dinosaur. His, but *not* his. Not in this place.

He'd taken it from his shelf

Ten years old

and put it in his pocket.

The dull thudding in the back of his head flared, the pain causing him to wince and take a quick breath, but it passed quickly. He put the dinosaur in his jacket pocket, pulled a dime from his pants pocket, and slipped it into the slot. He opened the box and grabbed the paper, checking the date.

Tuesday, November 12, 1968.

It was *always* Tuesday, November 12, 1968. Every, single, god-damned day.

He threw the paper on the ground and walked in the direction of the alley where he'd last seen Connie. *Connie from the future, a worker in an underground ark, whatever the hell that is, born in 2032, five years after the China War.* He wasn't sure exactly how she fit into this game, but she was the only person who seemed remotely real. Was she really from the twenty-first century, like she believed, or was she like him, trapped in some sort of made-up world? Maybe the war with China, the ruined country, and the underground facilities were all fake, too.

She'd only mentioned that single place, the Ark, and no others. There were four distinct places where his game was being played. He wondered if Connie was experiencing the same thing: different lives, ages, and events. If so, why hadn't she mentioned any of the other locales? Then again, their time together hadn't been long enough to have a real discussion about what was happening to both of them.

As he walked, he kept an eye on the darkened spaces between the buildings, watching for the shadow man to emerge. Brody had hurt him (as a ten-year-old kid, at that), and if the bastard did reappear, he'd probably be pissed. The important thing was, he'd actually *hurt* him. He remembered shooting the shadow man when he was in the firefight (someone else's, not his), when he appeared as an empty out-line of a man, a hole with nothing but blackness inside. The bullet didn't have any effect then, but in the school, when the shadow man was an actual *man*, the glass had cut him. He'd screamed in pain. If Brody saw him in this place again, and he appeared fully formed, as he did in the school, then a shot to the head might just kill him.

Brody hoped he'd get the chance to see what a 5.56 round to the visor would do.

All the alleys looked the same, and Brody had some difficulty finding the right one, but he recognized the dumpster he and Connie had hidden beside and found his M16 on the ground exactly where he'd left it, right after Connie had vanished. He sat down and laid the rifle across his legs and checked the magazine. He released it, and holding the gun against his thigh with his hand, he thumbed out the remaining rounds. There were seventeen rounds left, eighteen including the one still in the chamber. It made sense; he'd slammed a magazine into the rifle during the firefight (a made-up place), and fired one shot at the shadow man while still in the field. Then, he'd fired another single shot at him while he was chasing Connie on the street (here, another made-up place).

Eighteen would have to be enough. He slowly reloaded the steel twenty-round magazine, finding it extremely difficult to do with only one hand. The last time he'd done this, his left arm was still firmly attached.

Why the firefight? Brody wondered. Why would the shadow man have wanted him to relive his time in Vietnam and give him someone else's uniform (as well as someone else's fight)?

He reinserted the magazine, made sure the selector was set to SAFE, and stood.

At first, he wasn't sure, then he heard the sound again. He clicked the selector to SEMI, pressed the buttstock of the rifle between his elbow and ribs to hold it steady, and turned, index finger slipping from the guard to the trigger.

Someone was behind him.

He saw a shape in the alley, coming toward him. He squeezed the trigger.

She was in the darkness.

She was in the Ark.

She was in the darkness. A dream flashed by.

> *"Stay here, C Bear. Close the door and don't come out, okay?"*

> *"Mommy, don't—"*

> *"Listen to me. Stay in our room and don't open the door."*

She was in the Ark, hands over her mouth, muffling a scream. The *pain*.

She was in the darkness. Floating in the nothingness. Then—

She was in the Ark, huddled against one of the air purifiers on the eighteenth level. Everything was happening so fast this time she barely had any time to catch her breath and recover from the pain of slipping away. Her head felt as if someone had buried an axe blade in the back of her skull, right above her neck. A slicing pain, hot steel splitting her brain in two.

She held her hands tightly over her mouth as she released an agonized moan, the tears streaming down her dirty cheeks.

The smell of recycled air, oil, and solvents calmed her trembling body, and the pain in her head slowly began to fade. *Home. My God, I'm home.* It had been so long since she'd felt the familiar confines of her workspace.

Connie grabbed the side of the rusty machine and lifted herself off the floor, surprised at how weak she was. And hungry. She stood by the machine, listening to the comforting hum of the equipment she was tasked with maintaining. She felt the familiar thrumming of the massive generator on the lower levels through the steel floorplates, heard the whoosh of air through the ductwork and the clacking of automatic circuits opening and closing.

Home.

It had been a safe place, once. But not anymore.

This was where all the people she'd ever known had been transformed into unblinking robots and where the shadow man had killed her entire family.

She'd had the dream again while in the darkness. She'd been a little girl, terribly scared, hugging her mother, a woman whom she felt *was* her mother, but it wasn't really her. She'd seen her real mother, here, in the Ark, lying dead on the floorplates, the shadow man standing over her.

This time the dream had only lasted a few seconds, but it usually lasted much longer. The woman would disappear into the shadows, calling for Connie's father (not her *real* father). She would stand in the doorway, terrified, then, driven by some longing (Mommy and Daddy are hurt), she would walk down the dark hallway to the living room, where she would see them. *All* of them.

Then they would come for her. She felt herself slipping away, just as quickly as before.

She was in the darkness. Only for a second.

She was on an icy street during nighttime, and the air was cold. She knelt on the freezing asphalt for a few seconds, waiting for the pain to subside. She wrapped her arms around herself and felt her teeth begin to chatter. This was Brody's place. She was back.

Connie rose to her feet and looked around, trying to get her bearings, and saw two men peeking out from a nearby alley.

There are three of them. The other one was still out of view. She knew she had to go away from them and toward the last place she and Brody had been together. She'd told him that, right? If Brody was here, now, he'd be in the alley by the dumpster. And if not, she'd wait for him there. As long as she could.

Connie walked quickly, trying to stay out of the lights but watching the shadows for her tormentor. She'd managed to avoid the shadow man so far, and she wasn't about to break her lucky streak.

"I've got to figure out how to bring a damned *coat* with me next time," she whispered to herself, her breath curling into the air. She found the alley easily enough and turned the corner. She stopped in her tracks when she saw a shadowy figure rise in the dim light. Then she saw the rifle.

What do you know, a man who can follow directions. She stepped into the alley, relieved to see Brody again. The smile on her face faded as she watched him turn and point the rifle right at her.

X

Brody swung his body to the left just as the rifle fired, the bullet ricocheting off the building to his left and zinging into the air. At the last second, he'd realized who he was shooting at. *Jesus Christ, what did I just do?*

He tossed the rifle to the ground. He'd missed, but if the ricochet had hit her . . .

She was facedown on the ground, arms covering her head.

"Connie!" Brody skidded to a stop and dropped to his knees.

She looked up at him, a strange mix of surprise, fear, and *pissed-off* in her eyes. "What—the—*fuck*, Brody! You could've killed me!" She reached out and pushed him.

He couldn't keep his balance and fell to his side. "Are you hit?"

Connie stood and brushed the dirt from her palms on her coveralls. "*No*, I'm not *hit*, asshole. What the hell were you thinking?"

Brody was relieved Connie was okay, but he was so surprised he was fumbling his words. "I thought you were—I couldn't see—*Jesus*! Don't *ever* sneak up on a guy with a *rifle*!" He got to his feet as well.

"I wasn't sneaking."

"Then why didn't you say something? Anything? Like 'Hi, Brody, it's me, Connie!'"

She tilted her head and put her hands on her hips. "Hi, Brody! It's me, Connie! Hey, nice rifle! Don't blow my fucking head off, okay? Is *that* better?"

Brody laughed, which probably wasn't the right thing to do at the moment, considering he'd almost killed the only real person in this crazy place who was in it with him, but with her head tilted like that . . . Well, it *was* funny.

She stared at him for what seemed an eternity, then started laughing. "God, Brody, do I need to paint myself bright orange or something?"

He shook his head. "That was close. I thought you were the shadow man."

She picked up the rifle. "If the shadow man is here, he probably heard the shot," Connie said. "Not to mention the three guys who like to beat you up back there, or that fat-ass bartender with the cannon and all his angry buddies. We need to move."

Brody reached for the rifle, but Connie shook her head. "Uh-uh. If you think I'm giving this back to you right now, you're crazy."

Brody smiled. "Can you use it?" He was pretty sure she could.

"I guess we'll find out, won't we?"

※

They made their way through the darkened town, walking through the shadow-cloaked streets, until they found another boundary. The scene in front of them ended abruptly at a swirling black cloud, stretching from the ground and up into the night sky. They chose one of the nearby buildings to hole up inside.

"Hold this," Connie said, handing him the rifle. Brody watched as Connie pulled her sleeve over her hand, balled it up, and punched through a glass panel on a side door. She reached inside and flipped the lock.

"You've done this before?" he asked, more than a little impressed.

"Nope. Never." She opened the door and motioned him inside.

"Why didn't you use the rifle?" Brody asked as he walked inside.

"Because . . . it's plastic?"

"It's tougher than it looks, believe me." *And so are you.*

Connie shut the door behind them.

"Want to risk any lights?" Brody asked.

She shook her head. "If he's out there, we don't want to make finding us easier."

They used illumination from the streetlights outside and made their way to a pile of boxes on the far side of the mostly empty room. The space looked like a storage facility of some kind. "Have you felt it yet?" Brody asked.

"No, not yet. We've got some time, I think." Connie sat down on the floor beside the boxes. Brody sat down next to her and leaned the rifle against the nearest box, well within reach.

"I was in the dark, Connie, and I learned something about this place." Brody blurted it out but figured this was the way their conversations would have to be, since neither of them knew how long they'd have together.

"Did you dream?" she asked. There was an excitement in her voice that Brody hadn't heard before.

"No," Brody replied, "it wasn't a dream, really. More of an awareness of what's happening around me. There's *four* of me, Connie."

She was silent for a few seconds, and Brody could tell his revelation wasn't registering.

"Along with this place," Brody continued, "there are three others."

"What do you mean by *others?*"

He scooted closer to her and didn't like the way she recoiled. The withdrawal was minimal, a tiny movement, but he noticed it just the same. He stayed where he was. "Look, when I was in the darkness, I saw things. Remembered things. About me, but from other places. We're going through the same thing, Connie. I know we are. You've been there. I saw you."

She moved a few inches away. "What do you mean, I've been there?" she asked, her voice taking on an odd tone that Brody didn't particularly like. He heard fear in her voice. He'd thought she would tell him much the same thing, how she'd seen other versions of herself as well, but from her reaction, Brody began to think she had no idea what he spoke of.

"In Joshua, Maine," Brody continued, "you were there. In my house. You were dressed like my wife, same clothes and everything, but it was you, Connie."

She said nothing.

"I've seen you in Culver, Ohio. We're both little kids." Again, nothing but silence. "And in Colorado. West Glenn, Colorado. We're both teenagers."

Even in the dim light from the outside, Brody could see that she'd looked away from him and was shaking her head.

"Connie, we've talked to each other, run from the shadow man together, in all of these places, just like we've done here. And you—the different you—have asked me if I remember any of my dreams." He waited, the seconds ticking by as he gave her time to respond. Connie just sat there, her eyes fixed on a spot on the floor in front of her feet. "You don't have any idea what I'm talking about, do you?" Brody asked.

"I only know my home, in the Ark, and this place," she said softly.

He'd unloaded a new set of problems on her, and what he initially expected to be a moment for both of them to move forward, comparing their similar experiences and maybe finding some common theme they could use to their advantage, had instead turned into something different.

"When you're in the darkness, do you see yourself in any other places?" he asked.

She nodded. "In my dreams, I do, but *you're* never in my dreams, and it's only one place. I'm a little girl, like I've told you, and it's all terrifying." She shifted her gaze from the floor to him. "I've never seen you anywhere but here, Brody. Nowhere else."

Brody shook his head. Everything he'd felt so confident of began to shift. He no longer felt so sure of himself.

He glanced at the rifle. For a moment, the shifting stopped.

"The first time you saw me with this," he said, pointing at the M16, "was back there, where the three morons were, or are, right?"

She nodded.

"That rifle shouldn't be here, Connie. I was back in Vietnam, smack in the middle of a firefight with the NVA in some valley I don't remember ever being in, and I had *that* rifle in my hands. Both of them,

Connie. I had *both* of my hands. Then, all of a sudden, I was back here, in Garland Trail, with the *rifle*." He flicked his pinned-up sleeve with a finger. "And I was like this again."

"What are you trying to say?"

"I brought it with me, somehow. From one place to another. I don't know how or why, but it's here just the same." He reached into his pants pocket. "And then there's this," he said, holding up the yellow toy dinosaur. "I found this in my apartment just a little while ago, before I went looking for you. It's from my house in Colorado. It sits on my shelf right next to a model airplane in my room. I'm ten years old there, Connie. It shouldn't be here, either, but here it is." He handed it to her, and she reluctantly took it from him. "It feels real, doesn't it?"

"I don't understand."

"Squeeze it, Connie. Feel it. It's real, right?"

She nodded slightly. "Yes, it's real."

"I don't think I'm imagining all this, Connie. I really don't. I can't explain any of it, but I know what I've seen."

"Why am *I* here? And if I am in those other places, why don't I remember any of it?"

"I don't know," Brody replied. He gently put his hand on her arm, relieved to see that she didn't pull away. "We'll figure this out. You and me. Okay?"

Connie looked at the floor again. "My dream, Brody. It isn't like what you're saying. At all."

Brody remembered Connie saying she'd seen where it all started. "What do you see when you're dreaming?"

Her voice took on a detached quality, as if she was recalling something she'd rather not. "I'm in a house, like I told you before. I'm little, and my parents are there, but they're not my real parents. I feel close to them, like I love them both so much, but they're not my real mom and dad. It's hard to describe."

Brody gave her arm a squeeze, telling her it was okay to continue. He was here, and he would listen.

"I think there's someone breaking into the house, and I peek outside my door. My dad is there, and he tells me to go back to my room. My mom is in the hall, and I wait with her while my dad goes to see what's making the noises."

Brody felt her body tense. "It's okay, it's just a dream. It's not real." As soon as he said it, he realized how ironic he sounded.

"But it *feels* real, Brody!" she said, her voice shot through with emotion. "More real than any of this! Oh God, what's going on?"

"You told me you saw how this all started. Is it your dream? Is that where you see it?"

Connie nodded, and Brody thought he saw her quickly wipe a tear away, though it was difficult to see her face in the dim light. "After my dad goes into the living room," Connie said, continuing her description of the dream, "I hear a noise. It's his voice, like he's surprised, but then he doesn't say anything else. My mom calls for him—his name is Jack, she calls him Jackie—but he doesn't answer. Then she leaves me, goes into the living room, too."

Brody put his arm around Connie's shoulder. She leaned into him.

"I stayed in the room, like my mom . . . like she told me to, but they didn't come back. I waited, but they didn't come back."

Brody felt as if he were hearing the story from a child's point of view, as if she had really been there and felt the same terror that he could hear in her voice.

"I heard them, moaning or something. I went to see for myself and saw them in the living room. It was dark, but I could still see them. They were just standing there, not moving. Then I turned on the light."

Brody felt her body shudder. At first he thought it was the start of the pain that would take her away to the darkness, but it wasn't.

"There was something else, there, Brody. And one of them came after me."

"Who were they?" he asked softly.

She turned her face to his. "Not a who."

"What was it?"

"I can never see them clearly, just shapes, like people. I don't know, but I think my mind is blocking them out for some reason. I know I'm scared of them, not only because they were in my house when they weren't supposed to be, and they had done something to my parents—the man and woman—but there was something else about them that scared me so badly. I turned and ran, but they grabbed me. They took me away, Brody. They took me away." She moaned a little. "Oh God."

"And that's where this whole thing started?" he asked quickly.

Connie nodded, and her body began to shake. He held her more tightly, knowing his gesture wasn't going to make any difference. She would vanish from his arms no matter how firmly he held on.

"I think so," Connie said, her voice betraying the pain she was feeling.

Brody stroked her hair, knowing he only had seconds. "It's okay, we'll meet back here, right here, okay?"

Connie nodded, and then she wasn't there anymore.

✕

Brody sat there for the next few minutes, digesting Connie's words. Her dream sounded real. He could tell by the fear in her voice, the terror, and in the way she spoke about her parents. She wasn't convinced they were her real parents, but Brody questioned her assumption. If the moment she described was when this farcical mind game had started for Connie, then deep down she *must* know that the scared little girl taken away by someone who had broken into her house was *her*.

Brody felt the first twinges of pain as he watched the world around him begin to fade away, and he wondered if the same thing had happened to him. He'd had no dreams like that, no dreams at all, for that matter. His time here, in Joshua, and in both Culver and West Glenn, was part of a sick game. What troubled him was that Connie had no idea she was with him in those other places. He had met Connie elsewhere, but she hadn't made the connection. Yet.

He checked that the rifle was sitting where he could easily find it again. He took the yellow dinosaur from the floor and tucked it back in his pocket.

The pain in the back of his head exploded, and he let the darkness take him. Wherever he would find himself next, he would find Connie again.

They would fight the shadow man as best they could. And escape this crazy trap.

Chapter 30
BRODY16

West Glenn, Colorado
Monday, March 30, 1981

Brody was in the cafeteria again, sitting with his friends and listening to them discuss the assassination attempt against President Reagan. His time in the darkness had lasted only a few seconds, it seemed. And he remembered being there, right from the start. Moments earlier, he'd been in the warehouse, with Connie. Brody patted his pants pocket and couldn't feel the toy dinosaur. It didn't come with him for some reason. As he felt for it, he looked at his left arm, firmly attached in this world. He flexed his fingers.

"Dude, what are you doing?" Kyle asked.

Brody started to answer, then decided it wasn't worth the effort. None of this was real and talking to any of these people didn't matter. He stood up, leaving his books on the table, and headed for the cafeteria exit. The lingering smell of food from the previous hour's lunch made his stomach growl. He was starving.

"Hey, Brody, where are you going?" Kyle again.

Brody turned slightly and waved at him, remembering how the kids in Culver had reacted badly as soon as he stepped outside his scripted role. If that happened here, he wanted to be as far away from his "friends" as possible. The cafeteria was full of kids, and if they all reacted like those other kids had, he'd be in a world of hurt. Better to leave now, fast.

Brody spied Joan sitting at her table and noticed she was looking right at him, a questioning look in her eyes (not glassy, not yet). She was supposed to go to the table where he'd been sitting, open her notebook, and let him see his name (written in large, teenage-girl balloon letters) across the top of one of the pages. She'd find him in the parking lot and ask him to drive her home. And then, there would be an accident.

Sometimes she lives, sometimes she dies. He remembered it all.

Brody was surprised to see Joan get up from her table and move to follow him. He quickened his pace, but she actually ran after him.

He walked briskly out of the cafeteria and could feel everyone's eyes burning into his back. All the normal lunchtime noises suddenly ceased. He had gone off script, and his schoolmates had all noticed.

Brody ran through the halls, heading for an exit door. He would get to his car and drive to the last place he'd seen Connie.

It was a building, right? He tried to remember, as the memories slowly seeped into his mind. They'd been hiding in a gas station, then they ran to a theater, and Connie had opened the side door and slipped inside.

The shadow man had been there, too, following them.

Brody remembered going inside, and then—

A dark room, with a point of light at one end. He'd gone to the light, opened a door, and found himself in the bedroom. *Reba's bedroom.*

He'd opened a door in *that* place and found himself back home in Joshua, in *his* house, but he was still sixteen then, not fifty-two. Brody remembered feeling a gun in his hand and seeing Felix. He couldn't remember anything else from that point on. The theater was the key, though. It was the last place where he'd seen Connie, a teenager like him in this place, and it had a door through which he could make it back to his house in Joshua.

Brody pushed through the exit and ran toward his car.

"Brody!"

Joan was behind him. He glanced back and saw her standing in the exit, holding the door open.

"Brody? Where are you going?" she asked. Her voice was still the same, not flat and emotionless. Not yet, anyway. It would be soon. Brody still couldn't help but think about how pretty Joan was, and deep inside a little voice spoke to him, urging him to go to her, talk to her, drive her home (like he was *supposed* to). He blinked hard, trying to clear his head.

"Go back inside, Joan," Brody said. "You're going to get in trouble."

Get in trouble? Why are you talking to her? She's not even real!

Joan looked back inside the school for a moment, then walked outside, letting the door close behind her. "Where are you going?" she asked as she ran after him.

"I'm going home," he lied, but it wasn't really a lie when the person you lied to wasn't real, right? Joan slowed to a walk as she approached, and for some reason, Brody couldn't take his eyes off her.

"Can you drop me off at home?" she asked. "It's on the way. I think I'm done with this place today, too." Her smile was amazing, and Brody could smell her perfume on the breeze.

"What about your boyfriend?" Brody asked, wondering why his feet weren't moving and why he couldn't stop talking.

"Who, Todd?" Joan said.

The wrestler. Todd. "Yeah, him."

Joan looked down at her feet for a moment, then back to him. "He's a jerk. Don't worry about him." She stepped closer, and Brody felt the familiar electric shock coursing through his body. "I know you saw what was in my notebook," Joan continued. "I kinda like you, Brody Quail."

For a second, Brody's heart jumped. Joan had just said the words he'd longed to hear, at least as a sixteen-year-old kid, but then he remembered, this time he *hadn't* seen the page with his name written across the top. He had to get away from her.

"I'm sorry, Joan, but I can't take you home. You need to go back inside."

Before he could turn and run to his car, Joan grabbed his arms, pulled him closer, and kissed him, right on the lips.

The feeling was so strong, so overwhelming, that for a few seconds Brody completely forgot who he was. He was sixteen, getting kissed by a beautiful girl, and that's all that mattered. He didn't think about the accident. He didn't think about having to find Connie. He leaned into the kiss and put his arms around her.

The moment didn't last long.

He pushed her away, a little more strongly than he meant to. "Go!" Brody yelled, feeling a little guilty, but the regret he felt was fleeting as his senses returned. "Get away from me. Now."

And he saw exactly what he expected to see: the shock and hurt that erupted on Joan's face from being shoved away quickly vanished, and the life in her eyes faded. When she spoke, the girl he'd kissed just seconds before, so warm, so full of life, was gone.

"You have to take me home."

Brody turned and ran to his car. With each step, the urge to return to Joan, to kiss her again, grew weaker and weaker. The ache in his head was back, though, and it began to throb, a sign he'd come to realize as the moment when the game master knew his player was no longer playing. Brody pushed it away, locked it in a drawer in his mind, managed it.

He opened his car door and turned the key. The old Impala coughed, then started. The tires squealed as he gunned the engine and backed out of the parking space, then hit the brakes and slammed the shifter into first gear. In his rearview mirror, he saw Joan, still standing where he'd left her; she was moving her mouth and he could read her lips.

You're supposed to drive me home.

There were others there, too, walking up behind her. Kids *and* teachers, as if the entire school had suddenly emptied out.

They were coming for him, the hive-mind aware that a player had gone off script. Brody shuddered as he remembered the time at the elementary school when much the same thing had happened. When a mob of lifeless grade-school automatons had attacked.

Brody tore out of the parking lot and headed for the theater. And hopefully for Connie.

҉

As he drove, Brody kept an eye on the people on the streets, both pedestrians and drivers. Everything seemed normal (as normal as it could be in this crazy place); none of the people seemed to go out of their way to watch him or run out into the street to block his way, and none of the drivers grabbed their steering wheels and careened into his car to stop him. Maybe time was needed for the collective mind of these things to react, or maybe their communication was limited by distance, like a transmitter or something. Brody didn't know and didn't care. He had to get to the theater.

He would enter the building as he had before, from the side door. There he had entered a darkened room and found the door to his house in Joshua.

Reba's room.

Brody clicked his blinker on and turned the corner, the theater only a couple of blocks away. He'd avoided the intersection where the accident was supposed to occur, wondering whether it mattered if Joan was with him.

His head hurt, and his stomach was growling, but he'd turned on his radio to help keep his mind off the pain. The sound quality on the Impala's original AM radio wasn't very good, but when every station was talking about John Hinckley's attempt on Reagan's life instead of playing music, sound quality didn't matter.

Brody parked his car on the street beside the alley and walked toward the door. Before, it was unlocked, and he hoped it would be this time, too. Right before he reached for the door handle, Brody felt eyes on him. He turned and saw that others were now aware that he had gone off script. At the mouth of the alley, a crowd had gathered, staring. He grabbed the handle, pulled, and stepped inside.

🔾

A technician studying the readout said, "Sir, he's transiting. One of the junction points."

"How long until we're ready to intercept?"

The tech checked another part of his screen. "Injection point in ten minutes, sir. I have to recalibrate for the new environment before we send him in."

Lead checked his timer and sighed. Time was running out. "Do it as quickly as you can. The diver has to get in there fast."

"Copy, sir."

Every second that passed meant less time for an escape. He had hundreds of lives resting on his shoulders, and as Lead he wasn't going to let them all die. Years of hard work were coming down to this moment. He could stop the operation right now, and no sane person could blame him, considering what was going to happen soon, but he wasn't ready to give up.

Not yet.

"Sir, he's transitioned into the new environment," the tech said. "Recalibration in seven minutes." He paused, then said, "And there's another junction point now, close. If he finds it, we'll have to recalibrate again. Stability is fluctuating. It's getting turbulent in there."

"Where's the girl?" Lead asked.

"She's still off the grid, sir. We'll see her when she transits."

Lead glanced over to the corner. *The girl. A real wild card, that one.* He shook his head and checked his timer again. More drastic measures might be necessary when it came to the girl. And soon. "Send the diver at the first opportunity, copy?"

The tech nodded but seemed unsure. "If we insert the diver, and the target crosses the junction point, we'll lose—"

"More time. I *know*," Lead snapped, immediately regretting his shortness with a man who was only trying to do his job *and* let his boss know when things were about to be screwed up. They were all tired after months of nonstop work. Tempers were starting to flare. Time was getting dangerously short. As Lead, though, he wasn't allowed to let his temper get the best of him. He put his gloved hand on the tech's shoulder. "I know. First opportunity."

"Copy, sir. Insertion sequence for current environment will start in five minutes. I'll send the diver at the first opportunity."

Lead nodded, then turned toward the Last One. He liked to imagine there was sorrow somewhere in those empty eyes, maybe even a longing for forgiveness, but he wasn't sure.

"Recalibration in four minutes," the tech said, the glow from the screen reflecting on his helmet visor.

The diver was to his right, suited up and ready to go. The man's eyes were closed, his mind retracted deep within his own subconscious, spring-loaded, waiting to be released. At this point, he was cut off from the rest of his peers, unable to hear or speak. He was a round, waiting to be fired.

And by his order to the tech, Lead had already pulled the trigger.

Chapter 31
BRODY16

He was back in the house in Joshua, but something was different this time. The bedroom looked exactly as he knew it would, everything in its proper place, but *he* was different. Brody was viewing the room from an altered vantage point, as if he'd suddenly lost three or four inches in height.

Brody looked at his hands. They lacked the worn look he'd become accustomed to; rather, they were smooth and clear. He was clad in jeans, a blue-sleeved baseball shirt, and unlaced canvas high-top tennis shoes instead of his usual Italian loafers, dress pants, and button-down silk shirt.

He was sixteen.

The Brody Quail from West Glenn was here in Joshua, Maine. He hadn't returned to his older self after he'd gone through the theater door, apparently a portal between West Glenn and Joshua.

Brody's mind spun, trying to wrap itself around what he was seeing, what he was feeling. The knocking at the door began immediately. The two officers were back, exactly as they should be, following their parts in the shadow man's sick script.

He'd shot them last time, put a bullet into each of their heads.

Everything had reset to that penultimate moment, where he would learn of his son's death, and he would fight the urge to grab a bottle, or his gun, and deal with the pain in different ways, time and time again.

There would be no pain this time, though. He was here to find Connie, and that's all that mattered.

Brody slowly opened the bedroom door and peeked into the hallway. It was empty—no Felix yet—and cloaked in shadow. Just as it should be, except for one thing.

A bright light emanated from his office, halfway down the hall.

Much brighter than he would expect it to be.

The room had an overhead light fixture and a lamp on the desk, but even combined, the lights wouldn't have produced the amount of brightness he saw flowing from his office door. As far back as he could remember, the desk lamp was all he ever used. Something was odd here, which, as soon as he thought about it, seemed utterly ridiculous to ponder.

Brody stepped down the hall. He shifted his glance from the office door to the head of the stairway, expecting Felix to emerge at any second from either location.

In another instance, Felix had wrestled the gun away from him and fired just as Brody tumbled into the darkness in the open doorway.

He remembered the loud report and his ear stinging from the bullet's close (too close) encounter with his ear.

Brody stood just outside the office door, trying to decide whether he should rush in. Maybe Felix was there, which would explain the lights being on (but *not* the odd brightness). The gun might still be in the desk drawer. Or maybe Felix was already clutching the weapon in his hand, just waiting for Brody to expose himself in the doorway. Downstairs, the knocking continued, unabated. "Sorry, fellas," Brody whispered to himself. "Not tonight."

Brody moved into the doorway and saw another place, another time.

It wasn't his office.

It was his bedroom in Culver, Ohio.

Before he had a chance to absorb what was before him, Brody heard a creaking sound, weight on the stairway, and turned to see his Reba (*not* Reba) coming up the stairs. It was Connie, wearing Reba's dress as she always did in this house, looking much older, too. Felix was directly behind her, following her up the stairs. Brody couldn't see his hands and wondered if he already had the revolver, pressed against Connie's back.

Brody saw a strange look in her eyes, one of fear—and *confusion*? She was looking at him as if she had no idea who he was. "Connie?"

She didn't answer.

Brody quickly glanced into the office (his Ohio bedroom) and realized there would be no access to his pistol this time if Felix didn't already have it. He felt strange to be standing in the hallway and looking into a bedroom that he knew as well as he knew his Joshua house.

In that room, Brody was ten. He had a little brother named Murf. And it was 1975.

Here, it was 1974. And hundreds of miles away. Or was it?

Connie was at the top of the stairs now, standing perfectly still, staring at him, with Felix by her side. "Felix," Brody said, "show me your hands."

More knocking downstairs.

Felix ignored his request. "Do you require me to answer the door, sir?"

"I *require* you to show me your *hands*, Felix."

Slowly, Felix brought his left hand up, but his right hand remained hidden behind Connie.

"Does he have a gun?" Brody asked her. His blood ran cold when she nodded her head. "It's okay, Connie," Brody said. "He's not going to hurt you."

"She doesn't belong here, sir," Felix said, prodding Connie forward, taking a few steps down the hall, getting closer. Brody noticed his eyes were clear, his voice normal, which worried him. This time, Felix was operating off script and hadn't turned into some sort of emotionless zombie.

"She's not part of this place, Felix. *I* am. And *I* don't belong here, either."

"You need to answer the door, Mr. Quail," Felix said.

"And if I don't?"

"Then I will remove this woman from this place, Mr. Quail, and we will continue with our evening."

Brody watched as Connie squinted at him, as if she wasn't sure what she was seeing. "Brody?" she said, her voice timid, unsure.

He nodded. "It's me, Connie." This confirmed his earlier suspicions; Connie had no awareness of the fact that she had seen him like this before, as a sixteen-year-old kid in West Glenn, Colorado. *This* Connie only knew him as a fifty-two-year-old man living in an empty house.

"I—I don't understand," Connie stammered.

A dark shape, a hole in the twisted reality of this place, began to appear behind Felix, a grayish outline barely visible.

The shadow man was coming.

Brody reacted without thinking and rushed Felix, shoving Connie aside, waiting for the gun to go off and fire a bullet into his chest. But the revolver fell from Felix's hand as Brody slammed into him, sending Felix sprawling backward to land at the feet of the coalescing shadow man.

Connie was slumped against the wall, her eyes fixed on the shape at the head of the stairs. Brody grabbed her arm and pulled her up. He dragged her down the hall toward the bedroom, then stopped.

Behind them, the shadow man was there, fully formed, and stepping over Felix, his body lying crumpled on the floor. With glassy eyes, the butler looked up at the black-clad man. "You don't belong here," Felix said flatly.

Brody could feel Connie pulling against his grip, recoiling from the thing walking down the hall toward them. He looked into her terrified eyes. "Trust me," he said, then pulled her into the office, his bedroom in Culver, Ohio.

⋊⋉

The diver stood at the threshold, staring inside the brightly lit bedroom, knowing he couldn't follow. Not yet.

He stood still as the scene dissolved around him. He would be retrieved in a few seconds, then the chase would begin again.

In time.

Which was a commodity they just didn't have.

Chapter 32
BRODY10

Culver, Ohio
Thursday, May 15, 1975

As he crossed the threshold from the house in Joshua to this place, his bedroom in Culver, Brody felt immense pain rack his body, and his eyesight faded. For a moment, he was suspended in the black, so quiet and alone. He'd had hold of Connie's arm but didn't feel her now.

There was only the darkness, stretching out in all directions.

But it only lasted for a second.

He came to on the floor beside his bed, and the first thing he did was look at his hands. They weren't the hands of a teenager but rather those of a ten-year-old boy. This time, Brody was who he was supposed to be in this world. He looked at his door, and beyond the door frame lay not the hallway in Joshua, but the upstairs hall he was used to seeing here. The portal, or whatever it was, was gone. And so was the shadow man.

"Connie?" Brody said, his voice higher, not yet deepened by puberty. He whipped his head around as he struggled to his feet, grabbing the bedspread as he pulled himself up, but she was nowhere to be seen.

Brody was dizzy, weak, and had trouble keeping his balance as he quickly stepped around the bed. And then he saw her.

Connie was still unconscious, facedown on the floor, hair spilling about her shoulders. She wasn't wearing Reba's dress anymore. She was a kid again, too. Brody knelt down and gently shook her shoulder. "Connie? Wake up. Come on, Connie."

She took a gasp of breath and sat upright, turning herself over and kicking her legs, jumping away from him. Her eyes were bright with shock and fear.

Brody raised his hands and leaned back, sitting on his heels. "It's okay! It's just me, Brody!"

Quickly the terror in Connie's eyes faded, and she rushed to him, hugging him tightly. "He was there. He was there, wasn't he?" she sobbed.

"He was, but he didn't follow us through." Brody hugged her, remembering how it felt to hold her just like this in the janitor's closet, her body trembling before she disappeared into the dark. "We're safe for now, okay?"

Connie pushed herself away and looked at her hands. She turned them over in front of her face, then studied her dress, her shoes. "I—I remember, Brody. I remember who I was there, in that house."

"It's the same for me, Connie. In the other house, I'm a fifty-two-year-old man."

"But, you were younger, a teenager," Connie said.

Brody nodded and said, "I can't explain how that happened, but you're right. When I'm sixteen, I'm in a place called West—"

"West *Glenn*!" Connie said. "I remember!" Brody watched as she stared off into space for a moment, clearly recalling even more. "And

I've been there, too. With you." She looked down at her dress. "And I'm not like this, am I?"

"No, you're a teenager, just like I am." Brody wasn't sure how quickly he should dump the rest on her, about how she was also a grown woman in Garland Trail (who sure knows how to use a pipe to defend herself). He decided he would wait and see if she remembered the details on her own.

"You knew this already?"

"I did, but it hasn't been for long. Before I was in the house in Joshua, this last time, I was in the darkness. It came to me, Connie. I don't know how, or why, but I saw each of the places I live and who I am in each one."

Connie looked around the room. "I don't know this place."

"It's my bedroom. Right outside that door," he said, pointing, "and down the hall is my little brother's room. His name is Murf. My mom is probably downstairs right now, in the kitchen. At least that's the way it usually is when I'm in my room here." Brody stood, still a little weak and wobbly, and held his hand out to Connie. She took it, and he helped her stand.

Connie's eyes locked on a shelf, a few feet away. "I've seen that before."

On the shelf, right next to his Avenger model, was the yellow T. rex, sitting right where it should be. Brody's hand reflexively went to his pocket, as he remembered he had stuffed the toy there before. "I'll be damned," he said.

"What?"

"It was in my pocket, before. When we were in the warehouse, I had it with me."

"The warehouse in Garland Trail," Connie said, recalling that place as well. "I remember. There were people there, three guys, who were beating you up. And a bartender with a gun, and we were running." Connie abruptly covered her face with her hands.

"What's wrong?"

When she dropped her hands, Brody saw tears welling up in her eyes. "How many, Brody?" she asked, her voice cracking.

At first he wasn't sure what she meant but soon figured it out. She'd just realized that there were more than two versions of her. "There's four, Connie. Four places. Four of you and four of me."

The sadness and confusion evident in Connie's eyes slowly drained away, replaced with an acceptance of sorts. And determination. Odd, for a ten-year-old girl to exhibit that sort of emotional strength, but then again, Brody realized he didn't feel much like a kid anymore.

"And I've been with you in each of those places?" Connie asked.

"Yes," he answered. "In each place."

"Why didn't I realize that until now?"

"I'm not sure," Brody said. He walked over to his shelf and picked up the T. rex. "But I think I have an idea."

Connie walked over beside him and stared at the toy. "That's part of it, isn't it?"

"I've had this same toy with me in more than one place," Brody said, "and there've been other things, too. Things that have crossed from one place to another. Not to mention this room. There's some sort of portal in Reba's room, in the house in Joshua, which lets us cross from one place to another. The theater door, remember?"

She didn't, at first.

"We were running from the shadow man, in West Glenn," Brody explained, "and you ducked inside a theater. I followed you, but you were already gone. There was a door there, and it opened into Reba's room. I used it again right before you appeared in the house, except I was still sixteen, and you were much older. Just like you had always been when I'd seen you in that house."

"Why didn't you change that time? We're both ten now, right?" Connie asked.

"I don't know why. But tell me this. Do you feel ten?"

She thought for a second. "No, I suppose I don't."

"Neither do I. Not anymore." Brody put the T. rex back in his pocket. "I think things are starting to fall apart, Connie. I don't know *how* I know, but none of this has ever happened before. I just played my part, did what I was supposed to do, and then moved on to the next place. The next show for the shadow man." What he *didn't* want to say was how everything began to fall apart, go off script, when Connie started to appear. She very well might be the cause of all this madness.

"You think he's behind all this?"

Brody had to clear his mind before he answered, and he pushed his suspicions away. For now. "He's the common factor, isn't he? We've both seen him, and you even saw him in your *own* place." Brody didn't want to bring up her family in the Ark, again feeling it was probably better to let her remember that part on her own. And it didn't take long.

"He killed my parents."

Brody nodded slightly, searching her eyes for the emotions he hoped wouldn't come. He needed her to stay strong, mostly so she could help *him* stay strong.

"We need to kill him, Brody," Connie said, and Brody was surprised to hear the coldness that had slipped from the lips of such a little girl—little in body, anyway. Inside, though, the Connie he'd seen fight the three thugs was churning behind those green eyes, just as brave and capable as he knew she could be.

"That might be a little tough here," he said, looking around his room. "We don't have any weapons, and I'm not too sure how a ten-year-old kid could get his hands on an M16. The rifle is still in Garland Trail, at least I think it is, and the pistol is somewhere in the house in Joshua." He remembered how Felix had held the gun to Connie's back and had dropped it when Brody had slammed into him. "Unless Felix is going to keep it now. God, this is so confusing."

"Do your parents have any guns? Here?"

"No. Not that I've ever seen."

Connie thought for a second, then her eyes lit up. "This house has a kitchen, right?"

"Yeah, of course it does. Why?"

"Kitchens have knives, Brody."

And there she was. Connie was definitely inside that little, innocent-looking body. "You're damn right there is," Brody said.

"You shouldn't curse. You're ten, remember?"

"Oh shit. You're right."

"Nice. So do we just waltz downstairs and grab one? If your mother is down there, she'll know *I'm not supposed to be here*," Connie said. "And we both know what happens then."

"I'll get one. Hopefully she won't notice what I'm doing. Then we'll leave."

"While you're down there, could you maybe grab me something to eat? I don't know why, but I'm starving."

She's hungry, too? For some reason, that was important, but Brody didn't know why. In each of the four places, Brody had felt weak and incredibly ravenous, as if he hadn't eaten for days. Even when he *had* eaten, the food still didn't completely silence the tiger growling in his gut. He tucked the thought away for now, because he had the sudden feeling that they would have to move. And soon.

"I'll see what I can find. Stay here, and I'll be right back. We'll crawl out the window so you don't have to go downstairs."

Connie hugged herself. "Hurry, okay? I think we have to get moving."

"You feel it, too?"

"Yes," Connie said. "The shadow man is coming."

Brody put the T. rex in his pocket and closed the door behind him when he walked out into the hallway. He jumped when he saw his brother.

"Who are you talking to, Brody?" Murf asked.

"Nobody," Brody said quickly. "I had my radio on."

"It was a girl, wasn't it?"

His voice is wrong. Brody didn't have much time. "Go back in your room, Murf. Right now."

"She doesn't belong here," Murf replied, the twinkle in his eyes having faded.

"Please, Murf, go back in your room. Everything is just like it's supposed to be, okay? We're going to go downstairs after we wash our hands and eat some dinner. Just like we always do."

The line seemed to work, and the life returned to Murphy's eyes.

"Now go in your room and play for a few minutes. I have to go talk to Mom about something."

"Is it about what happened today at school?"

Was it the car this time, or some other crisis? "Yeah, I want to talk to her about that." *That* was general enough to avoid the mistake he'd made the last time he was here.

"Why can't I hear?"

"Because it doesn't concern you, okay? That's why." *No, too quick, that was wrong. If it was about school, then it* would *concern Murf.* "It's about something Mrs. Carlisle said to me. Now go on, and I'll be back up in a second."

Brody was relieved when his brother walked back to his doorway. But then Murphy stopped and turned around. His eyes were flat, glassy.

"He doesn't belong here, either."

It was then that Brody heard Connie scream.

Brody pulled his door open, and Connie came rushing out, her eyes wide with terror. Inside, a foot or so in front of the window, there was a hole in his room, black and empty. In the shape of a man.

The shadow man was here.

Connie grabbed Brody's arm and pulled him down the hallway toward the stairs. Murf stood there, watching them pass, and Brody felt a pang of emotion so strong, so sad, he could hardly bear to look at his little brother. *But he's not real, he's not real.*

At the foot of the stairs, Brody took the lead and headed for the kitchen, Connie close behind. His mother was there—he could hear her banging around in the kitchen, making dinner (like she always was). She looked up when they entered. Her eyes were happy and full of life, until she saw Connie. The transformation was nearly instantaneous, from mother to mannequin in the blink of an eye.

"She doesn't belong here," his mother said.

"Wait until you see what's upstairs, lady," Connie said.

Brody opened a drawer and selected two of the longest knives he could see, handing one to Connie. He didn't give his mother a second glance as both he and Connie sprinted for the front door.

You shouldn't run in the house with something sharp, Brody.

A voice he knew so well, a woman's voice, but not his mother. Not from this place.

Always point it down, and walk slowly.

The floor seemed to shift beneath his feet, and he had trouble keeping his balance.

You don't want to hurt yourself.

From the corner of his eye, he saw the shadow man at the top of the stairs, coming down. Murf was there, too, staring down at Brody, and for a moment his brother was alive again, the dolls' eyes gone. Brody almost wanted to run upstairs, shadow man be damned, and grab Murf and hold him close. Keep him safe.

"Brody! Come *on*!" Connie yelled, dragging him to the door.

The shadow man moved quickly, his boots thudding against the hardwood floor as he drew near. Brody felt the man's gloved hand brush his shoulder just as he and Connie rushed out the front door and onto a street that didn't belong there.

※

He slammed his fist against the console. "Dammit!" They'd just missed him this time, and as before, the girl had screwed their chances. "Time!"

The tech checked his readings. "Another seven minutes to recalibrate." He paused, then offered an apology to his boss that he knew wasn't necessary. "We didn't see that transition point until it erupted, sir. Stability is dropping quickly."

"I know, I know," Lead answered. "You're doing the best you can. Just keep at it."

"Sir, if it gets more unstable in there, we may have to pull the diver out."

Lead knew that fact as well as anyone. If he pulled the diver out now, though, that might be it. Failure. Something he wasn't ready to admit. "Is it stable enough for two divers?"

"Sir?"

"Is it stable enough for two!"

"Negative, sir. We can barely keep one in there, as bad as it's getting. The turbulence is getting stronger, and the separation protocols are failing."

His decision was an easy one. He might well be signing his own death sentence, but better him than anyone else. "Pull the diver. I'm suiting up."

Lead could feel the eyes of everyone in the room immediately shift to him.

"Sir, I don't think that's such a good idea," the tech said.

"Pull the diver, now," Lead repeated, "and these are your orders. If I don't finish the job before we reach the critical escape time, which is in"—he paused and looked at his timer—"three hours and forty-six minutes, you will abandon this place and get your butts home. Am I clear?"

The tech nodded grudgingly.

Lead turned his attention to everyone else. "All of you, is that clear? Three hours and forty-six minutes. That's *all* the time we have. Anything more, and everything we've done here for the past seven months will be for nothing. If I'm still in there, so be it. Copy?"

No one said anything, but Lead knew they would follow his orders. He turned his attention back to the console tech. "I'm going to need a weapon, son. Can you arrange that?"

"Yes, sir. I can."

Lead didn't want to do what he was planning, but he couldn't see any choice. The girl was a problem.

And she might have to be removed.

"All right, people, let's move! The clock is ticking!"

God, I hope I know what I'm doing.

Chapter 33
BRODY26

Garland Trail, Nebraska
Tuesday, November 12, 1968

Brody found himself in the darkness, swallowed up by the shadows as he and Connie ran out the front door of the house in Culver.

The pain passed quickly as he felt his body tumble onto something hard and cold. He lay still for a moment, his mind screaming at him to get up and run—the shadow man had nearly grabbed him—but he couldn't move. Brody opened his eyes and wondered why he was still in the darkness, then realized he had crossed over to one of the other four places. This time Garland Trail. It was wintry and nighttime. As always.

Brody tried to push himself up and fell onto his left side. His left arm was gone. He was *that* Brody Quail again, a twenty-six-year-old vet with a pinned-up sleeve. He glanced behind, remembering the position of the front door in Culver, but there was nothing there, no portal for the shadow man to pass through.

He hadn't followed them. *Or maybe he couldn't.*

To his right, Connie was on her side, eyes closed, but she was beginning to stir. She wasn't a little girl anymore. She'd changed into her character for this world, too. Brody crawled over to her as she opened her eyes.

"He's not here, Connie. He didn't follow us," Brody said, assuring her before she was fully aware of what had happened. Connie sat up and rubbed her head. There was a nasty scrape on her temple, but it wasn't bleeding.

"What happened?" she asked, looking at her hands again, realizing she had changed.

"We went through the front door and ended up here." Brody helped her up. "It's like I was trying to explain back there," he said, "the whole thing feels like it's falling apart."

"He got close, didn't he," Connie said.

Brody could still feel the shadow man's fingers sliding across his shoulder, trying to find purchase. "Really close. He almost grabbed me."

"Why can't he follow us?"

"I'm not sure, but that's the second time it's happened. We go through some sort of . . . door, and he can't follow us."

"Not right away," Connie added.

"Not right away," Brody agreed. "We have to assume he'll be back here again, too."

Connie glanced around, trying to get her bearings. "Where are we?"

At first, the street didn't look entirely familiar, but the scene slowly came back to him. Brody pointed off to their left. "There. That's where the warehouse is, just a block away."

"And the rifle, right?"

"I hope so. Wait." Brody looked down and searched the street, looking for the knives. "Do you remember having the knife in your hand when we went through the door?"

Connie looked, too. "I know I had it when I was running, but—there!" About ten feet away, a blade glinted in the streetlight's glow. "There's one. And there's the other one."

Brody patted his pants pocket. The toy dinosaur was there, too. They each grabbed a knife, and Brody tucked his under his belt. Connie slipped hers inside a zippered pocket on her calf. "If these came with us, then maybe the rifle will, too," Brody said. As he took his hand off the knife's wooden handle, he remembered the woman's voice telling him not to run with something sharp, to point it down at the floor. A comforting voice, so much so that it upset him a little. He could almost see the woman's face, it was so close, but he couldn't seem to picture her.

"Daydreaming?" Connie asked.

Brody shook his head. "It's nothing. Another memory, I guess. Can't quite place it."

"Another place? Apart from the other four?"

Brody wanted to say yes, but he wasn't sure. "It's nothing, really. We need to go get that rifle."

"Lead the way," Connie said, with a sweep of her arm. "Age before beauty, right?"

"You might be older than me."

"Maybe, but I'm definitely better-looking," Connie said, grinning. Brody wasn't about to disagree. She *was* pretty. Hopefully, when this was over, he'd be able to get to know her. But first things first.

They walked quickly, heads on a swivel to spot anyone who might be out and about. Few people were seen in this world because of the time of day, Brody supposed, but when they did show up, things tended to get violent.

"Are you still hungry?" Brody asked.

"I could eat my own arm," Connie said. "Oh shit. Sorry."

Brody smiled. "I'd offer you mine, but then I wouldn't be able to do any more one-armed pushups."

"You do one-armed pushups?"

"Hah! That's a no. I'm hungry, too. Want to try and find something?"

"The bar's out, I hope."

"Don't want to go back there, huh?"

"I don't like shotguns."

"Me neither. There's got to be something around here."

"I don't think I can just waltz in somewhere and sit down at a booth and order. The waitress would probably turn into a zombie and scream at me to get the hell out or something. I don't belong here, remember?"

"Yeah, I know. I was thinking more about taking something."

"I like the way you think, Brody Quail."

Brody and Connie searched the next block over, hoping they would have the time to get to the warehouse and grab the rifle before the shadow man made an appearance or they were both swallowed up by the blackness again and ended up somewhere else. They found a bakery on the next street, and Brody smashed the window with the butt of the knife handle. They would have to risk setting off an alarm, but their hunger was growing worse by the minute, their strength waning.

Brody took two boxes of donuts and stuffed them into his field jacket. Five minutes later, powdered sugar on their lips and chins because neither of them wanted to wait to eat, they stood outside the warehouse.

"This is it," Brody said. "Ladies first."

✗

Preparing for insertion took more time than he wanted, but then again, he hadn't personally done this for quite a while. In his headphones, he heard the tech give him the countdown.

"Insertion in thirty seconds, sir. Readings are good, environment stability is at acceptable levels. Bio readings are good."

"Copy," Lead replied. He fingered the weapon strapped to his hip. He hoped he wouldn't have to use it, but with time ticking down, he might not have a choice.

"Fifteen seconds, sir. Juices are flowing. See you on the other side."

He could feel the chemicals enter his arm, burning as they traveled up his vein, one of the joys of being a diver that he'd forgotten about. "Remember my orders. Not a second past the critical escape time."

The tech's voice was already fading as the insertion process took hold of his body. "Copy, sir," he heard the tech say, as if he were far away.

Then, for Lead, there was nothing but blackness.

 ✖

They found the rifle right where Brody had left it. They sat down on the concrete floor and ate more of the donuts, but for Brody the snack didn't seem to be doing much good.

She wiped her hands against her coveralls, leaving white streaks of powdered sugar. "So what's next? Do we wait for him here or track him down?"

"You told me before that he only showed up in places that you knew, not close to any boundaries, right?"

"Yeah," Connie said, "but I'm not sure if that's still the case. Like you said before, it seems like things are starting to fall apart. None of the rules are making any sense."

"*None* of this makes any sense."

"No shit."

"I say we go looking for him. Maybe back to where the three thugs are. We've seen him there a couple of times, right?"

"If you say so," Connie replied, tapping her head with her index finger. "I have a memory problem, remember?"

"Do you want the rifle?"

"Damn right I do. Want my other knife?"

"I still only have one hand, so . . ."

"Wow. I'm really stepping in it, aren't I?" She paused for a moment, then looked at him, her green eyes glowing in the shadows. "Do you think killing him will make this all stop?"

"I don't know. But if he's behind this, then I don't see any choice."

 ✖

The environment slowly came into focus through his mask as he transitioned in. For the first few seconds, he wasn't fully integrated, more of a shadow than anything else, an added layer on top of millions of others. He could move around, but couldn't interact fully with the environment. He couldn't speak, couldn't touch.

He moved, not willing to wait until the integration process was complete. He studied the grid projected inside his faceplate, then started following the path overlaid on the darkened streets to the point where the tech said Brody and the girl were located. With each step, he became more and more real, his form fully taking shape, until he could hear the crunch of his boots on the icy street, feel the cold air soaking through his suit. He reached down and felt the weapon on his hip.

"Diver is moving, grid five-one-five, heading for grid six-three-two," Lead said into his mic. "Confirm target location."

The tech wouldn't be able to speak to him, but Lead's words would appear on the tech's tracking console. The response came quickly, the text appearing at the upper part of his faceplate.

TARGETS CONFIRMED. STATIONARY. TRANSITION POINTS OPENING UP AT GRID LOCATIONS 516, 547, 548, 639. INSTABILITY WITHIN ACCEPTABLE LIMITS, BUT INCREASING.

"Great," Lead huffed. The whole thing was degrading to the point of being nearly too unstable to hold together. If he was still in here when it all went south, he'd lose both of his targets as well as himself.

"Diver approaching grid six-three-two," he said.

There was a warehouse straight ahead.

※

Brody had finished giving Connie another refresher on how the rifle worked when he felt the hair on the back of his neck rise. "He's here."

Connie stood, brought the rifle to her shoulder, and aimed it at the door they'd used to enter the warehouse. "Do we run or fight?" she asked.

The inside of the warehouse was dark, but if the shadow man came through the door, he'd be backlit from the streetlights outside. If they positioned themselves correctly, the plan Brody had formulated might work. "We're going to have to make a stand sooner or later," he said.

"I don't want to run anymore, Brody. I say we kill the bastard. Right now."

She was right. Soon, they wouldn't be in any shape to run. He was weak from hunger—they both were—and eating didn't seem to help. But even if he'd wanted to run, to find a better place to make their stand, he wouldn't have been able to convince Connie to follow. Even in the dim light, he could see her green eyes flashing with a vengeance that made him wonder what she'd seen the shadow man do to her family. She wanted blood. "Get behind the boxes and use them for cover," Brody said, placing Connie where she could stay (mostly) hidden and still be able to cover the doorway with the rifle. He took the kitchen knife from his belt. He told Connie the plan and then moved away, disappearing into the shadows.

Connie rested her cheek on the rifle's stock, peered down the iron sights, and with her thumb made sure the selector switch was set to "SEMI," just as Brody had shown her. One bullet per trigger pull.

Connie took a deep breath. And waited.

PART IV
THE UNRAVELING

Chapter 34

Lead knelt in the shadows, studying the building.

Communication was a problem. At times, when the environment was right (which it wasn't right now, just his luck), a diver could get a few words out, but usually, the external voice synthesizer wouldn't function properly. He wished he could stand out here and yell at both of them and explain what was happening, but then again, there was absolutely no guarantee they'd believe him.

He'd lost a diver in that exact way just two months back; thinking he'd gained the target's trust, he got a knife in the neck instead of the full cooperation he was expecting. The hold these places had on these targets—no, these *people*, he reminded himself—was sometimes too strong to overcome.

There had been a rifle in this environment, and one of the previous divers had barely escaped getting shot. One bullet had passed right through his helmet, but luckily the integration process wasn't fully complete, and the round passed clean through without doing any damage. It was the second shot, on the street, that had almost killed him. The tech had been on top of his game and pulled the diver out at the last possible instant before the bullet struck. Losing one man would be bad enough, but losing two would've been tremendously hard to bear.

If the rifle was still here (he had to assume that it was *and* that the targets—the *people*—had it in their possession), then Lead had to be extremely careful. He was fully integrated into this environment, and a bullet fired from an outdated weapon from an equally outdated time *would* tear through his flesh.

He couldn't see any motion within the building, and the last update from the tech indicated that the targets were still stationary on the main floor of the warehouse. They could be moving around inside now, but unless he *saw* them, there was no way to tell. Diver tracking equipment had a difficult time even when the environment was stable, but now, with the turbulence getting worse by the second, tracking was damned near impossible.

Lead inched closer, hugging the wall of the nearest building, cursing that they hadn't designed their visors with some sort of night-vision capabilities. When the mission started, they weren't sure they'd even need any divers, but over the last few months the divers had been getting quite a workout. Now there were just two left, and here he was, trying to finish their mission before the whole sickening mess was vaporized.

No, he'd have to do this the old-fashioned way: *look sharp in the dark*, as his old instructor used to say, which he hoped wouldn't end up with him on the ground, a rifle bullet through his skull.

There was one entrance in front of him, which they would expect him to come through. He'd lived long enough to know that doing what your opponent expected was the surest way to get killed.

He moved slowly and deliberately, crouching low, and headed for the rear of the building.

※

Connie shifted her weight, her arms and legs stinging from holding them in one position for too long, and looked away from the sights. She could feel that the shadow man was near, but she was getting more and more fatigued. Maybe it was the cold. Brody had found an old blanket for her in the corner, which provided some warmth, but her fingers were a little numb, and she couldn't feel her nose. Her hunger was growing worse, too, and her energy was slipping away, as if someone had opened a valve on her soul, and what was once a trickle was growing into a steady stream, her life draining out. She wouldn't be able to run away now even if she wanted to, at least not very far.

Brody was out there, waiting for the shadow man to appear, just as she was. If she didn't take the shadow man down with the rifle, Brody would take him with the kitchen knife. That was their plan anyway, and she really couldn't think of anything better.

She wondered if Brody was feeling as rotten as she was, and if he also had the sinking feeling in his gut that their time here was growing short. Connie didn't feel like she was going to go back to the darkness. This time was different. More final. Like she was dying.

Connie thought about closing her eyes in this cold, abandoned warehouse and letting go. But then she thought about her parents, and about how the shadow man had slaughtered them right in front of her, a bullet to each of their heads, and how she'd vowed to avenge their deaths.

No, she wouldn't quit.

"Come on, you bastard," she whispered to herself. "We're right here. Come and get us." She rubbed her eyes, then settled back down into firing position, cheek on the stock, right eye fixed on the front door, the front sight post hovering within the rear peep sight.

She swung the rifle slightly to the left as she sensed motion and dropped her finger to the trigger—and saw Brody emerging from the shadows, running at her, knife held high. Her mind began to race. Had he lost his mind? Was he coming at her? She tightened her pull on the trigger, then noticed his eyes.

He wasn't looking at her. He was looking *behind* her.

※

Brody was feeling worse. He hadn't felt the pain in the back of his head, the constant pounding and throbbing, for some time, and he supposed that was a good thing, but the rest of his body was so weak, he could barely stay awake. His stomach was growling so loudly that he was afraid it would echo in the darkened warehouse, but there was nothing he could do about it. Eating surely didn't help, and he and Connie had finished off both boxes of donuts anyway.

He'd been hiding in the dark to the right of the entry door for what felt like hours, though only twenty minutes or so must have passed. The cold was seeping into his joints, and he was fighting off the shivers. The shadow man was out there, close. Brody could feel him, but he hadn't yet made his presence known.

Why? Just come in through the door already.

He'd been watching Connie move every so often. There was enough ambient light that Brody could see her, hopefully only because he knew where she was. If *he* walked through the front door, Brody didn't think he would see her right away. If things went as planned, Connie would be pulling that trigger for all she was worth before the shadow man knew she was there.

And if she missed somehow, he would approach the shadow man from the darkened corner, from behind, and take him with the knife.

It would work.

It had to.

Brody was surprised that he and Connie had been in the same place, the same world, for so long this time. She hadn't shown any signs of being dragged back to the darkness (at least not while he was still close to her, before they took their positions), and he hadn't felt anything that would signal his time in this place would soon be coming to an end. In fact, he had a weird feeling that this was their last place.

Maybe he wouldn't ever see Culver again, or West Glenn. Or Joshua.

Maybe Garland Trail would be where this whole farce ended. Once and for all.

Brody heard Connie whisper something and looked in her direction. She was still hunched by the boxes, blanket over her shoulders and head, with the rifle pointing directly at the front door.

But he saw something else, too. Just barely, but enough to cause his blood to run cold.

The shadow man was behind her.

He'd come in through the back of the building.

In the moment before Brody sprang to his feet, he cursed himself for being so careless and not checking for any other entry points. A moment of stupidity, sure, maybe because he was cold, tired, and hungry. But his carelessness might have just gotten Connie killed.

He drew the knife from his belt, stood, and ran, hoping Connie wouldn't shoot him instead. He could yell at her, warn her, but that wouldn't do any good.

The shadow man was too close.

✗

Lead found exactly what he was looking for, another entry to the building that was far enough away from his targets that they wouldn't hear him breaking in. Some boxes were piled in front of a broken door in the back alley, and he gained access in a few seconds.

The warnings from the tech continued to pour in. The instability of the environment was getting worse, evidenced by the boundary walls he could see all around him. Swirling black shadows, stretching from the ground all the way to the sky. This place was contracting, positioned to collapse in on itself. The other three were almost gone, too.

Time was tight, but he still had to be patient and move slowly.

As he'd made his way around the side of the building, he'd risked peeking into a window; the darkness of the alley hid his movements. He thought if he crept slowly enough, they wouldn't notice any motion in the window. And he'd been right.

From his vantage point, he spied the girl easily enough. She was hiding behind boxes, covered in a blanket, the rifle pointed directly at the front door. He had to give them credit. Had he come through the front door, he doubted he would've seen her right away, and would thus have given her all the time she needed to put a bullet right through his facemask.

The man, however, was another story. Lead looked but couldn't see him anywhere. Unless he was hiding at the back of the building, possibly covering a rear door—*there*. A puff of breath in the cold air, floating from the shadows into the ambient light. The man was off to the side of the front door, out of sight. They only had the one rifle, but there was no telling what the man might have armed himself with. He'd seen what he did to one of the other divers with a piece of glass from a broken window.

Lead moved cautiously through the back room, carefully placing his steps in order to avoid any noises that would alert them to his approach. He'd go for the girl first, get the rifle away from her, then drag her into one of the boundary walls, take her away from the man, and break their connection.

It was easier to refer to both of them as targets, but they were still real people, even now, after all this time, who had God-given names. The man was Brody Quail. And the woman was Constance Drake. Two people from different places and different times, shoved into this crazy world with no idea of what was going on.

None of this was their fault. They were the innocents in all this, just like all the others.

And they were also the last two.

There. The doorway into the main warehouse. He stepped into the door, crouching low, knowing he was well hidden in the darkened space at the rear of the room. The girl, Constance, was directly to his front, maybe fifteen feet away, her back to him. He studied the lighting in the room. As soon as he moved toward her, there was a good chance that the man, Brody, would see him coming, *if* he happened to be looking in this direction. If he were concentrating on the front door, Lead might be able to get to Constance, disarm her, and drag her out of here before Brody could react.

Lead wouldn't use his weapon unless he absolutely had to, but it might be the only way he could break the connection between the two. Either he pulled Constance into one of the boundary walls, or he'd sever the connection the only other way he knew how.

Another message scrolled across his visor:

INSTABILITY AT CRITICAL LEVELS—ENVIRONMENT FAILING

That was it. He had to move now.

Lead bolted from the doorway and headed for Constance, stepping gently but quickly. She was moving a little, possibly shifting her weight. He had to get to the rifle, throw it away into the shadows, and buy himself enough time to get her away from Brody and end this.

Ten feet, five. Almost there.

Then he saw Brody bursting from the shadows with a knife held high above his head. He'd spotted him.

INSTABILITY THRESHOLD EXCEEDED—ENVIRONMENT COLLAPSE IMMINENT

Lead tried to ignore the flashing message and reached for the rifle—

—just as the environment blinked away, and a pressure wave sent him flying.

Chapter 35

Brody saw it coming but had no time to react before it slammed into him.

He saw the shadow man emerge from the darkened rear of the warehouse and head right toward Connie, and as he approached with the knife held high, the scene behind the shadow man changed. It was no longer dark and no longer the warehouse. A shimmering wall, a pulsing, sky-high picture of another place, rushed through the back wall of the warehouse and across the floor, like a tsunami. A distorted scene of another place, bright, with a blue sky, as if viewed through a wall of water. And soundless, except for a low hum that registered in the back of Brody's head. What he was hearing wasn't coming from the wall, but rather from his own skull.

The shadow man pitched forward as the scene enveloped him, and Brody watched him disappear behind the distortion's leading edge. Brody caught Connie's eye right before the wall rolled over her. She had no idea what was coming, and Brody saw confusion in her eyes as he ran toward her with the knife in his hand.

In a split second, Brody saw her confusion replaced by fear, as she realized the shadow man was behind her. Then the wall hit her, and she disappeared behind the distortion, her body tumbling forward and the rifle falling from her hands.

In the last moment before the wall hit him, too, Brody could see both of them through the pulsing distortion, fuzzy figures on the ground, one dressed in black, the other covered in a blanket.

Brody couldn't help but take a quick breath and hold it as the wave hit him. He closed his eyes and—

The pain.

A quick, brutal shock assaulting every cell in his body, from the tips of his toes to the top of his head, causing his body to convulse, seemingly every muscle contracting at once.

Brody screamed, but there was no sound.

He was in the darkness again, floating alone in the expanse.

Then there was sunlight, warmth on his face, and asphalt under his feet.

The wave had passed, and with one quick look at his surroundings, Brody knew he was back in West Glenn again. He was sixteen, in the intersection where he and Joan had been T-boned by a truck (over and over again). There were cars on the street and people standing around, but nothing was moving, as if he'd dropped onto a stage set with cardboard cars and wax figures.

Connie was facedown on the ground by the sidewalk, the rifle sitting in the gutter a few feet away. She was moving but not much. The blanket had slid off, and Brody saw that she had changed again, too.

She was the teenage Connie, the one he had always seen in this place. He watched as she looked at her hands and her body, the realization sinking in.

But there was someone else here, too, and he was already up and moving. Brody tried to stand, but his legs failed him. He was so incredibly weak, so weak that when he screamed at Connie to warn her, the words came out more as a sigh. "Connie, behind you!" The wave hadn't affected the shadow man in the same way it had affected him and Connie, Brody noticed.

Connie looked over her shoulder and saw the shadow man walking toward her, but instead of trying to stand, she began to crawl on all fours. Toward the rifle.

Brody crawled, too, hoping one of them could get to the rifle before the shadow man did, but he quickly realized the effort was pointless.

The shadow man stood over Connie, looking down at her as she clawed her way to the rifle. Brody watched, helpless, as the shadow man picked up the rifle and threw it away. The weapon clanged to the sidewalk on the far side of the street, which might as well be miles away, as there was no way either he or Connie could get to the gun now.

It can't end this way, no, please no. "Leave her alone!" Brody sighed, dropping to his chest, the strength in his arms fading away.

The shadow man looked away from Connie, no longer worried about her being a threat, and stared directly at Brody. Then he spoke. His voice hissed through the speaker at the front of his helmet. "You—eed to le—her go." The words were broken, flushed with static, but Brody knew what he'd said.

Brody shook his head. "No, I won't let her go. Don't you touch her." He was so powerless, watching Connie try to crawl away, the sheer terror in her eyes breaking his heart as the shadow man reached for her and grabbed her by the arm.

She tried to fight back, slapping at his arm, but was too weak to resist. Brody reached toward her desperately as the shadow man easily lifted her off the ground and turned toward the east to what was approaching.

Another wave was coming, rolling toward them fast, a huge wall of distortion passing through the houses and streets of West Glenn, soundlessly devouring them and leaving an entirely different scene in its wake.

Brody looked into Connie's eyes and saw acceptance there, a realization that this was the way it was going to end. He saw Connie mouth the words *it's okay,* and then the wave hit them again.

The pain wasn't as severe, nor did it last as long as before. In a flash, Brody found himself inside the house in Joshua, with Connie, dressed as Reba, hanging from the shadow man's arm at the end of the hallway.

"Please," Brody said, "let her go. Take me instead."

The shadow man shook his head and raised what looked like a pistol from a holster strapped to his leg.

Another wave hit suddenly and flashed past, leaving all of them in a grassy field, a school close by. Culver, and both Brody and Connie were little kids again. This time, the shadow man seemed to stumble as the wave washed over him, and Brody decided he had to act, no matter how weak he was.

With his remaining strength, Brody crawled toward Connie and the shadow man, just as he took his pistol and aimed.

He was going to shoot her.

Another wave.

They were in the warehouse. In their twenties. He was going to kill her, just as he'd killed her family.

Another wave.

They were back on the street in West Glenn. Brody continued to scrape his way closer to Connie, keeping his eyes locked on hers. She was smiling at him, knowing what was about to happen.

The waves were coming fast now, the scene before his eyes changing from West Glenn, to Culver, to Joshua, to Garland Trail, again and again and again, four places where Brody had lived his life as different versions of himself. False versions. Cruel fakeries created by the man who was going to shoot the only person he'd ever known who was *real*.

Brody cried out as the shadow man brought his pistol to Connie's head.

She was ten. A teenager. A twentysomething. A middle-aged woman. Her body changed and changed again, her appearance flashing away with each wave. But one thing about her didn't change.

Her eyes. So deep, so green, and so full of life.

Brody's outstretched hand changed—young to old and back again—with each wave. The pain was constant now, and Brody screamed, his voice changing in timbre as each wave relentlessly rolled over him.

The shadow man remained the same, though. A man in black, holding Connie, his grip steady even as her body changed furiously in his grip.

He placed the gun to the side of her head.

Brody willed himself to keep his eyes open, as he didn't want Connie to feel alone. She'd told him how scared she always was, alone in the darkness. He would never be able to reach her or hold her in his arms again, comforting her in the face of such terror, so Brody would do the only thing he *could* do. He would stay with her, staring into her eyes, until it was over.

The changes were coming almost too fast to discern, as if the whole world was nothing more than a series of four pictures being projected at an insane rate of speed, with his and Connie's bodies changing with them. But within the blurry cloud of motion that was Connie's form, one thing remained the same.

Her eyes. Two pinpoints of life, of reality, shining back at him.

The scene began to shrink as the swirling shadows pressed inward, erasing everything in their path. Eating the stage.

Connie closed her eyes, and Brody knew it was almost over.

And then, it was.

The shadow man's hand rocked as the pistol fired, and Brody watched Connie's head jerk to the side—as a kid, as a young woman in her twenties, as a teenager, and as a woman in the prime of her years, each with a fountain of blood issuing from her temple—and then the shadow man released his grip, allowing her body to slump over.

Brody felt his heart break, and he let his head drop to the ground, every bit of strength now sapped from his body, along with his will to live. Against his face, he could sense the ground shifting from asphalt, to grass, to a warehouse floor, and to a hardwood hallway . . .

Connie was dead, and this was the end.

Brody was alone now, alone in the darkness. The pain was gone.

And for the first time he could remember, Brody dreamed.

※

It's a hot, humid summer night.

He can't sleep, and it's late. Well past midnight.

He sees a bright light outside his widow, as if someone is shining a spotlight at their house. He goes to his window as the light fades. He sees nothing, at first.

There's something moving in the backyard, coming toward their house in the darkness. He can't tell exactly what it is, but it scares him. Deeply.

He hears a crash downstairs, followed by the muffled voices of his parents in the next room. Hears his father open their bedroom door. The floor creaks as his dad pads down the hall toward the stairs.

He opens his door slowly and peers into the shadows down the hall. He turns and sees his mother standing in their doorway. She looks scared.

The voice, telling him not to run with something sharp. It's her. Even though Brody realizes he's dreaming, he knows he's seeing the face of his mother—his real mother—for the first time in—

His father flips on the downstairs light.

He hears the sound of a struggle. Screams.

His mother runs downstairs, orders him to stay in his room and shut the door.

He doesn't want to follow her, but he does. He has to.

He stands at the top of the stairs, frozen by the scene below.

They're in the house. The things from the backyard. More than one.

Long, thin bodies, glistening. He sees their eyes.

His parents are on the floor. Not moving.

A pair of large, black eyes spy him at the top of the stairs. The thing comes for him.

He runs down the hall toward his parents' room, tries to slam the door, but the thing crashes through.

There's nowhere to run. No place to hide.

Its arms pin him down, and he feels the coldness seeping from the thing's hands into his shoulders. It leans in close. Soulless black eyes twitch in their sockets only inches away, reflecting the face of a terrified little boy. A little boy named Brody Quail.

It lifts him up.

And takes him away.

Chapter 36

Lead didn't wait for the tech to signal it was safe, and ripped the visor from his face. He sat up from the immersion pod, his head still spinning from the emergency retrieval. "That's it! Disconnect *now*!"

The techs were already working on it, severing the connection between Brody's pod and the main controller. Long, glistening cables—more biological than mechanical—ran from the far end of the chamber to the head of each of the pods, ending in a series of tiny filaments, which entered the bodies near the base of the skull, irrevocably intertwined among the sulci and gyri of the cerebral cortex, like the roots of a tree. A few feet away, the techs were doing the same with the other active pod.

These two were the last of the 756 people they'd found on this doomed, godforsaken rock, the fourth planet in the Argus system. They'd been able to successfully disconnect nearly 600, but the rest had been too far gone.

Lead swung his legs over the side of his pod and dropped to the floor a few inches below. He was breathing heavily, and his heart was racing. It had been close. "Time until critical escape?"

"Three hours, sir," one of the console techs answered. "You weren't in there very long. We've got more than enough time to reach a safe-escape distance."

At first, Lead was shocked that he'd been diving (the slang term for what they were doing when they inserted themselves into the grid) only for roughly twenty minutes. Then he remembered how time had a completely different meaning when one was swimming in the grid. Whole lives could play in one of the subject's minds in the matter of a few hours, and the diver would experience the same warped passage of time. "Were you the one who pulled me out?" Lead asked.

The tech nodded. "Barely. You cut it *very* close, Commander. The environment has completely disintegrated." He hooked his thumb toward the rear of the chamber, where the controller sat, a large, bulbous shape jutting out from the curved wall, with hundreds of cables running to each of the pods lining the chamber's cavernous interior, all but two of them now empty. "It's nonfunctional now. All the readings are flatlined."

Lead—Commander Demetrius Pitcairn—looked at Brody's pod. The team of experts was carefully cutting the neural connections between the controller and his brain, and at the same time preparing Brody for immediate transport. The body, after all these years, barely resembled a human being anymore, so thin and emaciated, but his mind was still in there, waiting to be freed. "Is he going to make it?"

One of the med techs looked up and gave the commander a thumbs-up. "We'll have him ready for transport in the next twenty minutes, Commander."

His people were good at what they did, unfortunately because they'd done much the same thing hundreds of times over.

Pitcairn stepped to the girl's pod. As he looked down at her, he whispered her name. "Constance."

"Sir?" a tech answered, not sure what his boss had said.

"Constance. That's her name. Constance Drake." He shook his head, wishing he hadn't been forced to use the weapon. The bond was so strong between her and Brody, though, so the only way to break Brody's mind away from the controller was to make him see her die. The girl's environments had collapsed a few weeks ago, and much to their surprise she had established some sort of connection to Brody's environments. They wouldn't be able to take one without the other. "When will she be ready for transport?"

"We're finishing up right now, Commander. Maybe ten minutes."

Pitcairn nodded and stepped away.

The mission he and his team had trained for, then executed over the span of the last seven months, was finally coming to an end.

Within the hour, they would have the last of the subjects onboard and be on their way home.

To Earth.

They would leave Argus IV, and its last inhabitant, to face the fury of a supernova.

As Commander Pitcairn stepped closer to where the Last One sat, he could feel the tingle in the back of his mind as the creature reached out to him.

It was weak, near death, and had resigned itself to its fate.

you take them

Pitcairn had never gotten used to hearing the creature communicate this way, speaking inside his own head. He had eventually learned how to communicate back: by *thinking* the words, not speaking them. *Yes, we will.*

that is sufficient

Pitcairn had always sensed a lack of emotion from the creature, a trait of the species and a reason behind their endless experimentation, but this time, he could almost feel a sense of relief coming from it.

you leave now

As he turned away, Pitcairn felt a pang of pity for the thing. It had been left alone here, tasked to keep the place running, keep the experiments going, until a more suitable location could be found. That's what it had relayed to him, anyway, and he saw no reason for the creature to lie. Still, what it and its kind had done over the course of *centuries* was sickening. Thousands, if not millions, of human beings—people just like him and his family, and the team here trying to save their own kind—had been taken, submerged in these pods, and forced to endure lives not their own. Experiment after experiment without end.

Some of the ones his team couldn't save had been here since the early 1900s. Both Brody and Connie had been taken as children, back in the latter part of the twentieth century. And many more had been taken after them, all the way up to the point that the aliens had to abandon their facility.

So many years had passed, so much had happened, and all the while, they'd been here, on this stinking rock, submerged in bio gel, kept alive, kept from aging as a normal human would, until the creatures had skipped town, left a caretaker behind, and for a reason that even *it* wasn't aware of, never returned.

The Last One was what Pitcairn and his team had called the creature. Fitting.

"Commander, we're ready to move them."

Pitcairn looked around the cavernous chamber for the last time, knowing that he'd done his job. He hadn't saved all the victims, but he'd saved the ones he could. "Get them on the shuttle and tell the pilot to prepare for immediate launch. Contact *Oneiroi* and let them know we're finished here."

"Yes, sir. Our equipment?"

Most of their equipment had already been transported back to the *Oneiroi*, except for what they'd needed to use for the last two pods. "Leave it."

"Roger, sir."

Pitcairn was the last to depart, and as he walked toward the exit tunnel, he could feel a slight tingle in his mind. The Last One was trying to reach out to him one final time.

not supposed to happen this way was all it said.

Pitcairn didn't look back.

Chapter 37

Brody was in the darkness again, floating, without feeling, without purpose. It was a familiar place, and yet different. He was suspended in an eternal expanse of nothingness, but the sensation was different from his time in the shadow. And then he heard a voice.

The sound was faint, as if coming from far away, and he couldn't quite make out what the voice was saying. He became aware of other sounds, too. Beeping, whooshing, and heavy vibrations, like machinery being pushed around, moved into place.

He was cold. Every inch of his skin was freezing. He tried to move and felt something warm grasp his forearm. The grip was firm, unyielding, and he couldn't move his arm no matter how hard he tried.

"He's starting to come out of it," a voice said, still so faint, and not a voice he recognized. Awareness came quickly. He could feel his limbs, his fingers, and his toes; he could feel his chest rising and falling, but he wasn't *breathing*, at least not on his own. There was something down his throat.

He panicked.

He tried to kick, but the same warm, firm hands kept him from moving.

They're holding me down! They're killing me!

"Keep him steady," the voice said. "Bio readings are improving. Get ready to remove life support."

Life support? Where the hell was he, and what were these people doing? For a moment, his eyelids parted, and bright light flooded his senses. Brody didn't understand what was going on—*it had never happened this way!*

"That's it," the voice said. "Remove the endotracheal, slowly."

Brody felt something slide from his throat, as if they were tearing his lungs out. It passed his lips, and he felt someone quickly wipe his mouth.

He heard new sounds, a strange gurgling, a choking, and realized it was him.

Something else was in his mouth, soft and flexible, and he heard sucking noises.

"Airway is clear, Doctor," a second voice said.

Doctor? Was he in a hospital?

"Looking good." The first voice again. "Patient is breathing on his own."

And he was. Brody could feel himself breathing, his chest rising and falling when *he* wanted it to. But even such a simple act was difficult, and his chest hurt terribly. His breaths were shallow, and he had to fight for every lungful of air.

He tried to open his eyes again and squinted into the brightness.

He felt a hand on his shoulder, this time warm and comforting, as opposed to trying to hold him down.

"Can he hear me?" someone asked.

"We think so," another answered.

Then the voice asking the question spoke again. "Welcome back, Mr. Quail."

Chapter 38

Three Weeks Later
On Board the Terran Transport Carrier **Oneiroi**

Every moment seemed to blend into the next for the first few days.

There were sights and sounds completely foreign to him, strange and confusing. There was pain, terrible bouts of unbearable agony coursing up and down his arms and legs, that seemed to last for hours. He couldn't speak no matter how hard he tried; his voice just wasn't there anymore. He couldn't even scream.

There were machines all around him, covering his mouth and his eyes, and wires and tubes that he was sure were sticking into his body, even though he couldn't feel them or raise his head to look.

Brody was in a hospital, and the people here, all dressed in white from head to foot, were working to keep him alive.

He'd been in the same room since he'd gained enough awareness to realize what was going on around him, the doctors coming and going all throughout the day, checking, poking, prodding, checking again.

There was no night and day here, just bright lights every moment he was awake. He would drift in and out of consciousness, but it was different from when he would go into the darkness. This was less frightening, even relaxing in a way. He was actually sleeping. The world around him didn't change every time he woke. It remained the same.

The day came when one of the doctors entered his room without wearing the all-white suit; his face was uncovered. He sat by the edge of the bed and told Brody that he was going to live. That he had a long, tough journey ahead, but he was going to be okay. And that he was going home.

Home.

A simple word, but one that didn't hold a lot of meaning for Brody. Was home in Culver, West Glenn? Was it Garland Trail or Joshua?

The memories of those places were still fresh in his mind, as were his final moments there, when the shadow man had taken Connie from him.

He sensed no ill intent from these people, none at all, but if they had been behind the shadow man and his games, then they were not to be trusted. Trouble was, he was in no position to resist. He had no strength; he would try to lift his arms, even wiggle his fingers and toes, but if he tried too hard, the pain would start all over again, and the doctors would press the buttons that would put him to sleep.

He wanted to ask so many questions: Who were these people, and where were they taking him? Better yet: Where had they taken him *from*?

In time, the answers came.

Brody was awake when a different man entered his room. Tall, handsome, and wearing some sort of uniform. He carried himself with authority as he walked to Brody's bedside and sat down, scooting his chair closer so Brody could see his face.

Brody's eyesight had improved quite a bit since the first few days. The lights weren't as bright and no longer made him wince. Some things were still fuzzy, at a distance, but the doctors had said that was normal and his vision would improve. Brody looked into the man's face. The eyes that stared back at him were warm, honest. The man was an impressive figure, but Brody wasn't scared by him.

"Mr. Quail, I'm Commander Demetrius Pitcairn. I know you can't speak—yet—but I wanted to drop in and see how you were doing. Is this a good time?"

Is this a good time? It's not like I have any choice in the matter. I certainly don't have anything better to do, now, do I? The doctors told Brody how to communicate by blinking his eyes once for *yes*, twice for *no*, and three times for *unsure*. Brody blinked once, and the commander nodded his head.

"One blink means yes, correct?"

Brody blinked once.

"I know this must be very confusing for you right now, and you must have a million questions, but I want you to understand that we're here to help you. We'll answer all your questions, in time, as soon as your strength improves. I promise."

One blink.

"In the next few days, the doctors are going to provide you with an implant that'll help you speak, and afterward, work to get you up and about."

Brody wanted to ask what had happened to him. Why couldn't he speak? The questions were too numerous to list, but he had no choice other than to wait. The frustration was beyond description.

"It's going to be a tough road for you, Mr. Quail. I'm not going to lie. But there's something you need to know that might make it a little easier."

Brody involuntarily tried to nod his head but couldn't. Instead, he just blinked. Once.

"I was with you during that last . . . day you were in your . . . worlds."

He's having trouble finding the right words, Brody realized. *And if he was there, then where?* He'd never seen this man before, at least he didn't think so.

"And I know there was someone else there with you. A woman."

Brody's heart began to beat faster. *He's referring to Connie.*

An ugly realization crept into Brody's mind as he lay in this bed, unable to move and unable to defend himself.

I was with you during that last day, he'd said. *And he knows about Connie.*

That could only mean one thing.

Brody blinked his eyes, twice. Again and again, two blinks.

The man sitting beside his bed, impeccably dressed and seemingly so willing to help, was not what he seemed.

This man—this Commander Demetrius Pitcairn—was the shadow man.

And he'd killed Connie.

The noises from the machines, the beeps, sped up as the fear within Brody blossomed into panic.

The man noticed and placed his hand on Brody's arm. "I know what you think you saw, Mr. Quail. Brody. But it was an illusion."

Brody kept blinking his eyes twice, over and over, until the man spoke again.

"Constance is *alive,* Brody. She's alive, and we're taking care of her just as we're taking care of you."

And then the shadow man spoke the words that gave Brody the strength to overcome the grueling days and weeks ahead.

"And when you're strong enough, I'll take you to see her. I promise."

Chapter 39

Three Months Later
On Board the Terran Transport Carrier **Oneiroi**

"This is me?" Brody asked. Being able to speak, to really communicate again, was a godsend, but it was going to take some time to get used to hearing his words issue from a voice synthesizer implanted on the front of his throat.

"It is, Brody," Commander Pitcairn replied. "We were able to gather photographic records of almost all the people we retrieved. This particular picture," he said, tapping the projection device with his finger, "was taken after you were . . . after you disappeared."

Brody couldn't believe what he was seeing. "This is a boy from one of the worlds they made for me," he said.

"Brody, I assure you, this *is you*. It's from an archived missing person report filed by your parents."

They'd already filled him in about what had happened, even though Brody knew exactly what had occurred the night he'd disappeared. He'd dreamt about it, relived every terrifying moment. The things had been in his house, immobilized his parents, and taken him away. Him, and countless others. As far as his parents were concerned, they'd woken up the next morning and found him missing from his bed. They didn't remember any part of the ordeal. They'd lived their lives, and died, without ever knowing the truth.

And Brody could only remember them via images from his dream, and his mother's voice.

But this image was almost too difficult to look at. He wanted to lean closer, and the exoskeleton reacted to his nerve impulses, acting in place of the muscles in his body, which had long since atrophied. The bio-implants in his eyes made it easier to see—he could actually focus on things now—and he stared closely at the holographic display.

He saw a young boy, maybe four or five years old, standing in a bedroom. The room itself wasn't familiar to him, but the boy surely was.

Brody was staring at a 3-D holographic image of Murphy, an exact copy of his little brother from Culver, Ohio. But in reality, Murf was *him*. There was one other familiar thing in the picture, though, in the boy's hand. *His* hand.

A small, yellow dinosaur. A T. rex.

The things, the *aliens* that had taken him, had constructed numerous worlds for their subjects to experience, crafted using some of the subjects' own memories and the memories of the others they'd taken. A huge data bank thrived, filled with the lives of countless people trapped within oval coffins, which kept their bodies alive and their minds functioning.

Pitcairn had told him the place—a massive alien lab, full of hundreds of *human* life signs—was discovered by a scientific probe sent to study the death of the system's star. More probes were sent to Argus IV, robotic orbiters and landers, and the scope of what they'd found became clear. Plans for a massive rescue mission were set in motion.

Brody learned he was reported missing on July 21, 1973. He was only five years old.

He'd been missing for almost three hundred years.

Brody leaned back from the screen. "I had a younger brother in one of my worlds, Commander. His name was Murphy. Murf. They made him look just like me." And that was the only part of his four worlds that was anywhere close to being true. All that time, he'd been staring into his own face whenever he looked at Murphy. It explained so much. But Brody also knew that every single detail of his other worlds, all the places and people, had been copied.

Felix, Reba, his friends at the elementary school, his teachers, Joan, and the bartender in Garland Trail . . . all culled from other people's minds, mixed together to form a suitable world in which the aliens would study the one thing they didn't understand and couldn't comprehend about the strange species they'd discovered on the third planet in a distant star system.

That one thing had been simple human emotion.

Fear, longing, happiness, despair, loss, heartache, love, hate, sacrifice, revenge, lust, even physical addiction. None of it made sense to them. So they studied it. Brody, and all those like him who were taken from Earth, were nothing more than subjects to them, lab rats to torture, to shock, to please, and caress, all to see how humans reacted.

But they were abandoned when the system's star entered its rapid death throes, left with only a single caretaker. The controller began to fail, the subjects began to die, and the caretaker could do nothing to stop it. For it had been abandoned, too.

Worlds—*environments*, as Pitcairn called them—collapsed in on themselves, leaving the subjects in a mental limbo of sorts, still alive, but with no sensory input. They were trapped within their own minds, floating in the darkness, until the life-support systems failed. One by one.

Alone in the darkness, they starved to death. Just as he and Connie had almost done.

The shadow man, or *men*, had tried to communicate with him, pointing, attempting to get him to go where he'd never been before in his artificial worlds so he could see a boundary for himself. So he could break the bond. By the time he'd seen a boundary, however, his bond with Connie was too strong.

In the end, the *last* shadow man—Pitcairn—had saved them both, by appearing to shoot Connie in the head, severing the last chains holding them inside the aliens' illusory world. Unlike the divers, who weren't protected from injury by the alien controller, the people trapped in the pods could suffer catastrophic injuries without any harm to their physical being. For the divers, though, because of the sheer invasive power of the alien simulation, a bullet to the head or a shard of glass in the shoulder *would* cause bodily harm. If they died in the simulation, they died for real.

"I can only imagine how difficult this is for you, Brody," Commander Pitcairn said, "but you'll get through it."

Brody wasn't too sure he *wanted* to get through it.

He was nearly three hundred years old. The world he'd experienced as a little boy was long gone, blasted apart by war, and then rebuilt.

Connie's story about the Arks and living underground was true, but not for her, as the war, fight for survival, and rebuilding had occurred long after she'd disappeared; the world she'd believed was her real life was nothing more than someone else's memory, used as another experimental vignette. Brody had seen the post-war world, too, he remembered. His single, momentary glimpse into that ruined world, when he'd awoken in the middle of the ash-covered landscape, was accurate, even though that particular scene had been inserted into his mind by the controller, furiously attempting to manage the millions of environments in its databanks as its subjects failed and died. Like the firefight in Vietnam he'd found himself in, a memory taken from someone named J O H N S O N.

Physically, Brody didn't resemble a human being anymore. The machines had kept him alive, nourished him, and kept the aging process from progressing at anywhere near a normal rate, but lying prone in a coffin for nearly three centuries had resulted in a myriad of physical abnormalities that were difficult for Brody to view.

When he'd seen himself for the first time, he didn't see a person. He saw a monster. His legs and arms were impossibly thin, his torso short and wide, and his head oddly elongated. Of the other victims, some were older and in much worse shape, but the crew of *Oneiroi* was helping them in the same way, replacing muscles with mechanical exoskeletons, replacing eyes with implants, and, just as Brody would be forced to undergo for the rest of his days, giving nourishment from a tube in much the same manner as the alien pods.

Brody was no longer a human being. He was the detritus from a failed experiment. Everything he'd ever learned, seen, or experienced from the time he was five years old was crafted inside someone else's head, changed to fit the aliens' experiments, and forced into his mind through a series of cables inserted through a port in the back of his skull, branching out into tiny nanofilaments, woven throughout his brain, spreading and growing as time went on. The techs were able to sever the physical connection with the controller, but the alien technology would always be inside him.

He would never be fully human. No one wants to live as a monster.

But there was one thing that gave him a purpose, a reason to at least try to live a life in the new world they were taking him to.

Connie.

She'd been taken in 1994, more than two decades after Brody's abduction. For reasons Pitcairn's people couldn't explain, her body was, compared to Brody's and those of some of the others who had spent roughly the same amount of time in the coffins, in much better shape. Brody hadn't seen her yet, but from Commander Pitcairn's description of her condition, Brody figured the doctors on Earth would be able to reconstruct her features much more easily than his own.

If, that is, she could be saved.

Connie's worlds *had* collapsed in on themselves, but Commander Pitcairn's people discovered that her mind had somehow reached out, making a connection with *Brody's* worlds. This feat was, they said, the only thing that kept her alive.

But now, they were struggling to keep her body functioning. She had woken, just as Brody had done, had been told what had happened, and had seen her own physical appearance. Pitcairn wasn't sure how much of it Connie truly understood, because her periods of consciousness were brief and getting more and more infrequent.

She was dying, and the medical teams weren't sure how to stop it.

Commander Pitcairn had promised Brody he could see her once he was strong enough, and that time was now. His appearance might make things worse for her, but he had to try to reach her, let her know there was something worth living for.

"I would like to see Connie now, Commander," Brody said.

"Are you sure?"

The exoskeleton whirred slightly as Brody nodded. "We need to bring this with us," Brody said, pointing at the projection device.

He explained what he wanted to do, and Commander Pitcairn agreed, but not before he placed his hand on Brody's arm and said, "You need to know one other thing, Brody. We're not sure how much she remembers."

"About the worlds?" Brody asked.

"Yes," Pitcairn replied. He paused then added, "And you."

Brody had asked about Connie as soon as he was able to communicate. He assumed Connie had done the same; she'd been fitted with her voice synthesizer a few days ago. "She hasn't mentioned me, has she."

"No, she hasn't. Not yet, anyway," Pitcairn added quickly. "Maybe seeing you, or this, will make a difference," he said, motioning to the projection device.

Brody's heart sank. Connie was his one reason for living, and if she didn't—or *couldn't*—remember him, then what purpose was there for him to continue?

"Maybe she needs a reason to live, Brody. We'll give your idea a try, see what happens."

Pitcairn was right. He had to try. She might view him as a deformed monster instead of the Brody Quail with whom she'd shared so much, and there wouldn't be anything he could do to change that, and all the effort Commander Pitcairn had made to rescue him would have been in vain, for Brody didn't see any place for a man like him. Anywhere. Pitcairn had said that Earth was a wondrous place now, where war, starvation, and illness had become, almost, a distant memory. *Oneiroi* didn't have the extensive medical facilities that Brody would experience on Earth; she and her sister ships, three of which had already arrived back home, held facilities only capable of handling the initial care and rehabilitation the abductees required. On Earth, however, technology had advanced to such a state that in time, Brody would be able to walk among his fellow citizens with barely any sign of how he appeared now. He would at least *look* human.

But still, without Connie, would it matter?

If she *did* remember him, though, that changed things.

He would have a reason to live. And hopefully, Connie would, too.

It was hard enough to look upon his own body, but seeing Connie nearly broke Brody's heart.

The general shape of her face and the strands of red hair that still clung to her scalp told Brody that the body lying before him was, in fact, the Connie he'd seen in his different worlds. Still, as Pitcairn had told him, her body's deformations weren't quite as extreme as his.

Her arms and legs were long and thin, but her torso still appeared remarkably human. Her eyes, hidden under a light-therapy device, fluttered beneath drooping eyelids. She was sleeping, but from what Commander Pitcairn had told him on the way to her room, she wasn't going to last much longer. Her vitals were failing for no apparent reason, as if she didn't seem to have a reason to live. The doctors weren't sure what else they could do.

The Connie whom Brody had come to know in his four worlds had been a fighter. Inside that ruined body was someone who should be *fighting* to stay alive, not giving up.

Brody stepped closer, the exoskeleton whirring and jerking with each step. "Connie?" He wished his artificial voice was soft, comforting, but the synthesizer wasn't designed to mimic the sympathy and caring he wished to convey. He sounded like a damned machine.

He gently placed his hand on hers, feeling the warmth of her actual body for the very first time. Slowly, her eyes opened, and Pitcairn slid the therapy device out of the way, stepping back out of view.

This was the moment Brody feared most of all. She would see him, the real Brody Quail, for the first time, and his appearance might be too much for her to bear.

He watched as she turned her eyes toward him, the green sadly lacking the fire he'd come to know. They were cloudy. Tired. Sad.

"Can you see me, Connie?"

She blinked once, then remembering the voice implant, she spoke. "Yes."

Brody was glad he didn't see the terror he expected to see in her eyes, but in a way, he would've liked to see some sort of reaction. Instead, she only stared. Her eyes held no emotion. They were just . . . vacant.

"It's me. Brody."

There it was. She would either remember him, or not. After Brody gave her time enough to answer, it was obvious she didn't.

"Brody Quail," he said. "I was with you, back in that . . . place. Do you remember me, Connie?" *Please say you remember me, please.*

"Quail," Connie said, the name screeching from the still-new voice synthesizer. She was silent for a moment, then blinked.

Twice.

Brody straightened and glanced at Pitcairn, who was close by, watching silently. "She doesn't remember me."

Pitcairn pointed at the projection device.

Brody placed it next to Connie's bedside and touched the controls. A 3-D holographic picture floated above Connie's bed. Brody had never seen the image before, but he recognized the person at the center.

"Connie," he said. "There's something I want you to see."

She shifted her eyes to the picture. The seconds ticked by, and it seemed as if she couldn't recall ever seeing what was projected above her. Then her eyes widened with recognition.

"Who?" she asked.

Brody leaned closer. "You once told me of your dreams. You were a little girl, with a mom and dad, and you were taken from them." He watched as she looked into his face, then back at the picture. "This is that little girl, Connie. Her name is Constance Drake, taken from Watseka, Illinois, on July 23, 1994."

Brody watched as a tear slowly spilled from her eye, and he gently wiped it away.

"I was so scared," she said.

"You don't need to be scared anymore, Connie. You're here with me, and you're safe. Those things aren't ever going to hurt you again."

She stared at the picture for the longest time, remembering. She finally looked at Brody again, squinting slightly. "Who are you?" she asked.

Brody touched another control, and the picture of a four-year-old boy appeared next to her picture. He watched her face and again saw some recognition.

"That's Murphy," she said.

Brody hadn't expected her to recognize his little brother—the real reason he wanted her to see the picture was in his hand—but figured she must've seen him as they ran from his room in Culver. She at least remembered part of the worlds. "No, Connie, that's me. As a little boy, about a year before I was taken on July 21, 1973. My name is Brody Quail." *Please, remember.*

Again, Connie paused, considering. Then she said, "No, his name is Murphy. I don't know you."

"Try to remember, Connie. I was in a place called Culver, Ohio, and you were there with me, in an elementary school. We hid in a closet, and I hugged you before—"

Connie shifted her eyes away from the images, focusing instead on the ceiling. "Please leave."

One of the med techs at the back of the room stepped forward. "Commander, I think it would be better if we stopped for now."

Pitcairn raised his hand, and the tech retreated.

Brody had one more chance. "Look at his hand, Connie. Look what the little boy is holding in his hand."

Connie continued to stare at the ceiling.

"Please, Connie. Look at his hand."

Slowly, she shifted her eyes back to the image of the boy. She looked intently at the little yellow toy clutched in the boy's hand.

When she looked at him this time, Brody could see a glimmer of the girl he knew in her green eyes, a fighter named Connie. Then he heard the one word that meant somehow everything was going to be okay, no matter how difficult the journey ahead would prove to be. Because they would be making the journey together.

She smiled at him and said, "Brody . . ."

Epilogue

Two Years Later
Walter Reed National Hospital
Western Confederation

The beeps were slow and steady, like the ticking of a clock.

They marked the inevitable passage of time, each beep another moment toward an outcome that none of the doctors had expected, and none could prevent.

Hundreds of abductees had been transported back to Earth, undergone extensive reconstructive and rehabilitative therapy, and become *human* again. But even with all the remarkable technological advances mankind had developed over the last three centuries, there was one thing they still hadn't conquered.

Death.

The mysterious manner by which the alien controller had kept the subjects from aging, extending their lives beyond any reasonable measure, quickly reversed itself once the abductees were removed from their coffins.

The abductees aged, incredibly fast.

And they were dying. All of them.

Brody had emerged from his reconstructive surgery as a middle-aged man, with an appearance that could pass for normal in all but the most scrutinizing eyes. Connie, too, had successfully undergone reconstruction, but the promise of a long life together now dwindled away with every tick of the clock.

Brody sat at Connie's bedside, listening to the monitor beeping in rhythm with her heartbeat. She was an old woman now, gray haired and twisted with arthritis. Her organs were failing, and she was slipping in and out of consciousness.

Brody looked lovingly at her face, so wrinkled and pale, hoping he would see her green eyes at least one more time. He had aged, too, and in Connie, was looking at his own fate. Soon, he would be in a hospital bed, awaiting the inevitable.

The doctors didn't expect Connie to last through the night.

He wouldn't leave her.

Brody wasn't sure what to expect from death, but he hoped it wouldn't be like what they'd both experienced in the darkness, floating without purpose in an expanse of endless nothingness. That had scared Connie so, and he didn't want her to be scared ever again. He gripped her hand in his and gently gave it a squeeze. "There's nothing to be afraid of, Connie," he whispered. "You don't have to fight anymore." He leaned over and kissed her cheek. "You won't be alone for long. I'll be there soon."

The beeping continued, and Brody wondered if he was imagining it getting slower. More ticks of the clock. More time spinning away.

Tick, she lives.

Tock, she dies.

Brody closed his eyes, her hand in his, and drifted off to sleep.

He woke with a start, confused, and turned toward Connie. The staff had turned off the lights in the room, and he had trouble seeing her. Her hand was warm, but it didn't feel right. He searched the wall for the monitor, and saw what he feared.

Connie was gone.

Brody knew she had passed, the machine's silence having woken him.

He was alone, once again.

But he didn't feel alone. He could feel eyes upon him, watching.

They were there. The things from his dream.

Long, thin bodies, glistening.

He sees their eyes.

They're in the shadows. More than one. The creatures that had taken them both so many years ago.

Brody feels no fear, not like he did when he was a little boy. Instead, he feels something else entirely, something from *them*. There is regret, regret for allowing something to happen that shouldn't have. An admission that a mistake was made and an urgent need to correct it.

They speak to him, in his thoughts.

They give him a choice. But he needs to decide quickly, before any more time passes. At a certain point, even they can't stop the inexorable finality of death.

Tick, she dies.

It would be different this time. They would have awareness. They could start over, live the lives that had been taken from them. They'd be actors in another stage play, but it would be *their* play, no secret audience, no tests, no scripted events to overcome.

The choice was stark: let Connie die, and soon follow, or go with the creatures who wanted to make amends. And live.

Brody looks down at Connie, and decides. For both of them.

Tock, she lives. And so will he.

Former captors become caretakers, and the hospital room stands empty.

X

Brody is sitting in a classroom, and his teacher is at the front of the class. The place is familiar, full of faces he knows, friends. Lance is there, along with Gary Thompson and Rich Gable. He's aware of where he is, and why, but there's no pain in the back of his head, and he doubts there ever will be.

His teacher walks to the classroom door and opens it, allowing another student to enter. "Class, we have a new student today. This is Constance Drake, and her family just moved here from . . . Where did you come from, dear?"

"Illinois," she says. Then to the teacher she whispers, "My name is Connie."

"Oh, okay, Connie," the teacher whispers back. "Everyone, please make your new classmate feel welcome."

The teacher guides Connie to an empty desk next to Brody, and Connie sits down. She has red hair and the brightest green eyes Brody has ever seen.

Brody smiles at her, and Connie smiles back.

ACKNOWLEDGMENTS

First off, thank you, my reader, for spending a few hours of your precious time inside the pages of *The Argus Deceit*. I hope the world I built for you (and for Brody and Connie, too) was to your liking. Those of you who have read some of my short stories might recognize where this novel came from; if you've read "More," I think you'll see the similarities. That little thousand-word flash fiction story sparked an entire novel, and when I talked about where *that* story came from, this is what I said:

> *When I was a kid, my parents took me to see a documentary titled* Chariots of the Gods. *If I recall, the movie was about how ancient civilizations mistook visiting aliens for gods, built pyramids, etc. At one point in the movie, there was a prediction about when the aliens were supposed to return to Earth. I believe the year they predicted would've been when I reached my late thirties or early forties.*

I remember my mom coming into my room later that night because I was bawling my eyes out, yelling "The aliens are coming when I'm forty-two! The aliens are coming when I'm forty-two!" (or something like that). Even though I was only eight at the time, the number of years between that night and my forty-second birthday didn't seem like too much time, at least when it came to aliens showing up and eating my eyeballs.

I was a weird—and apparently quite impressionable— little kid.

My wife would probably tell you I'm now a weird—and quite impressionable—adult. Bottom line is, what I said about "More" still holds true for this novel. The whole subject of alien abduction has creeped me out for as long as I can remember. Have I ever seen a UFO? Nope. Have I ever experienced an alien abduction? Nope—at least I don't think so (*gulp*). Do I believe there's other intelligent life out there? Sure, why not. I think it's pretty arrogant to believe there isn't some other life out there in the stars, and maybe, just maybe, they've been here (oooh, spooky). Anyway, it's made for some great movies (and one very terrifying documentary that scared the living kee-rap out of a certain eight-year-old kid)!

Flight 19, a group of five Grumman Avenger torpedo bombers that went missing over the Bermuda Triangle back in 1945, has always intrigued me as well. Sure, their disappearance was probably due to a navigational error, but it was always entertaining to wonder if there was a supernatural/alien cause behind it. (Think about that awesome desert scene from *Close Encounters*.) If you caught the mention of an Avenger model on Brody's shelf, or even the name of the high school he attended, then I guess you caught me hiding Easter eggs!

Connie, and her life in one of the Arks, really isn't an Easter egg per se, but rather a nod to Hugh Howey and his incredible Wool series, which I thoroughly enjoyed. If you haven't read it yet, do. (After you read my stuff, of course.)

I really enjoyed writing this particular story because I was able to include some of my own experiences (and no, I'm not talking about being stuck in a vat of goo for a couple of hundred years).

Brody's yellow plastic T. rex? Real. I still have it, as a matter of fact, except half of its tail is gone.

The non-PC game called Smear the Queer? Real. Yep, that's what we called it, and I'm willing to bet if you asked any kid my age or older, they called it the same thing. It was fun, physical, and it was the 1970s, so give me a break. ;)

Brody's POS Impala? Real. A guy I went to high school with drove a 1963 Impala, which was almost as big of a heap as my 1962 Chevy II (which had a steel plate covering a big rust hole in the floor pan right under my feet).

The balloon letters in Joan's notebook that Brody saw when he wasn't supposed to? Real. The actual balloon letters didn't spell out Brody's name, though. (The real name started with a C and ended with a HUCK.) I won't say who wrote said balloon letters either. (Her name started with an S and ended with an ECRET.)

And now, on to the thank-yous:

To my lovely bride, Nessa, who survived another time-sucking stretch of novel-writing. Thanks for making sure I ate, slept, stayed out of the crazy end of the plot pool (for the most part), and didn't drink *too* much coffee/beer. I love you more.

To my agent, Mark Gottlieb, and to Jason Kirk, Clarence Haynes, and the rest of the 47North team, as well as my copyeditor Ben Grossblatt, you all have my thanks for helping a weird, impressionable adult bring yet another story out of his misshapen noggin and into the light of day.

Lastly, I'd like to thank *you* once again, my reader. I truly hope you enjoyed the story. As always, if you keep bringing the popcorn, I'll keep bringing the pages.

Chuck Grossart
Bellevue, Nebraska
2017

ABOUT THE AUTHOR

Photo © 2013 Ashley Crawford

Chuck Grossart is the author of the #1 US Kindle bestseller *The Gemini Effect*, which won the 2014 Amazon Breakthrough Novel Award for Science Fiction, Fantasy & Horror. He lives outside of Omaha, Nebraska, with his very patient, understanding wife and a few too many dogs.